VOYAGE FOR THE SUNDERED CROWN

THE SUNDERED CROWN SAGA BOOK FOUR

M.S. OLNEY

MAP OF THE CONTINENT OF TULIN

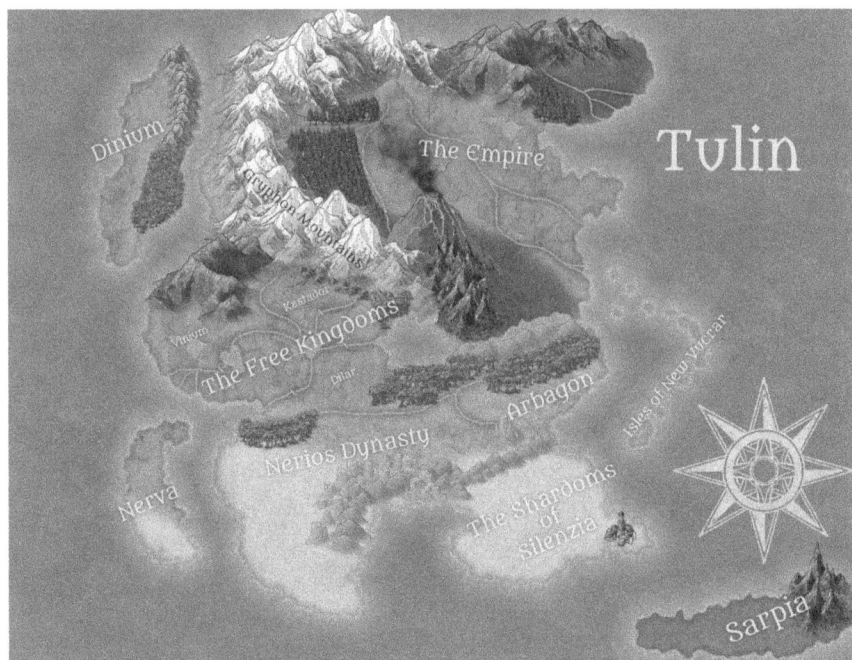

PREFACE

"The Tulins? Nothing but a bunch of decadents, all they care for is wealth and glory. The Yundols? A once proud race turned into savages who lust for war. The Sarpi? Don't even get me started on those foul beasts." – Tituss the scholar – First magistrate of the Golden Empire.

PROLOGUE

Caldaria

The view from the top of the mage city's crystal walls was breathtaking. Not just because of the views of the surrounding lands but of the vast horde slowly filling the plain below.

Kaiden lowered his spyglass and shook his head.

"I thought we'd have more time," he muttered.

In the city below cowered tens of thousands of refugees from across the Kingdom of Delfinnia. Danon's scourge had swept across the land until only Caldaria remained defiant.

The winter had set in with full force, and the howling wind only promised more ice. Already the once verdant plains surrounding the city were covered in several feet of snow, something that would have prevented a conventional army from laying siege. Danon's forces were far from that. The moans of countless undead and the growls of ravenous Fell Beasts carried on the frigid air.

"We always knew he would come sooner or later," replied the tall man at his side. The Archmage Thanos peered out over the plain, his bright blue eyes twinkling in the fading sunlight.

"He will not find Caldaria an easy prize to claim. Our defences are formidable," he said calmly, his golden cloak billowing in the wind.

"I'm pretty sure that's what the Baron of Eclin said, and the commander of the Watchers," Kaiden retorted.

Thanos smiled and placed a hand on the knight's shoulder.

"Have courage, Kaiden. Luxon and the others will return from their travels, and the help they will bring shall turn the tide."

Kaiden lowered his head and chuckled.

"I wish I had your confidence. We sent them out to sea in the height of winter with a map that is centuries old. Who knows what they will encounter on their voyage? Do the old alliances even still stand if there is no one left alive who remembers them? Have we sent them to their doom?"

Alarm bells began to ring out over the city, their mournful tones adding to the winds and howls of the enemy.

"They had better. All our lives depend on it," Thanos replied quietly.

Kaiden ran through the city's packed streets, careful not to slip on the ice that had formed in the bitter chill of the previous night. Snow flurries had gathered in large piles in some of the narrow streets and only the magical firestones set up by the mages kept the main roads clear. Panicked refugees from every corner of Delfinnia sought shelter from the biting cold wherever they could find it. Doorways, alleys, and every spare scrap of space were now occupied with terrified people all huddling together. The citizens of Caldaria had opened their homes to the masses, the Mages had opened the schools and dorms to as many people as they could, but even that wasn't enough to house everyone. Instead, most had to make do with hastily erected shelters in the city's streets or camp outside the city walls. People were streaming through the open gates as Nightblades shouted at them to hurry inside to safety.

Above the din of the city, came the mournful tone of the city's bell towers. The enemy was preparing to attack. Kaiden pushed his way through the crowds until he emerged into the city's Grand Plaza. There the last defenders of Delfinnia had gathered. Battle Mages and Nightblades mingled with the survivors of the King's Legion and the newly reformed Knights of Niveren.

A ragtag bunch of men and women armed with simple swords, axes, hammers, and bows had also started pouring into the plaza. They were the Refugee volunteers, thousands of them, and every single one would be needed. Kaiden strode through the ranks towards the platform that had been erected at the plaza's far end. Stood on it already was Grandmaster Thanos and the other Mage Masters. How the Arch Mage had beaten him to it was beyond him. A roar sounded from above indicating that Umbaroth and the other Dragons had spotted the danger. The gathered army watched in awe as the mighty silver dragon swooped down from the clouds and landed on the roof of a nearby building. Kaiden reached the dais and ascended the steps where he greeted the masters. It had been a month since Luxon had departed on his mission to find allies and Danon had appeared to have been in no hurry to assault the city. Instead, he had been busy consolidating his conquests from Sunguard where he had made the King's Spire his new dark fortress. His armies had spread across the land, but not all of Delfinnia had yet fallen. To the west, the city of BlackMoor remained defiant. Its strong walls and powerful navy kept the Sarpi at bay. To the east, Eclin was waging a guerrilla war in the vast mountain ranges, and in the south, Ricard of Champia had landed on the Marble Shore with an army.

"I'm surprised Danon has waited this long," he quipped weakly, unable to hide the concern in his voice.

Thanos nodded somberly.

"The dragons report that Danon is sending his undead and wolves against us. The Sarpi and mortal warriors are staying in the cities where they are sheltering for the winter," he said gesturing to the dragon looking down on them.

"A typical strategy from the N'Gist. They will use their more disposable troops to probe for weaknesses in our defences. I trust those defences are ready?"

"They are. I am hesitant to use them too early, however. Once they see what this city is capable of, they will become warier," said Master Ri'ges. Since the siege began, the powerful mage had proven to be an excellent strategist and one with a keen eye for defence. Kaiden was confident in the man's abilities.

"Wary is good,' said Thanos. 'we need to buy as much time as we can for Luxon. The city is prepared for a long siege. Unlike the other cities, Danon has conquered, we have magic as our ally. He will find it far harder to starve us out when we can magic up food and repair our walls faster than he can bring them down."

A Nightblade approached the dais and whispered into Ri'ges ear. The master nodded.

"They attack. Let's show the N'Gist what real mages can do."

Caldaria was unlike any other city in the realm. It didn't rely on stone walls but instead was protected by towering magic infused crystals that reached high into the sky. Crystalline platforms joined the individual 'wall' crystals together allowing the defenders to take up positions and fire down onto an attacking foe.

Kaiden led his Knights to their allocated positions and glanced at the wide range of people manning the walls. More snow was beginning to fall and swirl in the icy winds. On the lower tier stood his Knights, and the remnants of the King's Legion. They were considered the best at melee combat and so would be used to fend off any enemies that managed to reach the crystals themselves. On the level above them were the Battlemages and mages. The latter would be tasked with using magic to support the former and the other levels. With their combined might, they would rain death and destruction upon the N'Gist. Finally, on the upper level were the refugees, Fleetfoot thieves, rangers and Nightblades. From their vantage point, the expert marksmen of the ranger corps would be able to use their bows with deadly effect. The Nightblades were tasked with providing support to all the other levels whilst the refugee forces would act as runners and essentially be kept out of harm's way unless things went ill. Circling overhead were the dragons who would be used to strike at the advancing enemy from the skies. In short, Caldaria was the most heavily defended place on the continent. So much so, that it made the fortress at the Watchers look like a sandcastle in comparison. Kaiden drew his sword. No, Danon would not have an easy time of it.

The moans always made Kaiden shudder. The undead was a horror that he would never get used too. Once, the horde of snapping teeth and ripping claws had been human. Now, because of the N'Gists foul magics, they were shambling snarling beasts. He gripped the edge of the crystal platform tightly; there were thousands of them, more than he had ever seen before.

"By Niveren. There's so many," muttered one of his knights.

"Millions," whispered another.

Kaiden turned and placed a hand on the man's shoulder.

"They were once men, women and children, and they are what every soul within this city will become unless we stop them. Draw your sword and prepare my brother, for today we fight to avenge every single one in that army of the damned."

There were so many that the ground itself began to tremble. They drew nearer and nearer until their moans and howls became deafening. Some of the knights clutched their ears in a futile attempt to block out those torturous cries.

"They will surely bring down these crystals through sheer weight of numbers!" the knight cried. Kaiden watched as the first line of zombies pushed their way through waist deep snow that was quickly stained red as their rotting corpses fell apart as they moved.

The undead pressed on until they were within only a few hundred meters from the base of the crystal walls. Above, on the higher platforms, the rangers began to shoot their arrows. The projectiles lanced down, but just as they were about to strike, the mages used their magic to ignite them, turning them into flaming weapons of destruction.

Kaiden closed his eyes and whispered the old saying of the Nightblades.

"Only fire can truly destroy the dead."

The magic enhanced fire arrows struck, cutting down scores of zombies and burning them away to nothing. More volleys were shot, and more zombies fell, but it was nowhere near enough. Then the mages unleashed their magic. A wall of flame lanced downwards to engulf scores of zombies. From the sky, the dragons dived, and they unleashed their Dragonfire. Hundreds of undead were vaporized in an instant, but still, the horde pressed on. Kaiden bellowed at his men to ready themselves. At the base of the crystal walls, the zombies began to cluster. They clambered over each other to find a weakness. Within moments the piles of stinking, moving corpses had almost reached the lower defence level.

"Ready!" Kaiden roared dropping into a combat stance. All around him the other Knights and soldiers of the King's Legion raised their swords, spears, and shields.

A loud hum began to sound, and to the surprise of the defenders, the crystal walls began to glow. A bright light formed at the base before shooting upwards to the top. Then, with a loud zap, a beam of light shot out from the top of the crystal to strike the hordes below. The energy beam swept over the plain vaporizing hundreds of zombies and werewolves. All along the city's perimeter, the other crystals fired their beams. Kaiden lowered his sword and gawped in awe at the power on display. The crystal fired again, and this time the undead began to flee back whence they had come.

"Now that's what I call defences,' he whispered in wonder. 'Perhaps we can hold out after all."

CHAPTER I.

The Boundless Sea

Waves taller than the highest steeple rolled the ship *'The Agatha'* around like a toy in a bathtub, threatening to turn the vessel into a pile of matchsticks. The winter storm had struck without warning and so far, only the fast thinking and expertise of the ship's captain was saving them from destruction. In the distance and struggling in the furious storm were a half dozen Sarpi warships. As soon as they'd departed Caldaria and set out to sea, the enemy had been waiting. Only the *Agatha's* speed had allowed them to evade their pursuers.

Soaked and struggling to regain his footing on the slippery deck, Luxon Edioz did his best not to throw up the meal he'd eaten earlier that morning. Above, huge roiling clouds spewed snow and torrential rain, whilst thunder and lightning raged. His long leather cape coat was having little success at keeping him dry from the waves lashing the ship. Up ahead, and standing on the quarter-deck, was Captain Whitelaw 'The Mad' Weiss. The bald man had his arms spread wide and was cackling maniacally as seawater splashed over his bare torso. Luxon staggered over to him and the helmsman who was battling with the ship's wheel to keep the vessel under control.

"Aha! Master Wizard is this not glorious, does this not make you feel alive?" Whitelaw shouted over the howling winds and booming sea.

"That's not how I'd describe it, captain. We're getting tossed around like a rag doll, is there anything I can do?" Luxon shouted back as a wave broke over the deck.

A panicked cry came from one of the crewmen in the rigging. The sailor was desperately trying to pull in one of the sails but slipped. With a cry, he fell but managed to grab hold of a rope and cling on for dear life. Luxon crouched next to the helmsman and focused his magic, the storm made it hard to concentrate, but he quickly felt the tingling of his powers fill his body. He reached out with a telekinesis spell, catching the sailor just as a wave swatted him off the rigging. The spell caught him, preventing the screaming man from being thrown overboard and into the merciless water. With a movement of his hand, Luxon guided the floating sailor back to the relative safety of the deck.

"Nice catch!" Whitelaw cackled.

A worried shout came from the helmsman. Luxon followed the direction the man was pointing at. A massive wave taller than all the others was coming straight at them. It was the size of a mountain, and as it drew closer, its shadow loomed over the ship. Whitelaw grabbed a rope and began tying it about his waist, the other crew members on deck did likewise.

"I suggest you do the same Master Wizard; this is going to be a little rough," Whitelaw said with a twinkle in his eye. Luxon gulped and did as suggested. He took the rope offered to him by Whitelaw and rapidly began tying it around his waist. Water poured into his eyes, and he could feel it soaking through his overcoat. The massive wave struck, causing the Agatha to climb the wall of water at a near ninety-degree angle. On and on it climbed until it looked as though the wave would snap the ship like a twig. The magical runes carved into the ship's hull glowed brightly as the magics within did its work. Luxon cried out, expecting the ship to flip over. To everyone's relief, the ship crested the summit of the waves, only to plunge down the other side. The descent was a hundred feet, almost causing Luxon to spew his guts everywhere.

Another shout of alarm came from the deck. A fork of lightning split the sky, illuminating the giant waves. Even in the turmoil of the thrashing sea, the flash revealed a massive shadow moving against the storm. Luxon's stomach flipped at the sight; even Whitelaw looked afraid.

"Fell Beast!" the captain bellowed. He grabbed the petrified helmsman and set him back to his task.

"Don't make it easy for the bloody thing!"

Luxon staggered over to the deck's rail, his eyes fixed on the shadow. He couldn't make out any details of the beast, but it was massive in size. Giant taloned flippers were the only prominent feature. The ship began to rise again as it rode another giant wave. The Fell Beast, however, launched itself through the water to push its way through the other side of the wave. Luxon shouted a warning as the creature took up position right where the Agatha was due to fall. A long, lean snout, itself the length of a ship, burst out of the water and opened wide to reveal a cavernous mouth filled with razor-sharp teeth. Luxon turned his head to see Captain Whitelaw grab the ship's wheel to help the helmsman steer the vessel away from the monster's cavernous mouth. The two men strained, and the Agatha turned just in time, narrowly avoiding the Fell Beasts snapping jaws. As the ship turned, the crew hastily armed themselves with bows, crossbows and whatever else they could get their hands on. Luxon struggled towards the hatch that led below deck; he had to warn Ferran and the others. The Beast exploded through another wave, sending a wall of water smashing down onto the deck. Luxon was swept off his feet, only the guardrail stopping him from being tossed overboard. Other crew members weren't so lucky. Three sailors fell screaming into the icy cold waters of the deep. Luxon dared a glance behind them and saw their Sarpi pursuers trying to escape the storm and the Fell Beast's wrath. He watched in horror as a monstrous wave smashed one of the enemy ships, scattering men and material into the inky depths.

"Man the harpoons!" Whitelaw bellowed to his men. The Agatha was equipped with two large harpoon guns located on the foredeck. Fell Beasts of the Void were a terror the world over, and often ships were destroyed by their talons or tentacles. As a result, most merchant ships that dared venture into the deep ocean were armed with harpoons or ballistae.

The cyclone began to weaken just as quickly as it had arrived. The waves remained rough and tumbling, but the howling wind and rains were moving quickly eastwards towards the continent of Delfinnia, now a brown smudge on the distant horizon.

With the storm quickly passing overhead, the Fell Beast was revealed in all its horror. Luxon clung to the guardrail and gasped. He'd read tales of the Fell Beasts that used Esperia's oceans as their hunting grounds, but he'd never really believed them. The monster that was now stalking the 'Agatha' was larger than any creature he'd ever seen, including the dragons. Ferran and his fellow Nightblade Welsly emerged from below deck. The specialist monster hunters ran over to the rail and helped Luxon back onto his unsteady feet.

"What is it?" Luxon asked, unable to take his eyes off the beast pursuing the ship.

Captain Whitelaw hurled insults at his men as he ordered them to unfurl the sails. With the storm over, it was now safe to use the mainsails once more. The sailors moved through the rigging with incredible skill and agility as they unhooked ropes and pulled pulleys. Within moments the mainsail was deployed. The massive piece of blue fabric unfurled and flapped before catching the wind. With a whoosh the sail deployed, and with a jolt, the *Agatha* surged forward, picking up speed.

"It's a Leviathan," Ferran said in awe. "There are Void Rifts deep beneath the waves just as there are rifts on the land. No Nightblade has ever best one."

Suddenly, a melody began to play, causing everyone to look at the deck. The bard, Eripa stood there, her fingers playing expertly over the strings of her lute. Her blonde hair billowed, and her long red bard's cape whipped behind her in the wind. She began to sing. Her voice rose above the roar of the waves and pierced the hearts of every man on board. It was a song of the storms and seas, one of a tempest's passing. Her song was magical. Lightning lit up the sky, and the rain still fell, but the intensity of the storm began to fade.

Eripa winked at Luxon and the Nightblades as she continued to play her tune. With the storm weakening, the *Agatha* was able to pick up speed. The monstrous beast was now in pursuit, the waves parting as its enormous bulk barreled through the water. The *Agatha's* crew were shooting their weapons to try and scare the Beast off. Luxon watched as a harpoon struck the Leviathan only for it to spin wildly off its thick skin.

"I have an idea," Luxon said as he rushed to the hatch and clambered down into the hold where they were billeted. Next to his wildly swinging hammock was a chest containing his valuables. He opened it and reached inside. His fingers tightened around a long wooden object; the dragon enchanted staff Dragasdol. A whimper caused him to look up. Cowering in the darkness of the cabin was Alderlade. The boy king looked positively terrified. Luxon hurried over to him.

"Are you ok sire?" he asked. The words still felt strange to him knowing that the boy and rightful ruler of Delfinnia was, in fact, his half-brother. Kneeling next to the bleary-eyed lad, he took his hand in his own.

"It'll be over soon. Stay down here and keep your head down," he said. He looked over his shoulder to see Sophia staggering over to them. The Witch hunter looked wretched; the sea had not been kind to her stomach.

"I'll keep an eye on him," she said weakly.

Luxon nodded and picked up his staff. He ran back to the ladder and looked at them both.

"Stay strong," he added before climbing back to the deck.

Eripa was still singing, her voice somehow carrying loud and clear over the roar of the waves and Leviathan. The crew grew increasingly desperate as they continued to shoot every harpoon they had at the rapidly gaining Fell Beast. Luxon ran to the aft deck and raised Dragasdol high. He focused on the fading storm. He could feel its weakening power, and he latched onto it. With a loud crack of thunder, lightning split the sky and struck the tip of the staff. The hairs on his body stood on end as Dragasdol absorbed the power of the bolt. Electricity crackled and fizzed about him until with a shout he thrust the staff towards the approaching monster. Blinding white hot power lanced out from Dragasdol striking the Leviathan. Electricity mixed with seawater, vaporizing the tough outer skin of the creature. The beast roared in pain, but still, it came.

"Shoot everything you've got!" Luxon commanded the crew.

The sailors loosed a volley of arrows and harpoons, and this time the deadly projectiles hit their mark. The lightning, having exposed the soft tissue underneath allowed the harpoons to punch deep. Luxon ran to the ship's aft and watched in awe as the massive creature reeled back in agony. The Nightblades dashed to the rail and together pulled their banishing vials from the pouches on their belts.

"We could use a boost here Luxon," Ferran shouted as he arched his arm back ready to throw the vial. Luxon nodded and focused.

"Now!" he shouted.

Ferran and Welsly hurled the vials as hard as they could. Just as they reached their zenith, Luxon pushed with telekinesis to send the vials soaring through the air where they shattered against the writhing Leviathan. Instantly a blinding light flashed into existence as two portals to the Void ripped open. An unnatural wind began to blow, threatening to pull the ship and its crew towards the tear. Vast amounts of seawater was sucked into the powerful vortex, including the Leviathan. At first, it seemed like the massive creature would escape the pull of the magical portal, but the wounds inflicted upon it by the *Agatha's* crew took their toll, and soon its strength faded. With a last roar, the Leviathan disappeared into the portal with a flash. With its purpose fulfilled the portal collapsed in on itself to leave tumultuous waves in its wake.

The *Agatha* lurched forward once more as the pull of the void rift disappeared, and Eripa's strange song continued to calm the sea. The crew cheered and let out laughs of disbelief at surviving their encounter with a beast of the Void and the storm. Luxon couldn't help but laugh with them. Whitelaw clapped him on the shoulder and cackled before pacing down the deck to inspect the ship.

"I can't believe it. A Leviathan! I'd read about them in the old tomes from Caldaria's library, but never in a million years did I expect to ever set eyes on one," Welsly was saying to Ferran in excited tones as the two Nightblades walked towards the aft. In the days of the world-spanning Golden Empire, Nightblades had been common on the high seas, but after the Empire's collapse and the subsequent decline in global trade, ships travelling from one continent to another became rarer and rarer, until now, millennia later, the other lands were nothing more than a myth.

"It doesn't bode well that we encountered one so soon into the voyage. We've been at sea for what, a week? If the maps Thanos recovered from Caldaria's archive are correct then we have a long way to go until we reach Tulin," Ferran said with his arms crossed.

"We lost the Sarpi, so that's one positive," Welsly said, trying to brighten the mood.

Luxon looked to the horizon, not to the west where they were sailing, but back towards Delfinnia and the friends they had left behind. Dark clouds swirled in the far distance; he hoped they were not an ominous sign.

*

As evening fell, the waves remained large, but the *Agatha* rode them well. Below decks, Luxon and the others joined Captain Whitelaw in his cabin for dinner. The room was the largest onboard and dominated by a round wooden table that was firmly anchored to the floor. The walls were decorated with a range of exotic and bizarre items. On one of the shelves was a glass case containing a tiny human shaped skull. Luxon had asked Whitelaw about it their first night at sea.

"That there is a skull of what the Yundols call a Half man. I bought it from a bazaar on the island of Mizan. A strange land just west of Aniron's spine, that impassable barrier of rock that runs for thousands of miles south and a merchant told me of a chain of islands to the east of Yundolis that was home to all sorts of weird creatures. I sailed to them once, and by Niveren the tales were true. Half men are real! Whole tribes of them there are, nasty cannibals to boot!"

Tonight, Luxon and the captain were joined by Eripa, Welsly and Alderlade. Ferran meanwhile was tending to Sophia who was still suffering from seasickness. The food on offer was surprisingly extravagant, a plate of cooked salmon and crispy potatoes. Thanks to the magical runes carved into the *Agatha's* hull, the contents of the ship's larder was perpetually frozen in a time loop, resulting in all the food inside remaining as fresh as the day it was first produced. Such magical binding was hugely expensive, suggesting that Whitelaw was far wealthier than he first appeared.

After the food had been eaten, Whitelaw poured himself a glass of Robintan wine before passing the bottle to Eripa. Leaning back in his chair, he planted his booted feet on the table and belched loudly. Alderlade looked aghast at the captain's poor manners, Welsly chuckled and shook his head.

"So Eripa, it seems there's a lot more to you than meets the eye," the captain said with a twinkle in his eye.

A smile formed on Eripa's lips as she poured herself a glass. She took a sip before fixing the men in the room with a mischievous glint.

"I was born a Rurin somewhere in the Robintan jungles and spent much of my youth on the road. As you know the Rurin are nomadic people that never settle in one place for long. Famous for our music and as entertainers we would travel from town to town peddling our skills for coin."

"That explains why you're so...er...talented with a lute," Welsly said.

Eripa flashed the Nightblade a smile that would have sent most men weak at the knees and from the way Welsly's face flushed a deep red it appeared he was not immune to her charms.

"I played the lute in our family band with my brothers and sisters. We were famous in the east, for a time; at least until I discovered I was a wielder."

"How did you find out?" Luxon asked, intrigued.

Discovering that you could use magic was often a traumatic experience for the person and their family. With the laws of Delfinnia decreeing that no magic could be practised outside of Caldaria, many kept their powers a secret, often resulting in tragedy further down the road. Usually, as an untrained wielder grew older, their powers would manifest until either they hurt themselves, or someone close to them. Hiding the truth also meant that they would likely become a target for Witch Hunters or the Knights of Niveren. He had been fortunate that his mother, a powerful wielder herself, had recognised the signs when they had first manifested themselves when he was just ten years old.

"We were playing in Balnor for the Feast of the Brave Knight; I must have been twelve at the time. Anyway, as we were playing the 'Ballad of Estran,' the crowd began acting strangely. I was singing about Estran's fall, and as I sang those words, the entire crowd fell to the ground fast asleep. Naturally, we all panicked, not knowing what had happened, but there was one older man in the crowd still standing. He looked exhausted, as though he were struggling to stay awake, but he walked over to us and told us he was a wielder and that we had to flee the city. We ran and hid in the woods, but the strange man found us again the next morning."

Luxon leaned back in his chair and finished his glass of wine.

"Who was he?" he asked.

"He told us his name was Alther and that he was a Nightblade. He explained that one of us had used Song Magic. A very powerful gift. He asked each of my sisters and me to sing a song one after the other. Nothing happened when my siblings sang, but then it was my turn. As I sang, I could feel a tingling sensation pass through my body and as I sang the woods darkened despite the sun being high and bright."

"I've read about Song Magic in Caldaria's library. It's incredibly rare and recorded instances of it are even rarer. What did you sing to make the woods darken?"

Eripa brushed a stray strand of blonde hair behind her ear before answering.

"It was an old nursery rhyme about the Age of Darkness. You know, one of those songs intended to spook children into behaving. Once I stopped singing, Alther spoke to my parents and told them I had to go to Caldaria. Naturally, they were devastated but understood the law. Reluctantly, they handed me over to the old man. He took me north to the mages, and I then spent the next ten years in Caldaria learning to control my powers. The mages quickly deduced that I was no threat, as unlike them, I can only use magic through songs."

Alderlade raised an eyebrow and banged a hand on the table.

"But you're Eripa, the famous bard! You travel the kingdom singing your songs. Have you been bewitching people all this time?" the king demanded in his boyish voice. Eripa smiled at the confused and slightly annoyed expression on the King's face.

"I can control my powers now sire. I can sing normally, but if the need for it occurs as it did today, I can use my magic. I have never duped anyone into liking my voice. Perhaps one day you will ask me to sing at your wedding," she replied with a smile. Alderlade's face flushed.

"I am far too young for that nonsense," the young king grumbled.

Eripa reached for the wine bottle and poured herself another glass. "So, what about our fearsome leader, the mighty wizard? When did you discover you had magic?"

Luxon shook his head.

"It's a dull tale and one that cannot compete with yours," he said dismissively.

"Tell us, Luxon!" Alderlade pressed.

Luxon sighed and leant forward in his chair so that his hands lay flat on the dining table.

"The truth is I didn't know I was a wielder until my mother took me to Caldaria. Before that, I had no idea I could use magic. The mages took me in and over time and intensive study, I managed to tap into it gradually. Little did anyone know at the time that a Wizard's powers manifest differently to mages. As a Thaumaturgist, emotions tended to act as a catalyst to start with, but once I got them under control, it came to me as naturally as breathing. I think somehow my mother always knew."

"She must have seen your greatness," Eripa said.

Luxon nodded absently; a dark mood fell over him as he thought of his mother. The pain of her death was still raw and merely thinking of her almost always overwhelmed him with sadness. He put down his wine glass and excused himself from the cabin.

"Was it something I said?" Eripa asked as the door closed.

"Leave him be lass. There is more pain and sorrow in that wizard's soul than he lets on I think," Whitelaw said as he poured them all another round of drinks.

CHAPTER 2

Luxon stood on the *Agatha's* deck, his green cloak flapping gently in the chilly wind. The night sky was crystal clear, and Esperia's two moons cast the world below in an eerie glow. He breathed in the frigid salty air and sighed heavily. All he had felt since they had departed Caldaria was doubt. Were they doing the right thing? Should they have stayed? His thoughts went to Hannah. Was she safe?

Before they had set sail, Keenblade scouts had sighted a sizable N'Gist army advancing from the south. Had the army reached Caldaria? And then there was Yepert. His best friend had been used as a puppet by Danon. He had resisted the dark lord's presence to save Hannah's life and complete the quest for Asphodel, but the cost had been grave. In spite, Danon had destroyed Yepert's mind leaving him in a vegetative state, and the healers were powerless to help him. Luxon knotted his hands into fists as anger surged through him. Danon had taken so much from him. It was Danon's bride, the evil witch Cliria who had trapped him in the Void for what had felt like centuries. Danon had killed his mother, and now he was threatening to destroy his homeland.

The sound of footsteps behind him shook him out of his dark thoughts.

"Forgive me if I said something I shouldn't have," Eripa said softly.

Luxon shook his head and rubbed his eyes tiredly.

"There's nothing to forgive. I"-, he paused. There was a light on the horizon. He dashed to the rail and narrowed his eyes. Using magic, his vision became as sharp as that of an eagle's. Sure enough, he saw a ship; it looked damaged for its sails were torn and flapping uselessly in the breeze.

"Get the captain. It seems we may have more company."

Eripa turned and ran back towards the captain's cabin. A shout came from the *Agatha's* crow's nest as the on duty barrelman spotted the stricken vessel. A warning bell tolled, and the crew rushed to their positions. It didn't take long for the *Agatha* to move alongside the other ship. Now that they were closer, Luxon could see that the stricken vessel had been demasted and its hull was filled with holes. On the deck was a man, his clothes were torn, and a bloody bandage was wrapped around his head.

"Thanks to the gods!" the sailor shouted in relief.

With expert skill, the crew of the Agatha positioned the ship alongside the quickly sinking vessel. Luxon climbed onto the rail and jumped over the side. Using levitation magic, he floated gently to the deck below.

"Hail friend. Seems you could do with some assistance," he greeted. "Where's the rest of your crew?"

The sailor gawped at him for a few moments before shaking his head.

"I'm the only one who still lives. How-how did you do that?" the sailor said a look of fear in his wide eyes.

It was clear from the sailor's accent that he was no Delfinnian. Luxon thought of the map laid out in Whitelaw's cabin. The nearest landmass was the continent of Tulin, but surely, they were still many hundreds of leagues away.

"I used magic. I'm a wizard from Delfinnia," Luxon explained offering the now petrified man his hand. The sailor's distress grew at the words; he began to back away from Luxon, looking desperately for something to use as a weapon.

"Stay back! Wizards are evil!" the man shouted, close to hysteria.

Luxon looked back at the *Agatha's* crew who were watching the scene unfold with bemusement. Ferran shrugged his shoulders whilst Welsly was trying not to laugh. It was Whitelaw that spoke.

"We can't linger here for too long, lad. Use some of that fancy magic and get him onboard. From the looks of that ship, it doesn't have much longer for this world."

Sure enough, the deck shuddered as the ship began to list to port. The still heavy waves were beginning to cause it to capsize. A warning shout from Ferran caused Luxon to spin around. The sailor now held a heavy piece of wood in his hands.

"Stay back, wizard! You will not kill me without a fight!" the sailor raged.

The deck shuddered again causing Luxon to stagger.

"Enough of this. Sorry friend but you're coming with me whether you like it or not," he said. He raised a hand and focused on the sailor. The sleep spell took effect almost immediately. Before the man hit the deck, Luxon caught him with a spell and floated him gently upward to the safety of the *Agatha's* deck. The stricken ship shuddered, and the sound of water rushing into the hold below grew in intensity. He braced his legs and launched himself high into the sky before levitating gently to the *Agatha's* deck and safety. The unconscious sailor meanwhile was carried below decks.

"What do you suppose that was about?" said Ferran as he watched him go.

"No idea. Let's allow him some rest, and then we'll go get some answers," Luxon replied.

*

The mysterious ship quickly floundered and sank beneath the waves. By then the Agatha was back at top speed and gliding through the black waters of the deep ocean. Below decks, Luxon, Ferran and Whitelaw stood over the still sleeping sailor. Their new guest had olive skin, like that of a Yundol but his accent had been anything but. His had more of a twang to it whereas the Yundol tongue tended to be harsher.

"I looked at Whitelaw's map some more,' said Ferran breaking the silence. 'I couldn't make out where this man and his ship could have come from. We're still at least a week from Tulin if the winds are favourable. The only thing marked on the map was a small set of islands to the south."

"Perhaps they've been colonised since the map was created? Don't forget that the only maps we have are centuries old. Anything could have happened in the wider world since the fall of the Golden Empire," Luxon pointed out.

"Maybe so, but I'm curious as to his reaction to you being a Wizard. If everyone in Tulin is as petrified of you as this fellow is then it doesn't bode well for us finding support. Let's just wake him up," the captain grumbled.

"Wait a moment," Ferran said. The Nightblade reached down and lifted the sailor's right arm. Tattooed on the underside was a strange symbol. Ferran rubbed his chin.

"I swear I've seen this symbol before. Let me think a moment; ah that's it!" he exclaimed. He ushered for the others to follow him out of the cabin.

"That symbol belongs to one of the Great Tribes that fled the Doom of Vucrar before the rise of Zahnia the Great and the Golden Empire. The Vasin if I remember correctly. It's been a long time since I studied the tribes."

Luxon glanced back at the unconscious sailor. He too had read much of the Doom and the flight of the tribes. One of them, the Delfin, had been the tribe that had conquered the Golden Empire under the leadership of Marcus the Mighty and founded the Kingdom of Delfinnia.

"That's right. Six tribes are recorded as having fled across the sea when Vucrar was devastated by a massive volcanic eruption. The Delfin, Keenblade, Stormchaser, Rurin and Dafa tribes all crossed the sea and settled what is now the Great Plains, but there was another, one whose people were said to have been lost at sea during a mighty storm."

"The Vastar," croaked a voice from behind them.

They all turned to face the cabin. The sailor was stirring from his slumber and slowly sitting up. He shook his head and rubbed his eyes before looking warily at his captors.

"My people are the Vastar, not Vasin. We lived on the islands of New Vucrar. They are but three days sail to the southwest."

Luxon stepped into the cabin, the sailor flinched.

"Take it easy. I'm no threat to you, I promise," he explained, holding his hands up to show he was no danger.

"What's your name?" he asked.

The sailor watched him warily before answering.

"Lipur. My name is Luxon."

"You said your people lived on the islands to the south in the past tense. Do they not live there anymore?"

Lipur shook his head, angrily rubbing at tears that threatened to fall from his eyes.

"They-they took everybody. Burned all we had to the ground. I barely made it to the ships, but they pursued us without mercy, and now only I am left," he sobbed.

Luxon, Ferran and Whitelaw exchanged concerned glances.

"Who are they, lad? What happened to your people?" Whitelaw asked softly.

Lipur wiped his eyes again before pointing at Luxon.

"They came from the east. Black sailed ships. A people who will stop at nothing until all the world is theirs. Their fleet arrived before sunset, we tried to fight them, but their wizards set fire to our ships. Their eyes glowed in the darkness."

Lipur looked at them with desperation.

"Sarpi? Out here?" Luxon said, his tone full of concern.

"We have to sail away from here. Turn back whence you came for all you're going to find out here is death," the sailor pleaded. Ferran tugged Luxon's sleeve, and the two men stepped out of the cabin.

"If the Sarpi came from the east, then that means they're ahead of us. The enemy must know our plans," Ferran said.

"How? We set sail as soon as we could after acquiring Asphodel."

"Perhaps Danon has plans for Tulin. I doubt his ambitions will end with just conquering Delfinnia. That maniac won't stop until the whole of Esperia is his."

A sinking feeling wormed its way into Luxon's stomach. He stepped back into the cabin.

"You must turn back!" the sailor cried.

"We cannot do that Lipur. Our homeland is in great peril too. We had hoped to find allies on Tulin, is there no one there that could help us?" Luxon asked softly.

Lipur looked away and once more, angrily wiped away tears. He stared at the floor for a few minutes before nodding his head.

"Aye. There may be some. Despite what they claim, the Empire does not rule all Tulin. The Free Kingdoms oppose it, as do the Shars of Silenzia. Although" he paused "they were supposed to protect us. We were their vassals, and they did nothing," he finished bitterly.

"Do you think you could help us find our way to them?" Whitelaw asked. "I'm a stranger to these waters, so having some local knowledge would be a big help. At least when it comes to avoiding hidden reefs and rocks."

Lipur nodded his head slowly.

"I can help you, but only if you agree to help me."

"And how can we do that?" Ferran said, crossing his arms.

"These Sarpi took my people-I want your help to get them back."

"Attacking Sarpi forces wasn't part of our plan." Ferran interrupted an eyebrow raised.

"There was a big war between them and the southern realms for dominance of the seas. It ended in a stalemate with neither side gaining the upper hand. You must understand that the Shardom is no friend to the Sarpi. Although, I wouldn't put it past them to have bought slaves off the Sarpi. They don't care where the bodies come from, and they're more than happy to get rich from the trade."

"A lovely place we're visiting," Whitelaw said sarcastically.

Luxon excused them from Lipur's cabin and led the way to the captain's quarters to discuss what they had heard. Whitelaw threw himself into his worn looking armchair and placed his booted feet on his desk. Ferran paced the room whilst Luxon was sitting on one of the couches that were covered in opulent cushions.

"So," he began, "We now know that Tulin is a land divided and that there are various factions opposed to one another. We also know that the Sarpi are enemies to the peoples here, which can only work in our favour."

Whitelaw leaned forward and poured himself a glass of Robintan wine. He swished the liquid around before swallowing it in a single gulp.

"How does that help us? This Shardom may be powerful, but they sound just as bad as the Sarpi. Slavers? By Niveren, that barbaric practice was halted over three hundred years ago in Delfinnia."

"It helps us because we can potentially exploit those rivalries. We need allies, and to do that we're going to have to take sides," said Ferran. Luxon held up a hand and shook his head.

"Not necessarily. We need more information before we can even contemplate that. I want to learn more about these Kingdoms. If they are what Lipur says they are, they could be a great help against Danon. Then again, the Shardom must be powerful too. I say we go to this Silenzia and learn as much as we can about the situation on the continent. Perhaps an opportunity will present itself?"

Ferran stopped his pacing.

"Let's hope we've not left one war to find ourselves in the middle of another," he said ominously.

*

The *Agatha* glided through the bright blue waters of the Boundless Sea. Lipur had directed the ship to sail south, and within a few days, the cold weather turned warmer. The colour of the sea also changed as the dark blue of the violent northern seas gave way to bright aquamarine and calmer waves. With every mile travelled, the climate grew warmer and warmer, causing Luxon to surmise that they must be drawing close to Esperia's equator. No one from Delfinnia had travelled those waters in centuries, and he couldn't help but feel the thrill of adventure.

"Land ahoy!" shouted the lookout in the ship's crow's nest.

Luxon looked up and followed the direction the man was pointing. Sure enough, on the horizon and emerging through the morning mists was the shape of a landmass. Whitelaw moved to the rail to stand next to him.

"Well, slap me down and call me a kipper, Lipur was correct with his directions," the captain said before bellowing orders to the crew. "Hopefully, there's a port nearby where we can resupply."

Lipur stood on the deck and stared at the distant landmass. Unlike the jubilation of the *Agatha's* crew, he looked pale and more than a little afraid. Luxon walked over to him.

"I had hoped to never return to this place again," Lipur said. "My people thought they'd escaped the reach of the Tulin Empire and the Shardom's slavers. Now, here I am on a boat full of strangers sailing straight back into their clutches."

"I am sorry Lipur, but our homeland is in terrible danger, and if it should fall, that evil will come here too. We have to try and convince the peoples of these lands to help us."

Lipur leaned heavily against the ship's rail and sighed.

"Is fighting one evil with another truly going to save your home? The Tulin Empire has always sought to dominate the continent. Only the Free Kingdoms have kept it in check."

"Free Kingdoms? You mentioned them before. Tell me about them," Luxon asked, his curiosity piqued.

"Well, I say Free Kingdoms, they're just a bunch of squabbling realms that only hate two things more than they hate each other, and that's the Empire and the Shardom. Let me think; there's the Kingdom of Dilar that's ruled by Queen Merith, they're a strange bunch whose society revolves mostly around courtly love and chivalry. There's Vinium, more a collective of pirates than a kingdom and then there's Kastador. A realm that I suppose you could say is experiencing something of a golden age under the reign of King Thorn."

"You seem to know a lot," Luxon said, admiring the man's knowledge. In Delfinnia, it was rare to encounter such a well-travelled individual. Typically, only traders, adventurers and soldiers travelled extensively.

"Yeah, well, a life spent at sea will do that to a man, I guess. If I remember rightly, the land over there is Arbagon and to the west, up the great river is the Free Kingdoms. To the south is Silenzia and their accursed slave markets."

CHAPTER 3.

It took the *Agatha* another two days before it reached the seas of Silenzia. With Lipur's guidance, Whitelaw sailed the ship toward the Shardom's capital city of Shim. The sea was bright turquoise, and the sun beat down on the deck. Luxon surmised that they had sailed south of the equator. He stood on the ship's prow savouring the sun, and the warm wind assaulting his face. In his hands, Luxon held a notebook and pencil. He'd already made a few notes and sketches. If he closed his eyes, it felt like he was flying. Leaping and racing alongside the ship was a pod of dolphins with an infectious playfulness. He couldn't help but smile.

"You look happy," came a voice from behind him. He turned his head to see Sophia walking towards him. The witch hunter looked in far better shape than she had during the storm. Her black hair was tied up in a bun, and her grey eyes regarded him with amusement.

"I know I shouldn't be, what with all that's going on back home, but I can't help but feel excited. We are the first Delfinnians to reach the equator in what must be hundreds of years. We're rediscovering an entire world."

Sophia leant on the rail and took a deep breath of the fresh sea air.

"Ever the scholar. We should take these moments while we can. I have a feeling; we won't be getting much rest in the coming days."

Luxon nodded in agreement.

"After all we've been through, I think we can handle whatever this new land can throw at us," he said with more conviction than he felt.

A shout came from the crow's nest, causing them to look at the coast. The steep cliffs the *Agatha* had been following the past few days had given way to reveal a wide bay. On the shore was a city with its sandstone towers shimmering in the heat rolling off vast dunes that surrounded it. In the bay itself were dozens of small fishing boats and skiffs gliding through the water. The wide bay made the perfect harbour. Several piers reached far out to sea and docked at their side were several large ships with triangular sails.

"The city of Zlegend, the capital of the Shardom of Silenzia," said Lipur as he joined them at the bow of the ship. "A city of slavers, riches and the bizarre. You must be cautious."

The *Agatha* cut through the waters and turned towards the city. As they drew nearer, they could hear gulls crying on the gentle breeze and the ringing of bells. Under Whitelaw's skilful command the ship manoeuvred into the harbour. Several small skiffs came up alongside, on their decks were men with long beards and dark skin all trying to show off their wares in the hope of landing a sale. To Luxon's surprise, the men spoke a form of heavily accented Nivonian. He could just about understand their words. Finally, the ship slowed to a stop at one of the quaysides and Whitelaw gave the command to lower the *Agatha's* anchor. Once the ship had come to a stop and was safely moored, Ferran called Luxon and the others together. Lipur joined them; his knowledge of this strange land would be invaluable.

"We need to be careful here so we must be as discreet as possible. Me, Welsly and Sophia will check out the lay of the city and get our bearings. All weapons are to be concealed so only daggers for you, my love,' he said, looking at Sophia. "Luxon and Eripa, no use of magic. We don't know what the rules are here and the last thing we want is this land's version of the Knights of Niveren coming after us." Luxon and Eripa nodded in agreement.

"What about me?" asked Alderlade with eager eyes. Ferran and Luxon exchanged a look that suggested that they would prefer he stayed put. Alderlade noticed.

"No. I am not staying on this ship. I want to see this new world. As your king, I say that I will go with Luxon and Eripa," he said with hands firmly planted on his hips. Ferran was about to argue, but Luxon stopped him.

"You can come with me. But make sure you stay close and do exactly what I tell you." Alderlade whopped for joy and hopped on the spot excitedly. Ferran rolled his eyes.

"Right then, let's get back to business shall we," the Nightblade said, shaking his head disapprovingly. "We need to learn a few things. Firstly, who rules these lands and secondly the political situation here.   "

"An assessment of their military strength wouldn't hurt either not to mention whether they are capable of sending a sizable force across the oceans," added Welsly.

"I know this city pretty well,' said Lipur nervously, 'many of my kin have been sold here over the years."

*

Luxon and the others disembarked the *Agatha*. Each of them wore brown cloaks that they hoped would help them blend in. Captain Whitelaw had already set about finding supplies for the vessel and was haggling with one of the many merchants who set up shop on the quayside.

"We will meet back here at sunset," Ferran said. "If anything goes wrong, we head back here and hope that Whitelaw can get us away in a hurry. Good luck to us all and may Niverin watch over us."

With that Ferran, Sophia and Welsly said their farewells and set off towards the city. Luxon, Eripa, Alderlade and Lipur were left on the quayside.

"So Lipur, where should   go first?" Eripa asked. She too wore a brown cloak, but even with such a bland garment, she still stood out with her blue eyes and striking blonde hair. Already she was getting strange looks from some of the locals. Strapped to her back was her lute and on her hip was a dagger. Lipur too was armed, and Luxon had Asphodel in its scabbard attached to his belt.

"The Bazaar is a good place to start if you seek information. Travellers from all over congregate there to do business and trade."

"Sounds good. Lead the way," Luxon said.

Together they walked toward the city proper. It was protected by a massive sandstone wall that ran the length of the city's boundaries save for an opening where the harbour was situated. Wide circular towers were placed every two hundred meters, and each was topped with crenellations that provided excellent cover for the city's defenders in case of attack. A paved road made from sandstone led from the harbour up a hill to a wide squat gatehouse. The road was packed with men and women wearing a plethora of colourful clothing. Some wore long robes of patterned silks; others wore long capes and turbans that protected their heads from the sun. A wide variety of pack animals mixed with the people, the smell was almost overpowering and the noise near deafening. Alderlade kept close to Luxon as they moved through the bustling crowd. Eventually, they reached the gatehouse where two extremely bored looking guards kept watch. Both men wore gilded pointed helmets and mail shirts over a bright yellow cloth. Each held a ten-foot-long spear and on their belts hung exotic looking swords. Unlike Delfinnian longswords, these were curved and wider. They looked like the much smaller sabres used by the Yundol raiders. The guards paid them no heed, and they entered the city proper. Luxon couldn't be impressed at the sight that greeted them. The road split into three with the middle section sloping downward and the other two sections running to the left and right in wide semicircles. Along the side of the sloping road were tall structures that judging by the amount of washing hanging from lines was residential in nature. To the left were vast gated compounds that no doubt belonged to the city's nobles. Lavish gardens could be seen beyond tall iron barred fences. Trees covered in strange yellow flowers that smelt deliciously sweet lined each side of the road providing the city's residents with shade and refuge from the relentless sun. The road that split to the right curved as well but structures that were used for administration lined the pavements. One was a towering building covered in flags and banners of a multitude of colours and a massive statue of a woman her arms spread wide dominated the landscape.

"A statue to the Goddess Aniron," Lipur explained. "The Shardom of Silenzia worships the old gods still. They believe that men are not deserving of worship, even Niveren. To them, Niveren is a hero to be revered but nothing more."

Luxon took in the statue, his eyes filled with wonder. It was beyond anything the masters of Delfinnia could craft and made the statues in Sunguard look, well, pathetic in comparison.

"What do they think of Danon?" Eripa asked. The bard too, was admiring the city's architecture.

Lipur spat in disgust.

"He is evil, the great betrayer of all mankind. The Shardom has no love for him or his followers."

"Well, that's promising,' Luxon said, 'perhaps we can find allies here after all."

They moved on, choosing to follow the central road down towards what Lipur called the Bazaar district. Sure enough, the procession of pack animals increased dramatically as they descended. The noise grew in volume, and the smells of exotic spices grew in potency. Street entertainers plied their craft desperate to earn a coin from the passing shoppers. Alderlade stopped in front of one, a man who held a long sword in one hand and a flaming torch in the other. Luxon joined the boy and watched as the performer flicked his wrist to send the sword spinning high into the air. With the deadly blade soaring high, the man, much to the surprise and delight of the growing crowd raised the flaming torch and swallowed the flame. Then, with incredible skill, he spun, raised his free hand, and nimbly caught the sword by the hilt. The crowd cheered at the spectacle, Alderlade among them. Luxon too was impressed.

Once at the bottom of the slope, the road evened out, leading into a vast circular space that was packed with people. Tall, whitewashed buildings loomed over the Bazaar, and some were so tall that they reached the higher levels of the city that could be seen above. Tall wooden winches stood at several points overlooking the Bazaar and as Luxon watched a wooden platform filled with goods and pack animals was being lowered down from the top level. Market stalls of all shapes and sizes stood in groups at the side of the road selling a vast array of strange and exotic looking produce. At the center was a tall tower built from stone from which water poured from the top to fall into a sparkling lake at its base. Atop of that was a statue of a woman dressed in the garb of a Silenzian. Vegetation and spectacular flowers grew at intervals in the side of the structure and water poured majestically into vast pools beneath. Some children swam in the waters, and several dozen adults were sitting under umbrellas around the edges of the pool.

"The Fountain of Alize," Lipur said, noticing his companions' stunned expressions at the magnificent fountain. "Truly a wonder of the world no?"

Luxon couldn't help but nod in agreement. The fountain was truly spectacular, and as they walked closer, he could see that the tower was comprised of different rings. Into them were carved hollows in which hundreds of small brightly coloured birds used for nests. Stunningly beautiful flowers in which insects flitted to and fro grew on vines stretching from the top to the waters at the base. Alderlade brushed past Luxon and ran to the lake. A sense of panic filled Luxon as the boy disappeared amongst the crowd. He called after the King and shoved his way through the masses to keep him in view. To his relief, the lad was standing at the edge of the lake. He and the others hurried over to him.

"Don't do that again, Alderlade," he scolded.

"Sorry," the boy muttered sheepishly.

The clear glistening waters of the lake were filled with dozens of fish. Some were tiny, and others were huge, one was almost as big as a shark. All were brightly coloured. One that had scales that glistened luminous green in the light swam close to where they stood on the bank. It regarded them with huge bulbous eyes before diving under the water and vanishing from sight.

"How deep is it?" Eripa asked in wonder.

"Deep enough to drown in," came a gruff voice from behind them.

A man with brown skin and wearing the loose clothing of a local stood behind them. He bowed deeply in greeting.

"Forgive me for interrupting. I noticed your party at the docks and was hoping to speak with you. It is not every day that a vessel such as yours makes harbour in our fair city. My name is Yazid of the house of Shur."

Luxon stepped in front of Alderlade protectively, his hand moving to rest on Asphodel's pommel. Eripa too touched the dagger on her waist. Lipur meanwhile cowered behind the bard.

"Greetings,' Luxon said cautiously. "How can we be of service?"

Yazid smiled to reveal a set of pearly white teeth.

"I merely wish to speak with you. I can tell this is your first time in the city. Walking around wide-eyed and open-mouthed is a clear indication that you are not from around here no? Your attire tells me that you wished not to stand out, but the dourness of your cloaks makes you stand out even more. And your accent tells me that you are not from the south, north or perhaps not even from this land at all."

Luxon tensed as several burly men pushed their way through the crowds to take up positions around them. Some carried sabres, whilst others wielded spears.

"Who are you exactly?" he asked.

The fact that the men had not attacked them outright and whilst they'd be completely unawares made him hesitate. The last thing they needed was to cause a commotion in the first city they visited.

Yazid spread his arms wide, gesturing to the men to relax.

"Conversation is so much more civilised than violence. I thank you for realising this young man. As I said, my name is Yazid, and I am the chief Inquisitor of the city of Shim and captain of the Shah of Silenzia's personal guard. It is my job to question any strangers, such as yourselves in these ominous times. Please, come with us," the tall man said with a smile that didn't quite reach his eyes.

Eripa tensed, but Luxon gestured at her to stay calm. It was Alderlade who stepped forward. The small boy pushed his way past Luxon to stand before the surprised Yazid.

"I am Alderlade. King of Delfinnia and I demand you let us go," he said with his chest puffed out and hands on hips. Luxon couldn't help but smile at the sight and the comedic expressions of shock on the men's faces.

Yazid stared at the boy, but Alderlade's stern gaze did not falter. To everyone's surprise, Yazid stepped back and bowed deeply.

"Forgive me, King Alderlade. I assure you we mean no offence. Your companions may keep their weapons if that will set you more at ease."

Alderlade looked to Luxon, the nervous young boy once more. Luxon nodded.

"Er-I-yes that is acceptable. Lead on," he said.

Yazid faced his men and clapped his hands. As quickly as they appeared, they stepped back into the crowds and vanished from view.

"Please; your majesty, follow me."

CHAPTER 4.

The sixteen-year-old Shar of Silenzia, Yazim the twenty-third had a problem. Sitting on his ivory throne, he regarded the strange band of foreigners with curious eyes and hoped against hope that they could help him. He wore the ornately decorated robes of his office complete with a tall golden crown inlaid with dozens of precious stones atop his head. The crown looked far too big for the child wearing it. Around the Shar's neck was a thick golden chain and hanging from it a strange metallic disk inlaid with runes. Luxon frowned as he saw it, he could sense powerful magic radiating from it.

The palace's throne room was a vast vaulted chamber carved out of white marble. The bones of some of the desert's vast predators adorned the ceiling, and the banners of the hundred great houses of the Shardom lined the red carpet leading to the throne. Stood before the Shar was Luxon, Alderlade, Ferran and Sophia. The Nightblade and Witch hunter's group had also been apprehended during their explorations of the city. Their plan to blend in and go unnoticed had failed utterly. Now, here they were, standing in front of a foreign King and surrounded by potential foes. A full platoon of the Shar's bodyguards lined the throne room, their hands resting on the hilts of their sabres, ready to act at the first hint of trouble. Behind the guards were hundreds of men and women, the Shardom's nobility. All were there to see the foreigners. Lipur and Eripa were being held outside of the throne room under armed guard. An insurance policy Yazid had said, in case they proved hostile toward the Shar. In effect, they would have to do whatever the Shar commanded of them if their friends were to remain safe.

A few moments of awkward silence passed as the young King regarded his strange guests. Finally, he spoke in a voice that had not yet deepened to a man's. "I welcome you to my realm. My advisor Gatiz tells me that you have travelled from across the Boundless Sea from lands long lost to history. Judging by the weapons, you carry, I see that you are warriors."

Gatiz bowed at the mention of his name. The man was middle aged with a set of piercing blue eyes and a head of black curly hair that reached his shoulders. A smartly trimmed beard offset his handsome face, and he wore a brightly coloured robe as an indicator of his high office. He couldn't place it, but Luxon immediately disliked the man.

"Beware of Gatiz. The man is a snake," Yazid whispered from behind him.

Luxon stepped forward, he didn't want the Shar to have the wrong impression of them, but the Shar held up a hand.

"My lands require warriors," the Shar said suddenly.

Luxon glanced at Ferran. The Nightblade raised an eyebrow, he too was curious.

"Forgive me. May I speak," Luxon said politely. The Shar nodded.

"You may."

"We are from the lands that your history most likely records as Nivonia. We are on a desperate mission to seek aid. The armies of Danon have conquered our homeland; we cannot fight him alone."

The room filled with surprised gasps at the mention of the Dark Lord. To his credit, the Shar retained his composure. Gatiz approached the throne and whispered into his King's ear.

"Danon was cast into the Void by the great hero Zahnia. What you say is impossible," Gatiz said.

Luxon closed his eyes for a moment to gather his thoughts. If he were in their position, he too would be disbelieving. Danon had been nothing more than a myth to most of the people of Delfinnia until his minions were clawing at their doors.

"I wish that were so,' he said. He had to show them, prove to them what was happening. He focused and muttered an incantation. More surprised gasps filled the hall, and the Shar's bodyguards drew their swords as Luxon conjured a projection. Into it, he pushed his memories of all that had occurred since he first departed Caldaria all those years ago. Scenes, complete with sounds, showed the N'Gist, the brutal battles of Eclin and the fall of the Watchers and Danon himself at the head of his horde of evil flashed into life. The Shar and his people watched the scenes in horror. Finally, a stunned silence descended over the hall as the projection faded. The previously calm and composed Shar was now pale and grabbing the arms of his throne in a white-knuckled grip.

The Shar stared at Luxon, unable to hide the fear in his eyes. Gatiz leaned close to his liege and once more spoke in hushed tones. He too looked spooked.

"What you have shown us is most troubling,' the Shar said. "However, as my advisor says, the vision could just be that of magical trickery. I cannot commit to giving you the aid you seek without hard evidence."

Luxon's shoulders slumped in disappointment at the words. He turned as Alderlade tugged on his cloak.

"Show him the sword," the boy said his eyes bright.

A smile crossed Luxon's lip. Asphodel, the most famous blade in all history, now that would indeed be evidence.

"With your permission Great Shar I would like to show you something else," Luxon said.

The Shar exchanged a curious glance with Gatiz.

"Proceed."

Luxon took a deep breath and with one smooth motion drew Asphodel from its scabbard. Instantly, gasps came from the crowd as the golden blade caught the sunlight. The brightness of its glow filled the throne room, causing many to cover their eyes. As it always did, a sense of pure joy and tranquillity filled Luxon and all those close to the sword's influence. The Shar rose from his throne, his jaw-dropping in stunned awe.

"Behold Asphodel. Sword of Light, banisher of Darkness and the enemy of all evil. The blade wielded by Niveren, Zahnia and the Heroes of Old."

Some of the nobles fell to their knees; others stayed standing, openly weeping at the sacred blade's majesty. The effect Asphodel had on the righteous was one of euphoria, but for those with wickedness in their souls, it was like being held to a burning flame. Ferran shouted a warning as Gatiz screamed an inhuman screech. To the horror of the Shar, the terrible sound intensified as his advisor's skin began to blister and fill the room with the stench of burning flesh. The man fell to the ground to writhe around in agony. The Nightblade ran to the throne and stood over him. With a boot, Ferran pinned Gatiz in place and searched him. Sure enough, he pulled a dagger from the screaming nobleman's tunic and held it high for all to see. He then reached into his pockets and found a parchment of paper which he handed to the terrified Shar.

"Guards! Arrest Gatiz!" the Shar cried after reading the parchment. Two of the Shar's bodyguards hurried forward grabbing the now gibbering man and hauling him away. Luxon sheathed Asphodel, and the light dimmed. The feelings of euphoria faded too. Many of the gathered nobles shook their heads in confusion. Some remained on their knees with tears in their eyes. It was clear that what they had felt in the presence of the blade had been some sort of powerful religious experience.

"He was planning on assassinating me. This parchment proves it. The sigil: it is of the Morvan," the Shar said in disbelief. The crowd jeered the name.

"No, my Shar! I would never harm you!" pleaded Gatiz.

The man cried and sobbed, but the Shar ignored his begging. The room fell into stunned silence as Gatiz was dragged outside the chamber. The heavy doors slammed shut.

"Forgive me Great Shar, but who is the Morvan?" Luxon asked.

"They are a snake, a scorpion, a rival for my throne! A vile magic wielder who seeks to take my crown! Their people have been waging a guerrilla war against my realm this past year. Normally they keep to the desert vastness like the cowards they are, but now it seems they have sympathisers in my own court! You have saved my life master wizard from that traitor."

Hope grew in Luxon's heart that the Shar would agree to help them. Those hopes were quickly dashed when the King held up a hand.

"However, I cannot commit my nation to war across the sea. Not whilst the Devourer ravages my lands."

At the mention of the name the gathered nobles fell silent.

"For months now, it has made travel through the Silenzia Desert almost impossible. Entire trade caravans and even armies have been consumed by it. Until the beast is dead, I cannot help you."

Ferran perked up at the words. His trade was monster-slaying after all.

"Can you describe the beast? I am Ferran of BlackMoor, a Nightblade. I have hunted and killed many Fell Beasts of the Void over the years. Is this such a creature?" he asked.

Without his treacherous advisor at his side, the Shar looked lost and small sitting on his huge throne. He gestured to an elderly man standing amongst the nobles to step forward.

"This is Lord Yazti,' Shar introduced. 'Lord Yazti tell the foreigners what you know."

The elderly Yazti bowed deeply to his king before addressing Ferran. The man's dark skin was wrinkled like some ancient parchment, and the colour of his hair was that of freshly fallen snow.

"The beast moves through the desert sands at incredible speed. It is vast, taller than the highest of this city's mighty towers and its mouth is a vast cavernous maw lined with rows and rows of razor-sharp teeth. The desert has long suffered the Fell Beasts, but this creature is something else entirely."

"It cannot be killed," boomed a voice from the back of the room. Standing in the throne rooms doorway was a man clad in plate armour. His mantle embroidered with the emblem of a Blue bird-like creature was ripped and torn. His armour, too, was battered and dented. The man's face was covered in dirt and what looked like dried blood. The Shar rose from his throne and shook his head.

"Even the mighty Bannerlords of Kastador have failed me," the Shar moaned. "Lord Beric, what happened? You assured me that you and your company could slay the beast."

Beric looked away, unable to meet the young King's desperate eyes. He rubbed his shaved head and approached the throne. His long-tattered cape dragged on the floor as he went.

"The Devourer is a beast on a scale that I have never seen before. Giants and Striders, we can handle, but this thing? Our weapons might as well have been sticks for all the harm they did."

"Are you admitting defeat? If so, then the contract is forfeit, and you will not be paid as per our arrangement," the Shar replied, unable to hide a smirk.

'There's more to this relationship than meets the eye,' Ferran muttered into Luxon's ear.

Beric paced the floor in front of the throne. It was clear that admitting defeat was not something he did often.

"If I may?" said Luxon, interrupting the now heated conversation between the Shar and Bannerlord.

"Let us see this creature. Perhaps together, we can find a way to defeat it. That way, we all get what we want. Shar, your lands will be free from this beast. Lord Beric, you will have your honour intact and your contract fulfilled," he said.

The Shar and Beric looked at him for a moment.

"And what will you get out of this, stranger?" Beric asked suspiciously.

"If we help slay the beast, then we will want the support of the Shardom, and perhaps you could introduce us to your King."

Luxon exchanged a look with Ferran. He was utterly winging his way through these negotiations.

Beric regarded Luxon and the others for a few moments.

"My men need to rest and sort their gear. Meet us at the city's north gate tomorrow at dawn."

"Tomorrow at dawn it is," Luxon replied.

*

With the audience over, the Shar invited Luxon and the others to dine with him and offered to provide food and shelter for the *Agatha's* crew. Welsly returned to the ship to update Captain Whitelaw on all that had occurred. Within the hour the crew arrived at the palace. Now they found themselves in the Shar's private wing of the palace. As with the city beyond its walls, the architecture of the place was impressive. Intricate mosaics covered the floors, and monumental paintings adorned the whitewashed walls. The dining hall was filled with the city nobility, invited by the Shar to meet his strange guests. As they ate and drank the opulent food that was served to them by slaves, Lipur was quiet. He was too busy checking every man and woman in chains to see if they were one of his people. He rose from his seat and walked over to Luxon. He leaned in close so that he could be heard over the din of the partygoers.

"I cannot stay here. Seeing these people in chains makes my stomach turn. I will head back to the ship and stay there. Good luck on performing the Shar's errand," Lipur said with a hint of bitterness in his tone.

Luxon too felt no joy as his thoughts drifted to home, Hannah and Yepert. His best friend had always enjoyed such feasts; it felt strange to be at one without him by his side. He watched Lipur leave, and his mood worsened.

The *Agatha's* crew, however, were having the time of their lives as they were waited on hand and foot. Some of the sailors were being entertained by scantily clad dancing girls, their raucous cheers audible over the din of conversation. The wine was flowing, and it wasn't long before Silenzians and Delfinnians alike began to sing songs. The lyrics in many of them were surprisingly similar as they mentioned events from a time when the two lands had been in close contact with one another thanks to the Golden Empire. Sitting with the Shar was Ferran, who was deep in conversation with the young king. As the evening wore on and the stars began to fill the sky. The now rowdy crew of the *Agatha* called for Eripa to sing. The famous bard agreed, and soon her melodic voice enraptured the dinner guests. Her song was about Delfinnia and all that had occurred. It was the Ballad of the Sundered Crown. To Luxon's embarrassment, he was mentioned several times, but soon he too was lost in her voice. He wept as the song became a lament for the city of Eclin. He could still see the broken bodies of the brave men and women who had fallen in its defence when he slept. The song rose in tempo as Eripa sang of how the city was saved by the dragon Umbaroth and the Heroes of Eclin. She sang of the fall of the Watchers, of how Danon and his evil had swept across the land. It was a song that told of war, sacrifice, and despite everything, hope. It was a song to elicit emotion from all who listened; it was a song designed to get their desperation across.

When the ballad had ended, the room was silent as every person contemplated the words. Finally, the Shar himself began to clap. Others followed suit until the room was filled with thunderous applause. The Shar stood and banged his goblet on the table.

"My people. My new friends. I vow that if you can slay the Devourer, I will provide you with the Silenzia Fleet. Three hundred war galleys and an army to go with it. Also, if you can convince others to help you, we will provide enough ships to carry their warriors across the Boundless Sea," he said, slightly slurring his words.

Luxon couldn't help but join in the cheers at his words. Such a fleet would be a match for the Sarpi navy that had ravaged and strangled Delfinnia's coasts. The feast went on deep into the night, and it wasn't until the early hours that Luxon and the others found their beds.

CHAPTER 5.

The next morning Luxon awoke with a stinker of a headache. Groggily he rose from the comfortable bed and staggered over to the stained-glass window. The light of the early dawn filtered through the red and yellow panels to cast the room in fiery orange. He opened the window and breathed in the fresh air. The Shar had been generous to his guests, providing them with rooms in a wing of the palace. Below his room was the palace gardens, and the scent of hundreds of different flowers and spices wafted into his nostrils. He closed his eyes and focused and used his magic to clear the alcohol from his system. With the effects of the alcohol removed, he felt refreshed and ready to face the challenges of the day ahead. He went into the bathroom and to the marble sink. Running water was extremely rare back in Delfinnia, but here, in this palace built at the edge of a desert, he could turn a tap and water would flow. He splashed his face, marveling at the coolness of the liquid. He would have to ask the Shar how they kept it cool in such heat. The sun had only just broken the horizon, and already the temperature was beginning to climb. After washing, he put on his clothes, a light linen shirt and trousers and pulled on his boots. Finally, he took his green wizard's cloak off the peg in the wall and slid it over his broad shoulders. The garment was not ideal in such heat, but thanks to its ability to store magical energy, he was able to keep himself cool with a gentle enchantment of ice. Once dressed, he ate some fruit from the silver platter left at his bedside and prepared himself for the day ahead. Leaving the chambers, he found himself in a wide spacious hallway lined with arches that looked out onto the palace's interior gardens. Leaning against one of the arches was Ferran.

"Sleep well?" the Nightblade asked.

"Very well, I daresay it was the best night's rest I've had in months," Luxon replied with a yawn and a stretch.

"That Bannerlord is waiting for us in the outer courtyard. The Shar has insisted that Sophia and the others wait here until we return."

Luxon raised an eyebrow at that.

"Hostages?"

Ferran nodded and started walking towards the end of the hallway.

"That's my thinking too. Despite the young Shar's generosity, I don't think he's a pushover. We need to be cautious. All his talk of providing a fleet and troops means nothing until he delivers, and I suspect he won't unless we do what he wants."

Luxon nodded in agreement. Nothing in life was free. He'd met enough powerful men that talked the big talk and who often failed to deliver to not trust the Shar implicitly.

The two men walked through the palace and down a flight of sandstone steps leading to the exterior of the palace and into a large courtyard. To the right-hand side was a stable and to the left a series of workshops. The sound of hammering metal reverberated off the whitewashed walls and the smell of burning charcoal filled the air.

Loitering around the courtyard were a dozen men all dressed in plate armour. Each of them had a mantle over the armour emblazoned with a blue eagle-like creature that Luxon had never seen before.

The shaven haired Lord Beric hailed them and gestured for them to follow him and his men.

"Come. We have a short walk ahead of us."

Luxon fell into the step with the tall man.

"Forgive my ignorance Lord Beric, but what is that creature on your mantle?"

Beric looked at him in surprise.

"You don't have Gryphons where you're from? They are our King's sigil and no finer beasts could you hope to meet. Fierce in battle and loyal companions, a Gryphon will never let you down. They live in Kastador's Gryphon mountains and are very picky as to who they serve. Only a rare few people have ever been allowed the honour of riding them into battle. And what a sight they are," the Bannerlord said in a reverent tone.

"Have you flown one?" Luxon asked.

Beric's eyes looked distant for a moment before he nodded with a wistful smile.

"Aye, I did once. Sadly, my Elipsis fell in battle, and I've never been able to bond with another since. There's nothing like flying lad."

"Oh, I know. I've ridden dragons a few times," Luxon said simply. Beric stopped dead in his tracks.

"Dragons? They're nothing but legends," he said.

Luxon exchanged a glance with Ferran.

"No dragons have come as far as Tulin?" the Nightblade asked.

"Well, there have been stories from the north about great winged reptiles, but no one in Kastador has ever seen one. I imagine they're something special to behold indeed."

"You have no idea," Luxon said. "Forgive my asking Lord Beric, but I'm a bit confused as to what exactly a Bannerlord is?"

"You don't have warriors where you're from?" Beric replied.

"Well, yes, we have many, but none called Bannerlords."

"This-" Beric pointed to the sigil on his mantle. "- is the Banner of my lord. Each of my company serves King Thorn, but there are many Banners. We are elite warriors who above all serve Kastador, but in times of peace, our lords can seek service elsewhere. As King Thorn is currently overseeing a 'golden period' of peace and prosperity there hasn't been much need for us warriors, which is why he offered the Shar our services," he said unable to hide a hint of bitterness in his tone.

Luxon scratched his head.

"So, you're mercenaries? But really skilled ones," he added quickly so as not to cause any offence.

"You could say that I suppose," Beric chuckled.

After a few minutes, the small group reached the city's northern gate and stepped through.

Ahead of them for as far as the eye could see was sand. Giant sand dunes, the size of mountains loomed in the distance, and the horizon shimmered in the early morning heat.

"How are we supposed to traverse the desert?" Luxon said dumbly. He didn't fancy having to walk under the baking sun.

As if to answer his question, a cloud of dust and sand appeared on the eastern horizon. He narrowed his eyes and was stunned to see that the cloud was racing towards them. Ploughing through the sands as though it were water were three huge creatures. One leapt from the sand and high into the air eliciting a loud, mournful tone that swept across the vast desert. Great clouds of sand were thrown in all directions as it crashed back down.

Finally, the vast creatures slowed to a stop in front of them. Sitting astride their backs were men dressed from head to toe in bright yellow cloth, only their eyes could be seen, and a set of goggles protected those. In their right hands, they carried long curved poles that they used to convey instructions to the creatures.

Luxon approached the creature that had stopped closest to him awed by its size. A large eye filled with intelligence watched him.

"You are very impressive," he said in awe. He placed a hand against its grey skin and marveled at its texture.

"It's a Sand Whale. They live much like their cousins that rule the seas, only they live in the sands of the desert rather than the oceans," Beric explained as he and his men began to climb onto the other whales' backs. Luxon took the Whale Rider's offered hand and clambered onto the back of the whale in front of him. A harness ran down the length of its long body, and a series of seats was attached to it. Luxon sat down, and the Whale Rider strapped him in, Ferran took the seat behind him. The Rider then handed them both a pair of goggles like the ones he was wearing.

"Well, this is a first. I thought I'd seen everything there is to see," Ferran said as he put his goggles on. He'd been to every dark corner of Delfinnia and never had he seen such a beast.

The Whale Rider then tapped the whale's head three times, and with a lurch, they were off. The speed of the creatures was incredible. They glided through the sands like a fish through water. Luxon's hair flapped wildly, and he could not help but whoop in exhilaration. The desert passed by on all sides in a yellowish blur. As the Whale sped on it carved furrows in the dunes, piling up sand in towering piles either side of it. With a flick of his rod, the Whale Rider instructed their steed to rise, and with a loud songlike noise, the creature responded. It burst through a bank sending sand flying in all directions but once through they were now in the vast desert proper.

Similar furrows crisscrossed the landscape suggesting that the Sand Whales were common to this part of the desert. The ride was far from comfortable, Luxon's bum barely staying in the seat throughout. He glanced over his shoulder to see Ferran laughing in exhilaration at the ride. The Nightblade smiled a boyish grin. In all the years' Luxon had known the man he'd never seen him so happy. The city had now vanished in the distance, and only golden sand dunes could be seen from horizon to horizon. The wind whistled past Luxon so loud that he almost missed the warning shout made by the Whale Rider in front of him.

Suddenly, one of the sandbanks exploded outwards and a monster the likes he'd never seen before came screeching from it. It was like a giant worm covered in thick bony armoured plates and vicious razor-sharp spikes. The head was nothing but a cavernous maw of deadly snapping teeth. The Rider cried out, only just guiding the Whale out of the reach of the Devourer. With a thunderous boom, the Devourer crashed back down beneath the dunes sending clouds of sand flying in all directions. The whale sped on through the dunes, the Devourer hot on its heels. Luxon glanced over his shoulder and instantly regretted doing so. All he could see and gaining quickly was that cavernous teeth filled mouth. Ferran too was looking over his shoulder, but unlike himself, there was no fear on the Nightblade's face. Instead, his brow was knotted in concentration. The master monster hunter was studying every detail of the creature, analyzing it for any visible weakness. The Rider spurred the Whale to veer sharply to the right causing the less nimble Devourer to speed past. It let out a frustrated screech before arching around in an attempt to re-engage its prey. Luxon pushed himself up in his seat, his arms trembling against the forces trying to pin him down. Ahead was a rocky outcropping. The Devourer couldn't travel through stone.

"Head toward the outcropping!" he shouted to the panicking rider.

With a crack of the rod, the Whale veered to the right and sped toward the rocks.

"Get ready to jump!" Luxon shouted. He followed words with action and unsnapped the harness holding him into place. Ferran likewise detached himself. It was hard to move as the speed of the Sand Whale threatened to pin them into their seats. Luxon narrowed his eyes and channelled his magic into creating a shield that enveloped him, Ferran and the rider. The G-forces immediately eased, allowing them to move more freely. He grabbed the rider's hand, and Ferran gripped onto his cloak tightly. The outcropping approached, and Luxon jumped. With masterful skill, he cast a levitation spell that launched them high into the air and off the terrified Whale's back. They floated across the sand and onto the high rocky cliff. A solitary dead tree stood on the peak to offer some much-needed shelter from the blazing hot sun. Once they were safely on the rock, the Whale dived beneath the sand desperate to escape the monster. Strangely, the Devourer allowed the Whale to go; its attention was fixed on them.

"I can't be the only one who thinks it strange that such a beast would be more interested in us than such a large potential meal," Ferran remarked.

Luxon crouched and watched the Devourer as it circled the outcropping. In its huge armoured head was a solitary red eye that was fixed on them. He closed his eyes and focused on the monster. There was a familiar presence emanating from it, one that he'd hoped they would not encounter so far from Delfinnia.

"N'Gist magic," he muttered. There was no mistaking it. The gnashing monster below was one made from the darkest sorcery.

A shout came from below. Sir Beric and the other Bannerlords had arrived. Hastily they disembarked their Sand Whale and hurried toward the rocks. To Luxon's surprise, the Devourer ignored them.

"Er, it seems to like you, Luxon," Ferran said.

The Bannerlords clambered up the outcropping and joined them at the top.

"There's the hideous beast," wheezed Beric. Despite the desert heat he and his companions were wearing their plate armour. On their backs in packs was an array of weaponry.

The Devourer's red eye stared unblinking at the outcropping it's body eerily still.

"I trust it didn't do this when you first encountered it?" Ferran asked Beric.

"No. When we faced it, the beast attacked without mercy. It ate our horses first and then two of our squires. The poor sots didn't stand a chance. Ah well-"

Beric said as he took a spear from one of his comrades "it's still as a rock now. Let's kill this thing."

His squire handed him a spear. Creeping to the edge of the outcropping, he drew back his arm and hurled the weapon with all his might. Just as the spear looked as though it would strike its intended target, the eye snapped shut. The spear struck an armoured shell to spin wildly and harmlessly off its surface. Beric swore loudly.

The eye opened again, and it stared at Luxon.

"What's up with this thing?" Beric grumbled, taking another spear from his comrades. The four Bannerlords stepped to the edge, and all hurled their spears. Again, the weapons bounced off its armoured shell.

"Let me try something," Ferran said as he conjured a fireball into existence. With a flick of the wrist, the magical projectile shot downwards to strike the Devourer. The flame engulfed the monster, but instead of it retreating in pain as expected, it began to vibrate.

To their surprise, the creature absorbed the flames, and with a sickening crack, the shell split, and it began to grow in height. It grew so high that now it's snapping jaws were just a few feet from the top of the outcropping.

"Er, let's not do that again," Beric cried.

Luxon stroked his chin in thought.

"It's an elemental," he said finally.

"A what?" Beric asked bemused.

"It's made from fire magic. Whoever created it used a fire spell, which means that heat. instead of harming it, will only make it stronger."

"So, logically the opposite of flame will be its weakness," Ferran added, stroking his chin.

"What we need then is water!" Beric exclaimed. "Except, we're in the middle of a desert...," Ferran pointed out.

"We could use the water in our drinking gourds," offered the Whale rider who had introduced himself as Nafir.

"We don't know if the water is definitely the way to fight this thing and I don't fancy our chances if we have no water out here," Ferran replied.

"Hmm, aha I have an idea! Eustice come here,"

Beric said gesturing for his steward to step closer.

"Now lad, this might hurt a bit," he said mysteriously before suddenly kicking the young man squarely and harshly in the balls. The lad crashed to the ground clutching his nether regions, but sure enough, tears sprang from his eyes.

"Nothing can guarantee a man to weep than a blow to the knackers!" the Bannerlord cackled. Ferran exchanged a bemused look with Luxon.

"I think we're going to need a bit more than what poor Eustice here can produce," Ferran chuckled.

"Why don't we piss on it?" offered one of the other Bannerlords.

Luxon shook his head, unable to stifle the smile on his lips. These Bannerlords were undoubtedly creative. He edged closer to the ledge and peered towards the horizon. The sea was many miles away and judging by the clear blue cloudless sky the chance of rain was nil.

"What about magic? Could you not summon a storm or something?" Beric suggested.

"Unfortunately, no. In theory, I could, but to do so, there still needs to be water close by," Luxon explained.

"There's moisture in the air," Ferran offered. "During my Nightblade training, we were taught how to capture moisture and turn it into drinking water. It may not feel like it now, but when night falls, it will get cool enough to create dew."

Luxon nodded.

"I could then use magic to draw it from the air."

They all looked up at the merciless sun. Nightfall was still a long way off.

*

The bare branches of the dead, dried up tree atop the outcropping barely provided enough cover from the sun. As the day worn on, the Bannerlords removed their mantles and draped them across the branches to provide some semblance of shelter. They were also dangerously close to using up all their provisions of water. The Shar had provided them with just enough supplies to last a day or two max; after all, it was supposed to have just been a scouting mission. All the while, the Devourer had remained unmoving, its red eye fixed on the outcropping and Luxon. Finally, the sun began to set, and with it, the temperature plummeted. Luxon sat on the ledge, his legs dangling over the side and just out of reach of the monster. He stared at it. Somehow, he knew that it was of the N'Gist; he could feel it in his bones. If he was right, then the enemy had reached Tulin before they had. The implications were troubling. Had Danon's servants established themselves here? Were they already too late?

"Quite a sight isn't it?" Ferran said from behind him, his breath emanating as mist in the near freezing air. Luxon turned and saw the Nightblade looking at the sky. He did likewise and gasped. The night's sky was spectacular. Millions of stars glinted against the blackness, and Esperia's two moons glowed brightly. Never had he seen them so clearly and in such detail. The desert sky was devoid of all clouds, and there was no light to dull the view. The darkness was everywhere; the stars just bright points of light like islands in a vast ocean. Luxon shuddered at memories of his strange journey on the Isle of Magic. He had seen the Goddess of Darkness in the flesh. Judging from the night's sky, she was winning in the eternal struggle between the light and dark.

"The old stories tell that other worlds are out there. Places like our own with peoples and creatures beyond imagining," Ferran said softly his eyes fixed on the twinkling points of light.

"I think I visited one," Luxon said.

Ferran looked at him and blinked. Luxon shrugged his shoulders.

"Whilst on the Isles of Magic I experienced something. It was as though Magic itself was showing me things, strange places. One of the portals took me to a place that at first looked like home. Green fields of grass, high mountains and a blue sky filled with white fluffy clouds. I encountered a woman there and creatures that looked like goblins."

Ferran crouched in front of him, fascinated by his tale.

"There was a dragon too, but it was different from Umbaroth and the others we know. It was more beast like and even more vicious."

"What makes you think it was another world?"

Luxon pulled his cloak tighter around himself and sighed heavily.

"There was only one moon, and when I tried to use my magic, it felt different somehow. It is hard to explain. I also went back in time, -I think—right to the beginning of mankind. I saw Niveren in the flesh and Danon himself as a younger man. I saw what happened, the wars at the beginning of time, his fall, all of it."

Ferran stared at him for a few moments. Sympathy was in his eyes.

"I know that sometimes I've been hard on you, Luxon. I cannot imagine the things you have been through and seen, but I want you to know that I will always have your back."

Luxon smiled. That was the first time the gruff Nightblade had ever shown some semblance of affection for him. A thought entered his mind and his smile faded.

"Are we doing the right thing, Ferran? Our friends are back in Caldaria at the mercy of Danon, and here we are on the other side of the world."

Ferran placed a hand on his shoulder.

"It's the only way. We need the help of these people if we're to have any chance against him. The mages will hold. They must."

"Forgive me for interrupting," said Beric. The Bannerlord approached them and offered them a bread roll each. Luxon took one gratefully, as did Ferran.

"It's not luxury, but it's better than nothing. I couldn't help but overhear your conversation. It sounds as though things are bad in your homeland. I cannot imagine what horrors you've encountered, but I reckon King Thorn will want to hear your tale."

"Your King would help us?" Ferran asked.

Beric shrugged his shoulders.

"I cannot speak for Thorn, but I've known him since we were boys. He's the best man I know, and he has a lot of pull with the other Kingdoms. Once this beast is dead, I'd be honoured to introduce you."

"Thank you, Beric," said Luxon. He stood and shook the warrior's hand. "Speaking of the beast, let's see if the cold has done its work."

He walked to the tree and the mantles hanging from the branches. He touched one. It was damp with moisture.

"Okay, this should do. Get the others and bring them to the edge of the cliff."

The other Bannerlords did as commanded and gathered on the cliff edge.

Luxon took several deep breaths, closed his eyes and channelled the magic within himself. He could sense the water trapped inside the cloth and with a spell drew the liquid out. The Bannerlords gasped in surprise as the water began to float in the air. Still concentrating, Luxon touched Asphodel's hilt to draw upon the power within the sacred blade. Once he'd drawn out as much moisture as possible, he thrust his hands upwards, sending the water high into the sky. Keeping the magical link with the liquid, he drew upon the dust and other material floating in the air and within moments clouds began to form. At first, they were thin wispy things, but as he focused harder, they rapidly grew.

"And now for the final ingredient," he muttered through gritted teeth. Focusing his magic, he created a spark and lightning shot from his other hand to strike the cloud. The clouds expanded until within a few short moments; they filled the sky. Flashes emanated from within and then with a loud rumble of thunder, it began to rain. A few drops fell to strike the dusty ground, and then it became a deluge.

"Rain in the desert! It's a miracle!" cried the awestruck Whale Riders. Luxon ignored the whoops and cheers of the others. His attention was fixed on the Devourer.

Rain struck the beast. At first, it looked as though his theory had been wrong, but then he noticed plumes of steam begin to rise from its armoured plates. A few more moments went by, and then the Devourer emitted a howl of pain. The rain was like acid to it.

"You were right, look, the water is melting away its armour!" Beric yelled over the noise of the increasingly violent thunderstorm.

Ferran clapped Luxon on the shoulder.

"My turn," he said before stepping to the cliff edge. With a snap-hiss, he ignited his Tourmaline sword. The magical blade shimmered brightly in the rain to drive back the darkness. Then, with the skill of a master monster hunter, the Nightblade leapt from the cliff. The wind whistled in his ears as he fell, but that didn't bother him. Instead, he was focused on the Devourer. Pulling back, he avoided the pained creature's snapping jaws, gripped his blade in a two-handed grip and stabbed it into the monster's now exposed flesh. Immediately, the impact slowed his descent, but barely as the blade carved downwards. Warm blood sprayed and agonized screams boomed until, with a thud, he landed on the sand below. Ferran turned to see his handy work. He'd carved a huge mortal wound into the Devourer's worm like body, which now writhed and twisted, until, with a screech, it crashed to the ground.

With a casual grace, he walked over to the wounded creature and stood in front of its large eye. Without remorse, he plunged his sword into it, and with a final shudder, the Devourer was dead.

CHAPTER 6.

As the sun began to rise, Luxon and the others spotted a plume of sand on the horizon. It grew closer until they could make out the form of a Sand Whale. The mighty creature slowed to a stop at the base of the rocky outcropping where they had spent the night. On the creature's back were Sophia and Captain Yazid. A squad of six Silenzia warriors were with them. At seeing the corpse of the Devourer, the captain and his warriors cheered.

Luxon and the others descended the steep outcropping and walked over to the new arrivals.

Sophia slid from the whale's back and ran to Ferran. She threw her arms about his shoulders and kissed him.

"I'm so glad you're all safe!" she cried. "When you didn't return, we feared the worst."

Ferran laughed.

"No giant sandworm thing is a match for Luxon the Legendary," he chuckled.

Yazid walked over to the dead Devourer and clapped Luxon on the shoulder. He shook his head in disbelief.

"For so long that monster has plagued our realm. The Shar will be delighted to hear of its demise. Who struck the killer blow?" he asked.

"That would be Ferran. I've never seen skill like it," Beric enthused as he joined them.

"You have done well. The Shar will be delighted. Come, you must be tired after your ordeal. My men shall escort you back to the city," the captain said.

Luxon thanked the captain and together with Ferran and the others gratefully clambered aboard the Sand whale. Within a few moments, they were on their way back to the city.

*

Drums and trumpets played, and people cheered as the Devourer's huge corpse was dragged through the city streets. Hauling it down the wide avenues were huge creatures with massive ears and long tensile snouts. The Elephants, as the Silenzians called them, were just another exotic sight to Luxon and the others. He and Ferran had been hailed heroes by the Shar and were now guests of honour at the riotous celebrations. Upon their return, they had feasted like kings, and now the Shar wanted to demonstrate to his people that he could get things done. They now stood on a balcony at the front of the Shar's palace. The young King was waving to his people and loving their adulation.

"The beast is dead, and now the way is open for my armies to destroy the villainous Morvan," he laughed. Luxon looked at Ferran.

"Forgive me Shar, but I thought you wanted the Devourer destroyed to reopen trade routes across the desert?"

"Oh, yes that too," the Shar said, not taking his eyes from the crowds.

*

The Crimson Blade assassin moved through the crowd, his distinctive cloak just another amongst the colourful attire of the Silenzians. Other Blades had infiltrated the city, waiting for their moment to strike. Men, women, and children were all cheering and dancing in the streets. No one noticed as he reached into his cloak and drew out the long blowpipe. To an observer, it would look like a flute or some other musical instrument, after all plenty of musicians mingled in the delighted crowd. His target was above him standing carelessly at the railing of the palace's balcony. The assassin placed the pipe to his lips, lined up the shot and using magic enhanced his breath. He blew and quickly dashed back into the crowd. He didn't need to see him fall; the shouts told him he'd succeeded.

*

"In the morning I will assemble my-" the Shar choked, his eyes widening. Sophia shouted a warning. Luxon looked on in horror. A dart had struck the Shar in the throat. He rushed forward, catching the young King before he fell to the ground. He pulled the dart from the Shar's neck and passed it to Ferran.

"This is a toxic dart. One used by the N'Gist!" the Nightblade snarled.

The Shar was turning blue, and blood began to pour from his nose and then his eyes.

"Assassin!" bellowed Captain Yazid, who rushed to his fallen King's side.

Luxon closed his eyes and placed a palm to the Shar's now violently shaking head. He rifled in his memory for anything Hannah or Master Ri'Ges had taught him about healing spells and toxins. He swore as he came up with nothing. He longed for Hannah to be with him; she would have known what to do.

"Is there nothing you can do?" Yazid cried, panic in his voice.

"Move him inside and send someone to find Eripa!" Luxon shouted.

"I'll go back to the ship. I might have something that could help," Sophia said before sprinting off through the palace.

"Hurry!"

The crowd below was none the wiser to what had occurred, the celebratory music and cheering a stark contrast to the horror taking place within the palace.

The guards carried the now unmoving Shar to his chambers and placed him carefully on the bed. Ferran rushed to his side and felt for a pulse.

"It's very faint and weakening with every passing moment."

Luxon leapt onto the bed and knelt over the Shar. He placed a hand to the boy king's forehead and muttered an incantation. He focused his magic into the Shar and tried desperately to neutralize the poison rushing through the boy's bloodstream.

"I can't stop the spread! It is moving too fast. Whatever it is, it's resistant to healing magic."

Ferran moved to the bedside and pulled a small vial containing a blue liquid from a pouch on his belt.

"Here, try this. It's the antivenom from a Puck bite, but it has other properties. It might slow the poison's spread and stop the bleeding."

Luxon took the vial and pulled out the stopper with his teeth before placing it to the Shar's now deathly pale lips. Tilting the Shar's head back, he parted his lips and poured the thick liquid down the boy king's throat.

"You're going to have to massage his throat to trigger the swallow reflex," Ferran instructed as he rooted through other pouches on his belt. A Nightblade always carried several healing potions and anti-toxins. Many of the Fell Beasts of the Void were venomous after all.

Luxon pulled the heavy golden necklace from the boy king's throat and did as instructed. The Shar swallowed. A few seconds passed, and then he began to cough violently. Blood erupted from his lips, and his eyes rolled back into his skull until only the whites could be seen.

"That didn't work Ferran!" Luxon cried. Desperation was threatening to overwhelm them. If the Shar died, then all their efforts of eliciting support from the powerful Shardom would be for nothing. Immediately he felt ashamed for his selfishness.

With one last violent spasm, the Shar let out a choked gasp before falling still. Eripa and Alderlade hurried into the chamber, but it was too late, the Shar had stopped breathing, and his eyes were wide open in a death stare.

A commotion came from the hallway and through the doors charged the Shar's advisor Gatiz. At his back were four Crimson Blades. Yazid drew his sabre.

"You should be in jail," he said, confusion in his voice.

The advisor smiled cruelly.

"Please, Yazid, drop your weapon. My allies freed me the moment these absurd celebrations began. The destruction of the Devourer has forced our hand. Now that the brat is dead, the N'Gist will take this realm."

Ferran ignited his Tourmaline blade.

Gatiz smirked.

"I wouldn't do that if I were you. Get the amulet and bring it to me," the treacherous advisor ordered. One of the Crimson Blades stepped forward, picked up the Shar's strange amulet and handed it to Gatiz.

"She will be most pleased," he said with a cruel chuckle.

A cacophony of swearing came from the hallway and then Eripa was shoved violently into the chamber quickly followed by a bloodied Welsly. Ten heavily armed Silenzian soldiers followed, their spears aimed menacingly at them. Yazid tried to reason with them, but Luxon knew they were lost. Their eyes were now nothing but dark slits; their minds lost to Dark Magic.

Cries and screams began to sound from outside the palace. Yazid rushed to the room's balcony. In the streets below were dozens of Crimson clad figures hacking and slashing their way through the now panicking crowds. He watched in horror as a squad of his men suddenly burst into flame. A tall woman wearing a bright yellow cloak advanced upon them, her hands raised. N'Gist were in the city and using magic!

"How could you do this?" Yazid cried.

"The Lord Danon cannot allow these foreigners to gather allies. They must be destroyed,' Gatiz replied his eyes fixing on Luxon 'and the sword retrieved.'"

"Not if I can help it," Luxon said defiantly. He drew Asphodel, its power immediately surging through him. As before, a blinding light filled the room, causing those tainted by the N'Gist to retreat in terror. Gatiz among them, the advisor fled the chamber screaming. The corrupted soldiers staggered in a daze but were quickly recovering. Now was their chance. Ferran dashed forward and engaged the stunned soldiers. He impaled one on his sword before they could recover their wits. Eripa got back to her feet and joined the fray. She threw herself at one of the soldiers and tried to wrestle his spear from his grip. Yazid hacked down one of the soldiers, his eyes filled with fury. Luxon knelt next to Welsly, but the Nightblade was concussed, and his eyes dazed.

"We need to get out of here!" he shouted over the sound of combat. Eripa swatted aside an enemy's spear with her short sword before Ferran impaled him on his blade. The bard dropped the spear and rushed over to help Luxon lift Welsly, and together they dragged him out of harm's way. Alderlade meanwhile watched the carnage with his mouth agape.

Ferran parried a spear thrust, grabbed the shaft, and pulled its wielder onto the tip of his sword. Shouts of alarm now came from within the palace as those untainted were mercilessly cut down. Yazid cut down the last corrupted soldier, and the way out of the chamber was now clear.

"Let's go!" he said, leading the way, sabre held at the ready.

Luxon passed Welsly to Ferran and took Alderlade by the hand.

"Stay close to me and whatever you do, don't run off," Luxon ordered. The boy nodded.

They exited the chamber to find the hallway empty save for the bodies of two of Yazid's men. Screams came from deeper within the palace, and outside it sounded like the end of the world. It was the sound of a city being sacked by a savage enemy.

*

They ran through the palace's marbled corridors towards the main hall and passed scenes of horror. N'Gist and Crimson Blades were moving room by room and slaying, anyone, they found within. Finally, they reached the top of the staircase that led down to the tall mahogany doors that barred the exit. Ferran led the way down the steps his sword held at the ready, Yazid following close behind. Luxon and Eripa took up the rear as they helped the still dazed Welsly and the boy Alderlade.

The hall appeared empty, and Ferran ran to the doors. With a grunt, he tried to open them but to no avail.

"They're locked!" he growled.

"Can't you cut through with your sword?" Luxon asked.

"No, it would take too long. To cut through wood that thick, even a Tourmaline blade would take hours."

Luxon stepped forward and rubbed his hands together.

"I might be able to blast them open with a spell," he said, his eyes narrowed in concentration.

The sound of dozens of running feet put an end to that thought. Crimson Blades appeared at the top of the steps, and too many corrupted soldiers emerged from the ground floor corridors. On the landing above appeared the tall woman, Yazid had seen in the streets. Now that she was closer, they got a clearer look at her. Her long black hair fell to her waist. She would have been beautiful save for the fact she only had one eye. The other was hideously scarred and an empty husk. A cruel smile was on her lips.

"You!" screamed Alderlade in fright. "You killed Elena!"

"It's Yinnice, the High Witch of the N'Gist," Ferran shouted in warning.

They were trapped. Luxon drew Asphodel once more, but to his surprise, no light emanated from it and even the power he usually felt when wielding it felt diluted. He looked at the sword in confusion. Beside him, Ferran staggered, and his skin paled.

"N'Gist amulets," he groaned.

Luxon's eyes widened. The amulets were often used by the enemy when they battled magic wielders. They were extremely effective against most as they fed off the magic they used. Luxon, however, did not feel the effects due to being a Thaumaturgist. He drew his magic from within and not from the world around him as most other wielders did. His bond with the Dragon, Umbaroth also provided him with protection from such magic as the Dragon shared his power with him. It seemed Asphodel was not immune.

"You think that sword will save you? Our Lord Danon has faced that blade many times and has learned to thwart its power. The Darkness no longer fears the light," mocked the witch. Around her neck was one of the amulets.

Luxon sheathed Asphodel and stepped forward, his hands ready at his sides. He focused his magic until electricity began to crackle between his fingers. Yinnice raised a hand in warning. The N'Gist tensed and the Crimson Blades stopped their advance.

"You know who I am and what I can do," Luxon said, sounding more confident than he felt.

Tension filled the hall as both sides sized each other up. Luxon was sure he could handle the N'Gist, but even he would struggle to deal with the witch. Ferran was visibly fatigued thanks to the amulets, Welsly was in no condition to fight and Eripa, though determined with a sword in hand, was no match for the Assassins. Suddenly, the doors at the top of the stairs burst open to reveal Sir Beric and his Bannerlords. They wore their full plate armour and had swords and maces in hand. Some were covered in blood, suggesting that they had already slain a few of the enemy.

"Charge!" Beric roared, following his words with action. He ran forward and cut the surprised N'Gist closest to him nearly in two. The assassins wheeled to face the new threat, and soon the hall was filled with battling figures. Luxon blasted two Crimson Blades into atoms with lightning to leave two smoking piles of ash on the red carpeted floor. The Witch advanced down the stairs. A Bannerlord charged at her, his sword aimed at her heart. With a casual gesture, the Witch blasted the man backwards across the chamber where he crashed with a sickening crunch against the wall.

Eripa helped Ferran and using the Bannerlords distraction they began to break open the doors leading to the outside.

"Now's our chance, get those doors open Luxon!" Ferran shouted. The Nightblade still looked pale, but nonetheless, he threw himself into the thick of the fighting. Luxon faced the door while Eripa took up position behind him.

"I'll cover you as best I can," she said.

Luxon once again tapped into his reserves of magic and funnelled heat up his arms until his hands began to glow molten hot. He thrust them against the door, and immediately the wood began to smoke and crackle. Behind him the Bannerlords were being pushed back, three of them lay dead or dying whilst Beric's helmet was dented and his chainmail torn. Their skill was impressive as they fought toe to toe with the Crimson Blades. The fighting was frantic with blades slashing. Even fully trained Nightblades often fell to their daggers. Luxon renewed his efforts and then with a loud snap, the doors began to splinter. Satisfied that he had weakened them enough, he stepped back and unleashed a telekinetic blast that ripped them from their hinges.

"Come on!" he yelled.

Just as he was about to lead the way out of the palace, an invisible hand grabbed him by his cloak and yanked him violently backwards. He flew through the air and crashed to the ground. Quickly, he got to his feet and summoned flame into his hands. The Witch stood before him, unafraid.

"It's only a matter of time until I get my hands on the sword, boy," she snarled.

Luxon stared her down and slowly shook his head.

"If you want it, come and claim it."

Yinnice advanced, but Luxon unleashed the flames to create a wall of fire between them. The witch screamed in frustration.

"I WILL FIND YOU!"

Luxon scooped the crying Alderlade up in his arms and ran outside. The others followed, with the surviving Bannerlords acting as a rear guard.

"This way to the harbour, follow me!" said Yazid. They hurried through the gardens that thankfully were empty of the enemy and emerged onto one of the main roads that led downward to the Bazaar. Dozens of bodies lay like scattered dolls on the paved street and ahead they could see Crimson Blades moving from house to house. What resistance there was had fallen back to the city walls. Yazid led the way, only once did they have to fight, but the Bannerlords and now revived Ferran, quickly dispatched the N'Gist who tried to stop their escape. Finally, they reached the city walls, and there they discovered Captain Whitelaw and Sophia commanding a few soldiers who had escaped the N'Gists corruption. At seeing them, Sophia ran to her husband.

"Thank Niveren you're all safe," she cried, throwing her arms around Ferran's shoulders.

"It was touch and go for a while," he replied. "What's the situation?"

Whitelaw joined them; his one good eye focused on the street ahead.

"When we realized what was going on, me and the lads seized control of the gatehouse. We knew you would need an escape route. They were in the harbour too, but we dealt with them," the captain explained. Luxon could see many of the *Agatha's* crew in position around the gatehouse. Some wielded swords. Others were armed with crossbows.

"I cannot just abandon my city," Yazid growled his eyes fixed on a column of black smoke that was now rising from the direction of the palace.

"I'd say your city is lost, captain. Come, depart with us and live to fight another day," Beric said as he cleaned blood from his sword with his tunic.

"And where would I go? I cannot abandon Silenzia to the enemy," Yazid snapped back.

Luxon sighed. He'd seen too many places lost to the N'gist. Eclin, The Watchers, Bison, all had been sacked and ravaged by the enemy. He understood what Yazid was feeling.

"Beric is right, captain. The Shar is dead and your realm now leaderless. What you need is a plan and help if you're to retake this place. Live and fight another day."

Yazid nodded, pain was evident in his eyes. More columns of smoke had begun to rise from within the city.

One of the *Agatha's* crew shouted a warning from the gatehouse's tower.

"Black sails sighted sir!"

Ferran swore loudly.

"The Sarpi! Come on Yazid; you're no good to anyone here now."

"It's time we leave," said Whitelaw before bellowing orders to his men to head back to the ship. Together they passed through the gate and down the hill to the harbour. Several other ships were rapidly preparing to way anchor and others were already pushing out to sea. On the horizon, they could make out several dozen black sails heading towards the coast.

Luxon and the other bounded up the gangway and onto the *Agatha's* deck.

"Raise anchor and set the sails. We need to leave here with all haste!" Whitelaw commanded. The ship's crew set about their tasks with efficient discipline. For all his tall tales, Whitelaw was one hell of a good sea captain.

"Is there anything we can do to help, captain?" Luxon asked.

"Aye lad. Get yourself and those strong buggers there below decks and take an oar. We're going to have to row out of the harbour."

Luxon did as he was told and followed the Bannerlords and Ferran below decks. Sophia meanwhile took Alderlade and the still groggy Welsly to their cabins and safety. They clambered down a wooden ladder and into the cramped rower deck. A dozen sailors were already in position and getting the long oars ready. Lipur was among them.

Wooden slats were pushed aside, and the oars were funnelled through them until they touched the water. Luxon took a seat next to Lipur and gripped the oar.

"Have you ever done this before?" he asked uncertainly.

"Many times. Just follow my lead until you feel the rhythm. Least if you get tired you can always use magic to revive us all," Lipur replied with a chuckle.

"All right, you bastards, row!" came Whitelaw's command from the deck above.

Beric and the surviving Bannerlords were in front of them whilst Ferran was behind with Yazid. They all gripped their oars and pulled. With a jolt, the *Agatha* began to move, and once clear of the docks, the mainsail was unfurled. Now it would be a race to escape the arriving Sarpi.

*

Gatiz knelt before Yinnice. The N'Gist's high witch sat in the throne of the now dead Shar and smiled.

"I believe you have something for me?" she said.

Gatiz bowed and shuffled to her, in his hand was the amulet the Shar had worn about his neck. Yinnice smiled wickedly and took it from Gatiz.

"Lord Danon will be pleased. If those Delfinnian fools only knew what they've allowed to fall into our hands."

CHAPTER 7.

The ship sped through the clear turquoise waters; its sails were stretched to their limit thanks to the magical winds provided by Luxon. He stood next to Whitelaw, who was at the helm and took another deep breath before blowing. The wind spell had been one he had learned during his time in the Void.

At the time he would never have believed he would be using it to power a ship in a life or death race. Behind them, the bulk of the Sarpi fleet had arrived at Shim's harbour and had begun to disgorge troops. Only a handful of vessels had changed direction to intercept the *Agatha*. He blew again and the magical wind caught in the sail, causing the ship to move ever faster.

"All right lad I don't think they'll be catching us anytime soon. Let nature take care of the sails," Whitelaw said as he lowered his spyglass from his eye. Sure enough, the pursuing ships were now nothing more than tiny black dots on the horizon. Luxon stepped back and leant against the deck rail. He was exhausted and panting slightly. Whitelaw offered him a waterskin which he took gratefully. The cool liquid went some way to revitalize him.

Beric and Ferran emerged from below decks and approached. The two men had become fast friends with the Bannerlord fascinated with the Nightblade's Tourmaline sword. They waved in greeting and then climbed the steps to the upper deck.

"We've just been discussing what our next plan of action should be," Ferran explained. "Beric here has kindly offered to introduce us to the King of Kastador who he claims will be inclined to offer us aid."

Luxon drank from the skin again and wiped his mouth with the back of his hand. He offered it to Beric who took it with a nod of thanks.

"That is a generous offer, but who's to say the N'Gist like in Silenzia haven't infiltrated Kastador? We were so close to gaining their aid and now," he said, knotting his hands in frustration, 'we're back where we started. If the N'Gist   s   High Witch is here, then Danon knows our plan. It's hopeless."

"I wouldn't say that master wizard. You now have allies in the form of the most fearsome bastards on the continent of Tulin, not to mention you now know some of the complexities of the politics of this land," said Beric who clapped Luxon on the shoulder.

"We were so naive to think that Danon hadn't learned the lessons from the past. It took a unified world to defeat him before. We should have known he'd do all he could to prevent that from happening again."

"You can't blame yourself for what happened. Perhaps we will discover something in these lands that we can use against Danon, after all, according to the texts, Tulin is just as full of mystery and magic as Delfinnia," Ferran said.

Luxon nodded at Ferran's words. He was right. Before setting sail across the Dividing Sea, he'd spent several days and nights in study in Caldaria's library. The Prefect had been most displeased when he had asked to see all the information they had on Tulin. To his surprise, the Prefect and his small army of helpers had ended up dumping hundreds of books, scrolls and maps at his feet.

The sound of approaching footsteps caused them to look at the main deck. Striding towards them was Yazid.

"I have a favour to ask of you," the tall Silenzian said. "There is a small Silenzian settlement a day to the north on the coast. I ask that you drop me off there."

"For what purpose?" Ferran asked, folding his arms.

"The Shar may be dead and the capital lost, but the people of Silenzia are fighters. The Morvan has a strong army, and perhaps they will be willing to fight the N'Gist."

"I thought the Morvan was your enemy?" Beric said.

"With Shar Yazim dead, there is no other to contest the Morvan's claim to become Shar. The people will rally to their banner if they are willing to fight the Old Enemy. Let me disembark at the settlement, and I will do all I can to fight back and get you the fleet that Yazim promised you."

Luxon and Ferran exchanged a look. Perhaps things were not as dire as he'd feared.

"If you can convince the Morvan to fight the N'Gist then I promise that I will speak with King Thorn about sending aid in your struggle," Beric offered. "Thorn has a lot of sway with the other Free Kingdoms, perhaps enough even to revive the Old Alliances."

Yazid smiled and embraced the Bannerlord.

"I would appreciate that muchly."

He looked at Luxon and took his hand in his.

"To you, my foreign friend, I believe in your fight and cause. We must unite if we are to defeat the darkness. I will do all I can to make it happen, this I promise."

"Thank you, Yazid."

*

The small settlement was exactly where Yazid had said it would be. It consisted of a collection of ramshackle huts built on wooden stilts that jutted out into the sea and were tucked between two monolithic cliffs. The *Agatha* sailed into the bay and set anchor just off the shore. Yazid waved them goodbye as he clambered aboard one of the *Agatha's* small rowing boats.

"Good luck Yazid. If all goes well, try and send word to the Sentinels on Dilar's frontier. Kastador will come to your aid, even if it turns out to just be me and my Banners."

The Silenzian captain smiled and clapped a fist to his chest in salute.

"Until we meet again, my new friends. Where will you sail too now?"

Beric smiled.

"Back to Kastador and home."

Yazid paled slightly at his words.

"What is it, my friend?"

"You must be careful on such a journey. Recently, our ships dare not venture beyond the red cliffs," Yazid replied, pointing to the cliffs just visible to the north.

"Monsters dwell there. Inhuman beasts that lure men to their deaths. Be careful."

*

With Yazid now ashore the *Agatha* once more set out to sea. This time Lipur was at the helm with Captain Whitelaw. The man's knowledge of the local seas was invaluable as Beric, and the other Bannerlords were no sailors.

"We traverse north for another day, and then we will reach the Straits of Arbagorn. To the east lies my homeland of New Vucrar, but to the west is the mouth of the great River of Talas. We then follow its course for another day, perhaps two and we will arrive in the Free Kingdom of Dilar," the sailor explained to Luxon who had joined them on the upper deck.

"Is there anything we need to worry about? I didn't like what Yazid said about monsters," Luxon asked. He'd done much travelling and encountered too much peril to know that nothing was ever plain sailing.

Lipur leant back against the deck rail and squinted his eyes in thought.

"The coastline can be tricky to navigate, and the Arbagorns can be a dangerous lot if riled. As we're heading back north, we might encounter Empire vessels, but they rarely venture so far south, save for when they raid my islands for slaves," he said bitterly.

"We will do what we can to help your people Lipur," Luxon promised.

"As for monsters? I don't know about that. The only one I ever saw was a mighty beast, the size of a mountain it was with tentacles lined with blades as long as a man."

"Let's pray that we don't encounter one of those."

Lipur nodded in agreement before asking,

"What do you know of the Sarpi? To us, they've always been like wraiths that strike without warning from the Cursed Sea."

Luxon closed his eyes and breathed in the sea air before replying. According to the maps given to him by Grandmaster Thanos, the Sarpi homeland was not far from the continent of Tulin.

"All I know are the legends. That during the Age of Darkness, Zahnia the Great traversed the world in his bid to seek out allies to defeat Danon and the N'Gist. The peoples of Tulin followed him to war, but the Sarpi refused, for they worship Danon as their saviour."

Lipur's eyes widened at his words.

Luxon stared at the horizon, memories of what he saw on the Isle of Magic flooding back into his mind. He had seen Danon before his fall, had seen how once he had been a hero himself before being corrupted.

"The Sarpi tried to kill Zahnia,' he continued, 'but he escaped their trap and as punishment, he used his magic to blot out the sun and cast them forever in the darkness that they so loved. As the centuries passed, they were forgotten by the wider world, where it is said they lost their vision and became mindless beasts. The legends go, that the surviving N'Gist found them and made them an offer. If they were to serve them and their master Danon again, they would return to them their vision. The Sarpi agreed, and the N'Gist used dark magic to enable them to see once more, hence their glowing eyes. As for the land itself, we know virtually nothing. Just that the Sarpi possess a powerful army and fleet of black sailed warships."

"Saviour? How can Danon be a saviour?" asked Lipur in disbelief.

"They believe that Danon is the avatar of darkness and that only he can destroy the God of Balance, and free the Goddess of Darkness, Esperin."

Suddenly, an icy cold blast of air whipped over the ship. The sails fanned out violently, and the rigging jiggled noisily. An unearthly groan filled the air causing the ship's crew to cry out in fear and stop their tasks. The groan grew louder and then, abruptly, it ceased.

"By Niveren, what in the Void was that?" shouted a panicked crewmate. Everyone on the ship looked spooked. Captain Whitelaw spat over the side of the ship to ward off evil.

"I'd use that name sparingly master wizard. The old gods still have some power in this world it seems," the captain warned before shouting at his men to get back to work. Luxon nodded in agreement and wrapped his cloak tighter about himself. The strange wind and sound had shaken him. He excused himself and hurried to his cabin.

                                        *

Once inside his cabin, he walked over to the chest he kept under his bunk and pulled it out. He opened it. Asphodel lay safely inside. He sighed in relief and placed a hand on the golden blade. He could feel the power emanating from within. It was like standing too close to a roaring fire. The hilt was like no other sword he had ever set eyes on. On each side, a face was carved into the surface. It wasn't a human face; of that, he was certain although it had similar features. One of the faces was cheerful in appearance, whereas the other was locked in a perpetual look of anger. He placed it back and climbed onto his bunk.

'Beware the Goddess'

Luxon cried out and fell out of the bunk with a thud.

"Who said that?" he said his voice filled with panic.

'I did. In the chest.'

He scrambled to his feet, his heart racing. He shook his head in disbelief.

"Nope. This isn't happening. As if I didn't have enough to deal with, now I'm going mad. I mean, I knew it'd have to happen eventually, especially after all the craziness I've experienced. That's it. It's just stress. Get a grip, Luxon."

'Hey, kid. Stop talking to yourself and take me out of this damn chest.'

Luxon slapped himself. Pain lanced through his cheek.

"This is real," he said in surprise. He had hoped that he was dreaming. Cautiously, he approached the chest and opened the lid. Asphodel looked back at him. Then the face on the hilt blinked.

"Argh!" Luxon cried.

'Charming. I speak to a mortal for the first time in aeons, and this is the reaction,' the voice- Asphodel said.

Luxon got his rapid breathing under control. He was a wizard; he was used to dealing with crazy stuff. He could handle a talking sword. He reached into the chest, picked up the blade and leant it against the trunk so that the face on the hilt was facing him.

'That's better. Now, kid, I'm sure you have a lot of questions, but for now, I need you to keep your mouth shut and listen.'

"Er, okay-"

'I said shh! Flipping heck, I made you humans dumb, huh?'

Luxon's mind raced. It couldn't be. The face on the hilt smiled broadly as though it were proud of itself.

'Yes, it is I the God of Light, the mighty Rindar in the flesh- err, well I guess as close to flesh as I can get. In the metal doesn't quite have the same ring to it. Yes, I know what you're thinking, I'm a handsome creature.'

"Well, I-"

"I said shhh! Anyhow, where was I? Oh yes, I am speaking, a strange sensation after all this time, but it's necessary as I fear time is running out! My dear other half is growing in power, for real this time and I fear what will happen if she attains her full might. You simply said her name out loud and look what happened!'

Luxon watched the sword in amazement. A thought came to him, and he raised his hand as though he were back at the Mage school in Caldaria.

'You may speak.'

"Thank you- how can you be the God of Light? I thought you and the Dark Goddess-,' he said, being careful not to utter her real name, '-merged to form the God of Balance, Chiaroscuro to defeat Vectrix. Then later, I saw you depart the world. It sounds crazy even to me, but I saw what happened a hundred thousand years ago."

Asphodel's eyes widened at his words.

'How? Oh right. I sense the Waters of Magic on you. Did you know that they are the tears of my long dead mother, Aniron the Goddess of Creation? Yes, yes, I sensed you then. You were watching from a hiding place, weren't you? You must understand that my sister is a very tricky creature. She is of the darkness and has been hoping to rid herself of me for time immemorial. She twists and lies and wriggles and corrupts. I fear that this time unless her servant, Danon is stopped for good, she will be strong enough to destroy me fully, and if that happens, the entire universe will be in peril!'

"Oh great, more stakes to add to my already nigh impossible quest," Luxon muttered. "And you didn't answer my question."

'Hmm? Listen, boy, the pieces are aligning, but it is good that you are here. This land, this Tulin, is an important part of his plans. I sense the realm of Vectrix on you, the Void. It is that which is key. If he succeeds in bringing that here all will be lost, and seeing as I helped create you, humans, I'd be a bit vexed with such an outcome. As to your question, you have that pesky wizard, Zahnia to thank for that. That wizard was too smart for his own good. He correctly surmised that this sword, my gift to you lot, by the way, contained some of my powers, a fact that he used to summon me and then trapped me within! Little did he realise that by doing so, he split me from my sister, unleashing her to play mischief across Esperia. Also, how else do you think he was able to banish Danon to the Void in the first place.'

"Zahnia, bound you to the sword?" Luxon asked in bemusement. The man's powers seemed limitless.

'Oh, -you know what? I truly cannot remember. One minute I was whole and doing God stuff, and the next I was ripped apart and stuck inside this sword. I left Asphodel in Niveren's hands, and the silly sod gave it up and sealed it away. A brave Knight found it, a chap named, Estran if I recall, and he used it to fight Danon. He died sadly and then the sword was taken and hidden by the mages of the Isle. For countless years it lay hidden, and then Zahnia got his mitts on it to fight Danon. Never did I expect to be trapped within my own creation! I knew giving you lot magic was a bad idea, but dear old sis insisted. Anyway, since then, I've been locked away in various places for safekeeping. There was that brief time when that chap used me to bring down the Golden Empire, but that was so long ago. If I recall correctly that didn't end well for the poor chap.'

Luxon blinked. The sword was talking about Marcus the Mighty. He shuddered at the memory of witnessing the first King of Delfinnia and his lovers' demise.

'The most important thing is this. You must stop Danon. He seeks the power needed to tear open reality and bring the entirety of the Void and all the horrors within it to Esperia. If he achieves this, then he will use his power to empower my sister and make her strong enough to manifest in her true form. If that happens, then, well, it's game over for the light. What do you know of the Portal Towers?'

The question took Luxon by surprise. He tapped his chin as he wracked his brain.

"They were built by the first wizards after Aljeron during the height of the Second Age. There are supposed to be eight of them scattered across the world, but only one is known in Delfinnia. The citadel at Tentiv that was used by the Diasect as their fortress, -but the portal itself doesn't work," he said after a few moments.

'The Isle of Magic is also home to a portal, which of course you know, seeing as you used it. There's one beyond the spine of Aniron, but funnily enough, I can no longer sense it. There are two here in Tulin. You must find them and the channelling key. The portal towers possess incredible power that Danon will use to achieve his goal.'

Luxon sat heavily on his bunk.

"And how am I supposed to find it? The portal towers have been inactive for a millennium, I wouldn't even know where to start, and in case you're not aware there's a lot of other things happening right now."

Asphodel scowled.

'Are you always this whiney? Trust me on this. Just do what you're doing, and you'll find it, or at least a clue. I should know. I am a God, after all. Oh, and another thing. I'd keep this little conversation to yourself. We wouldn't want everyone thinking you're mad now would we!'

*

Luxon jolted awake with a start. He sat up to find himself in his bunk and rocking gently from side to side as the Agatha cut through the waves. He looked over at the chest. Asphodel wasn't leaning against it. Cautiously, he got up and approached it. Lifting the lid, he sighed. The sword was inside and safely in its sheath.

He rubbed his eyes tiredly.

"Thank Niveren for that. That was the weirdest dream," he chuckled in relief.

A knock sounded on his cabin door. It was Sophia.

"Luxon, sorry for waking you but Captain Whitelaw says we're about to sail past the Red Cliffs."

"Thanks, I'll be right there," he said. He pulled on his boots and cloak and walked to the door. He glanced over his shoulder at the chest and shook his head.

"It was just a dream. I hope."

CHAPTER 8.

The *Agatha* sailed north unhindered for much of the day, and the weather was bright and sunny with a strong breeze. As they reached the Red Cliffs that marked the beginning of the route that would take them inland toward the River Talas, a mist had rolled in. The breeze had dropped, causing the ship to come to a crawl.

Luxon joined the others on the main deck.

"Do you hear that?" Welsly muttered.

Luxon tilted his head. He couldn't hear anything except for the clinking of the ship's rigging. A cold shiver went up his spine, and the hairs on his hand stood on end. Something was terribly wrong.

"I hear nothing," he replied his voice barely louder than a whisper.

"Listen harder," the Nightblade said.

Luxon was about to insist he heard nothing, but then to his surprise, he heard music. At first, it was faint but as the Agatha sailed on it grew in volume. A female voice was there too, a voice more beautiful than any he had ever heard before. Around him, the ship's crew walked like zombies to the deck's rail, and there they stood with their eyes closed.

Ferran and the Bannerlords were among them. Sophia hurried to her husband and tried to pull him away, but he shrugged her off without a word. Sophia faced Luxon with a look of confusion on her face.

The music and song were impossible to resist. He stepped forward towards it. Sophia walked over to him and placed a hand on his chest.

"What is this?" she asked.

Luxon blinked. His thoughts were muddled, as though invisible fingers had entered his brain and were messing with his thoughts.

"Magic. I think," he mumbled. He took another step, and this time pushed Sophia away. He wanted to be close to the music. To see the women singing the melody.

*

Sophia watched Luxon join the other men at the deck's rail where they all stood like swaying statues. Each of them was glassy eyed with dumb smiles on their lips. She called out to Welsly, but now he too had succumbed to the song. Only she, Eripa and Alderlade seemed to be unaffected.

"What's going on, Sophia?" Eripa said with fear in her voice. At the ship's wheel was Captain Whitelaw, a similar expression on his face. He gripped the wheel and turned the Agatha towards the direction of the music. Sophia bounded up the steps leading to the top deck and pulled him away from the wheel. He resisted by clinging to the wheel.

"We must go to them," the captain whined.

A cry came from the deck. Sophia ran back to the deck to find Alderlade, pointing at the water.

"There are dead people in the sea," he cried. She followed where he was pointing and gasped. The sea was full of corpses floating face down in its inky depths. On the rocks, at the base of the Red Cliffs, she could see piles of human bones and rotting bodies that seagulls pecked and tore at.

"We're in trouble."

She dashed back to the ship's wheel and called for Eripa to join her. She tried to pull the captain away, but again he resisted.

"Sorry about this," she muttered. She looked about and saw one of the oars used for one of the ship's rowboats. She picked it up and smacked the captain over the head, knocking him out cold.

"Eripa, take Whitelaw and lock him in his cabin," she ordered the bard.

"What's happening?"

"At a guess, some type of Fell Beast is luring us towards it. We're in its feeding ground, and it seems men are its prey," said Sophia, gesturing to the crew.

Eripa's eyes widened.

"A singing Fell Beast?"

"I've never heard of such a thing either, but they come in countless forms. Take the captain and get Alderlade to safety too."

Eripa gripped Whitelaw under his armpits, and Alderlade helped with his legs. The boy looked petrified, but there was a determination on his face to not show his fear. Sophia felt pride in the lad as he helped carry the captain below decks. She looked up to the crow's nest and could see Lipur in the basket. He too was swaying to the melody, his eyes closed. She ran to the rigging and climbed. She'd never been much of a fan of heights, but she pressed on. The man was close to falling. She climbed and climbed until she reached the mast and crow nest. Next, she carefully edged along the mast pole and climbed into the nest next to Lipur. There was no doubt about it. He too was under a spell. She picked up a rope at the bottom of the nest and forcibly tied him up.

"This is for your own good," she said as she finished tying a knot. She then tied the rope to the mast to ensure that even if he should climb over the side of the nest and fall, he wouldn't splat onto the deck below. With Lipur secured, she grabbed one of the rigging ropes and jumped. She slid down to the deck. The whole crew was now gathered by the rail, and the song had grown in volume. They were now a danger to themselves as it looked as though each of them was about to leap overboard and no doubt land in the Fell Beasts hunting ground. She glanced to her left as the *Agatha* drifted past the wreck of what looked like a Sarpian ship. Its hull had been smashed against the rocky cliffs and was split in two. Amongst the wreckage and debris were what was left of the crew. Skeletons bleached white by the sea and sun lay scattered all over the place and floated in the water. Eripa returned from below decks.

"Help me tie up these idiots," Sophia said scowling at her husband who looked as though he was about to climb over the ship's side and chuck himself into the sea. Together they found one of the spare ropes and carefully nudged the mesmerized men together. They then wrapped the rope around them until they were all secured around the main mast. Despite being tied up, they still tried to shuffle towards the railing and the sea beyond. Sophia hurried back down to her cabin and took her bow and quiver from the chest. Back on deck, she readied the weapon.

"We need to silence whatever these things are," she said.

Eripa nodded.

"Let me try something."

The bard took a deep breath and then began to sing herself. Her powerful voice filled the air, and using magic; she amplified it. Her beautiful voice began to drown out the other, and the men began to regain their senses. Ferran shook his head.

"What are you doing woman? Why are we all tied up?" he said, confused. Luxon stirred, his eyes dazed.

"You're all under a spell. Shut up and let us deal with this," Sophia snapped back.

"Sirens, they must be Sirens," Welsly said groggily as he too regained his senses. "Their song lures ships to the rocks and men into the sea where they devour them. They were cleared from the main shipping lanes of Delfinnia years ago, but I remember stories of them."

"How do we kill them? Eripa can't keep this up forever, and the ship has drifted off course. We need Whitelaw and the crew."

Welsly rubbed his eyes and shook his head to clear it of the Siren's song.

"Bronze coated with the blood of one of its victims, which in this case would be any one of us," Welsly replied.

"Bronze?"

"Yes, they are one of the few Fell Beasts that's not harmed by silver or magic. I always carry a Bericze dagger. Here-" he said, shifting so that his belt was reachable. Sophia drew the Bericze dagger from its sheath.

"Take some banishing vials too," he added.

A frustrated shriek filled the air, and then the Siren's song grew in volume as the monster competed with Eripa who also raised her voice. The sky filled with song, one promising death the other life. The mist surrounding the ship began to thin to reveal a small rocky island dead ahead. Sophia dashed to the rear of the ship and hurled herself against the anchor mechanism. She had to bring the ship to a stop; else it would be dashed upon the rocks. Using all her strength the anchor wheel began to turn until with a final roar of effort it rotated fully and deployed the iron anchor. The Agatha juddered violently, but the ship slowed. There, through the mist and sat on the rocks were three humanoid figures. She narrowed her eyes and tightened her grip on the dagger. The mist cleared to reveal the Fell Beasts in all their horror. The Siren's were abominations of a kind only a deranged mad God could hope to conjure into existence. Sophia cursed Vectrix and the Void. The Siren's were a hybrid. Their top halves were that of beautiful naked women with long flowing red hair. Only their eyes betrayed the monsters they were. Yellow and glowing with evil magic. Their bottom halves were that of a fish and covered in thick scales that glistened in the dull light. Out of their backs were large wings like those of some sort of monstrous bird. Their haunting song now began to drown out Eripa's, and once again the men fell under their spell. With their prey so close, two of the monsters slid into the water. They beckoned to the men who were now struggling to free themselves and go to their doom. Eripa ran to the rope and held it tight to pin them in place. The Siren's in the water hissed in frustration, and then they began to clamber up the side of the ship. Sophia stood in front of the men and drew her bow. The monsters pulled themselves over the rail to land on the swaying deck. They looked hungrily at the men.

"Just try and take them," Sophia snarled.

The Siren's advanced, and as they did, so their heads began to vibrate violently. Sophia stepped back in horror as the heads that had been of beautiful women snapped backwards with a sickening crack to reveal the real beasts beneath. Where the women's heads had been was now a salivating maw filled with snapping teeth and oozing mucus. Sophia shot a silver tipped arrow that struck the nearest of the Sirens. It emitted an unearthly howl as the arrow punched deep into its flank. It's snapping jaws spun to face her, and awkwardly it came at her. Sophia lowered her bow and drew the Bericze dagger. She hurried to the mesmerized Welsly, held up his hand and drew the blade over it.

"Sorry," she said, making sure the blade was covered in his blood. The second Siren was now close to the crew, but Eripa stepped in front of it and defiantly began to sing once more. This time she put all her magic behind the words causing the creature to pause and stagger backwards. Sophia dashed forward, easily avoiding the Siren's cumbersome flailing limbs and with a shout, stabbed it deep in its chest. The Bericze dagger pierced flesh and black blood burst from the wound. The Siren arched back and emitted an agonised scream. Sophia struck again, this time punching the blade into the monster's throat. It collapsed to the deck unmoving. She moved onto the second Siren. It was fixated on Eripa and didn't notice Sophia creep up behind it. It screamed as the Bericze dagger punched through its torso as the Witchhunter plunged into the beast's back. Eripa jumped out of the way as the Siren crashed to the deck.

"Get back!" she yelled as she took one of the banishing vials and tossed it onto the deck. The vial shattered in a blinding flash as the magic within created a portal to the Void. An invisible wind began to blow, and the Fell Beasts were pulled inside the portal to be sent back to the foul realm from whence they came. That left the last Siren. It had stayed on the rocks, but now, at seeing its sisters slain, it flapped its wings and took to the sky. It continued to sing as it swooped down on the Agatha. Eripa shouted a warning, but Sophia was too slow.

The monster attacked and swatted her aside. She crashed to the deck, the dagger spilling from her grip. Her vision exploded with stars and pain lanced into her chest. Eripa was now alone to face the monster. Its womanly half was a horrific mimic of a human. It moved unnaturally, and its eyes were dead and devoid of life. Even so, the men reached out to it wanting to be close. Eripa planted her feet and held her ground. Her throat was sore, but her magical song was the only thing keeping the Siren at bay. She looked at the unmoving Sophia desperately, but the witch hunter remained unconscious. Her voice wavered, and the Siren sneered. It advanced like a cat about to eat a mouse, but just as it was about to strike it jerked upright and screeched in pain. Stood behind the monster, Bericze dagger in hand was Alderlade. The boy stabbed, again and again, forcing the Siren back.

"Get off my ship!" the boy yelled, waving the dagger.

That was the chance Eripa needed. She ran to where Sophia lay and picked up one of the Banishing vials. She hurled the vial at the Siren, and it shattered against its scales. As before, there was a flash and the Siren screamed as it was dragged back to the Void.

Alderlade stood panting on the deck, his hands trembling, and his eyes were fixed on the spot where the Siren had vanished. Eripa rushed to his side.

"You saved us, my King," she said before pulling the boy into a tight embrace.

With the Sirens slain, the crew were free from their song's influence.

"Ere, let us go!" moaned the sailors who'd finally recovered their wits. Sophia stirred and slowly sat up.

"Quit your bellyaching," she groaned back.

Eripa smiled and took the dagger from Alderlade. She cut the rope that had bound the crew, setting them free.

The sailors rushed to their stations as they noticed the ship's precarious situation and Captain Whitelaw emerged from below decks bellowing orders. Ferran rushed to Sophia's side and helped her stand.

"Are you okay?" he asked his voice full of concern.

"Nothing we couldn't handle. Isn't that right, Alderlade?" she said winking at the boy. He looked pale but nodded and smiled.

"Just another day at sea."

*

The River Talas

Luxon joined the others on the *Agatha's* deck and stood in awe at the vast mountains that towered over the River Talas. The snowcapped peaks of stone behemoths that made the mountains of Eclin look tiny in comparison reflected in the crystal clear water.

"We sail for three days up the river keeping the mountains to our right," Lipur was explaining to Captain Whitelaw.

"And what can we expect on the river?" Whitelaw asked his eyes fixed on the lands on the left hand bank. That side of the river was flat with thick jungle reaching the water. If anyone was watching them, then they had plenty of cover to do so. This part of the land was hot and humid with a vast array of brightly coloured and exotic birds flitting between the towering trees.

"On that side of the river is Arbagon. The people are merchants and traders mostly, but they can be a bit finicky with strangers."

"Could they be worth speaking with?" Luxon asked. They needed allies wherever they could find them.

"They're not a united land. The Arbagon are often too busy plotting against each other to be of much assistance realistically. It is a land divided into a wide array of systems and the thick jungle makes it a difficult place to traverse, which is why it's been left alone by the other powers that surround it."

Luxon raised a questioning eyebrow.

"What do you mean systems?"

Lipur scratched his chin as he thought how best to describe the strange land.

"Well, some of what you would call Kingdoms aren't ruled by a single King or Queen. Some are ruled by a collective of the people who vote for who will lead them. Others are ruled by tyrants or by systems where all people are considered equals. It's often these different systems that cause the Arbogans to quarrel with one another constantly. They like to try and prove their systems are the best ones."

"Sounds confusing," Ferran muttered from nearby.

"Do they have any magic wielders?" Luxon asked, his curiosity piqued by Lipur's description. The philosopher in him was fascinated by this new continent.

Lipur grimaced.

"They do, but they're not mages or wizards. They call themselves shamans and some of their practices are barbaric. They use blood magic, human sacrifices, that sort of thing. They're rarely seen but are most often used by the various city states in times of war, which is pretty much all the time-"

The sound of an animal came from deep within the jungle. It sounded massive, and some of the treetops swayed as whatever it was lumbered through the undergrowth.

"I dread to think what Fell Beasts stalk that place," Ferran muttered.

                                            *

The *Agatha* rowed up the wide river for another two days and beside sighting some small fishing rafts manned by the tall Bericzed skinned men from Arbagon the journey passed without incident.

The mountains had been at their side throughout, but now, as they rounded a wide bend, the landscape changed dramatically. The mountains turned into hills and then into rolling plains, whilst the jungles gave way to forest and flat terrain. In the morning of the second day, they followed the river's course to see two massive statues in the image of men wearing plate armour and wearing crowned helmets emerge from the mist. The figures stood with one arm thrust outwards whilst the other gripped the hilt of their sword. Luxon and the others looked at them in amazement.

"They're like the statues of the three kings on the borders of Eclin," Luxon said. The river was funnelled between them, and a stone archway joined the two statues together.

"Truly a wonder of this world is it not? Built over five hundred years ago, they depict the Kings Kastor and Dilarus. The men who founded the Kingdoms of Kastador and Dilar. They united to battle the Empire to the north and the Shardom to the south for the freedom of their land," Beric explained.

He turned to his men. "We're almost home."

The Bannerlord and his men cheered as the ship passed under the archway.

"We follow the river for another day, and then we will reach the inner sea. From there we sail northwest up the River Siren and then the Asphodel River to reach Kastador City."

Passing under the arch, the Agatha now found itself in the centre of the river. On the left hand bank stood a small settlement and they waved in greeting at a group of small children playing in the shallow water. Fishing boats were further out, and the fishermen called out in greeting.

Beric walked to the rail.

"Hail good folk of Dilar, what news of the Free Kingdoms?"

One of the little boats changed course until it was close enough to the *Agatha* for its crew to speak. From their expressions, it was clear that they were fascinated with the ship. From what they'd seen in Silenzia, the Delfinnian designed vessel stood out from the Tulin built crafts they had seen. Those had mostly been long squat galleys that relied on rowers rather than the enormous sails of the *Agatha*.

"We hear grim tidings, my Lord. Raiders from the Nerios Dynasty have pillaged the Southlands. The Dilar Banners have been raised, and men are being rallied at the stones of Trist. I'm afraid war is on the horizon," one of the fishermen replied.

Beric frowned at the news. He faced Luxon and the others.

"That's grim news indeed. The Nerios often raid but for Dilar's Queen to have summoned her banners means that it must be a large incursion. We should hurry to Kastador. King Thorn might be sending aid to Dilar."

He turned, reached into a pouch on his belt and tossed the fisherman a silver coin.

"Thank you for the information. Stay safe."

CHAPTER 9.

Kastador

The fast-flowing waters of the River Siren sped the Agatha onward towards the Kingdom of Kastador. The landscape was now one of temperate forests and farmers fields. They passed numerous towns and villages and even an ancient looking temple that loomed over the waters. Its sweeping arches reached towards the sky, and huge wide marble steps rose into a tower that dominated the skyline. Beric explained that it was a temple dedicated to the Goddess of Creation, Aniron. It was strange to Luxon and the Delfinnians to see the Old Gods still being worshipped. That practice had ended long ago in their homeland as the Cult of Niveren had grown in prominence. Kastador seemed like a peaceful place and one that was well guarded against the dangers posed by the outside world. Regularly they spotted patrols of heavily armoured warriors on the roads and bridges along the river.

Ferran stood on the *Agatha's* deck with Sophia in his arms. He'd spent much of the morning on the rowing deck, and it was his turn for a rest.

"I can't remember the last time we just stopped and enjoyed a view like this," Sophia said with contentment. She nuzzled her head against her husband's broad chest, savouring the comforting feeling.

"We shall enjoy these moments when they come. We all should," Ferran replied. He tilted her head back and kissed her. Sophia sighed, and her eyes settled on the boy King sitting on the gently rocking deck. His short legs dangled over the side of the ship, and his big eyes were wide with wonder. Dolphins had followed the *Agatha* for much of its journey through the wide river systems of Kastador. The playful creatures had kept them all entertained with their acrobatics.

"It must be so hard on Alderlade. The poor boy has been through so much and to see that Witch again, after what she did to Elena," she said softly.

"It's a good job we have the world's best Witch Hunter with us then," Ferran said. "I worry about Luxon. He's what? Barely nineteen years old and he has the weight of the world on his shoulders. I admire the lad for his bravery. Rarely does he show his doubts and fears even when men much older than he would be soiling their drawers."

Sophia slapped her husband playfully on the arm.

"You know that's not true. He may look like a young man, but his time in the Void changed him. Hannah told me that he once said he felt as though he was more like a hundred years old rather than nineteen, and I believe it. Sometimes when you look at his eyes, it's obvious."

Ferran nodded. He too believed it.

"Do you think they're okay back home?" Sophia asked.

"They'd better be, or all this will be for nought," Ferran answered.

"I'm sure Kaiden will be putting up a fierce resistance. Who knows, perhaps by the time we return he'll have liberated Delfinnia already," Sophia chuckled. Both had faith that the Knight would stand his ground. After all they had been through together they trusted him.

They looked up as a panicked shout came from the barrelman high up in the Agatha's crow's nest. Ferran frowned and gently moved Sophia aside. Just as he was about to shout up to the lookout, a shadow fell over the ship. In the sky and flying fast against the wind, was a creature the likes of which he'd never seen before. The beast had the body, tail, and back legs of a giant cat, yet its vast feathered wings, claws and head were the shape of a bird of prey. It swooped low over the water, moving with speed and stunning agility. The stunned crew of the Agatha watched it in awe, Ferran among them. It spun before arching high into the sky where it emitted a high-pitched call.

"Is it a Fell Beast?" Sophia said, her hand dropping to the hilt of the dagger on her belt.

Captain Whitelaw shouted at his men to prepare the harpoons and Alderlade clambered away from the ship's side to cling protectively to Sophia.

"Hold your men, captain!" shouted Beric, who had emerged from the lower decks. Instead of showing fear, the man looked delighted.

"It's a Gryphon. It is no threat to us. Though what it is doing so far from the Gryphon Mountains is a mystery. Is it not magnificent?"

The other Bannerlords cheered as the creature soared over the ship.

"It's magnificent," Ferran said, unable to take his eyes off it. It looped around one last time, emitting an almost deafening screech as it did so. They watched as the beast moved on and flew north.

Beric walked over to Ferran a broad grin on his face.

"You rode one of those things?" Ferran asked in disbelief.

Beric chuckled and clapped the Nightblade on the shoulder.

"I did indeed. Being a Banner Rider was the highlight of my life. The Gryphon is the most sacred animal in all Kastador. To see one at all is an immense gift from the gods. I'd say that it bodes well for your time here. Perhaps you will get the chance to ride one."

Ferran watched the Gryphon until it flew out of sight.

"I hope you're right."

*

The rest of the journey went by without incident and just as Beric had predicted they reached the capital city of Kastador on the third morning. The river widened and was filled with ships of all shapes and sizes going about their business. Some were colossal merchant vessels; others were small boats used by fishermen. Luxon recognized the design of some that must have come from Silenzia. Trade flowed along the Kingdoms river systems, and vessels from across Tulin plied their wares in the city's markets. The city itself was built on top of a hill that dominated the land around it. The colossal palace sat shining white in the rising sunshine. Below it, the city was laid out in a series of different levels each protected by a curtain wall that ran right around the city. Beric explained that King Thorn had kept the walls well maintained and that he was always expecting trouble.

"It's to do with how Thorn became King really,' he said as the *Agatha* lined up to wait to be assigned a place to dock.

'He took the crown by force of arms. For you see, the previous King had been usurped and killed by wicked men who sought power for themselves. Thorn never wanted the crown, but alas when there's no other choice he did what needed to be done and saved Kastador."

Another hour passed until finally, the *Agatha* was granted permission to dock. The harbour, like the lower levels, surrounded the city in all directions. A single stone bridge providing the only access by land, which made the city a tough place to attack.

"It was built by the first Emperor of the Golden Empire to defend the riverways. You'd need a huge army and navy to take it," Beric continued after Luxon asked him about the city's layout. "When Thorn did it, the populace was on his side, and they opened the gates for him."

As the ship moved to the quayside, a contingent of knights and a woman sat astride a black horse was gathering to greet them. At seeing them, Beric waved and commanded his men to gather their things. The anchor was dropped, and the gangplank lowered. Beric and his bannermen led the way off the ship with Luxon and the others following close behind.

"Queen Nix, you shouldn't have, we've not been gone that long," Beric laughed with a bow.

The Queen was a tall woman with long brown hair that reached her shoulders. She wore an outfit of a white silken shirt and green velvet trousers offset by a pair of tall black riding boots. Only the crown sitting on her head revealed her status. Her green eyes radiated with intelligence. She smiled at Beric.

"Welcome home, Sir Beric. I trust your contract in Silenzia was completed?" she asked, casting a wary look at Luxon and the others.

"It was, although we did have some help from my new friends here. Your Grace, allow me to introduce you to them. They hail from far across the sea, and they are here to seek an audience with King Thorn."

Queen Nix slid from her saddle and approached Luxon. He bowed deeply, as did the other Delfinnians.

"You come from across the sea? How can that be? No ship has made such a voyage in centuries."

Captain Whitelaw stepped forward and gestured to the *Agatha*.

"Aye, your grace, you are correct. Many have tried such a journey over the years, but the waves created by the two moons make the sea nigh impossible to traverse unless you have an exceptional ship. This vessel is one of a kind. It was built using ancient designs and crafted by the finest carpenters. Its secret is the magical runes built into its frame and the shape of the sails."

Queen Nix stepped closer to the *Agatha* and looked at where Whitelaw was pointing. The runes carved into the ship's hull glowed softly.

"Fascinating. My brother Meric would love to study such a vessel. For many years I've pestered my husband to look to the seas, but alas, events at home have always gotten in the way."

Whitelaw smiled with pride.

"I would be honoured to show her off to your people. She has served us well thus far."

Nix turned from the captain and looked Luxon up and down.

"I'd guess from your cloak that you are some sort of mage. And you-,' Nix said pointing at Ferran and Welsly, '-are monster hunters. I haven't seen your like for many a year. Your services are rarely required in Kastador."

"Forgive me your Grace, but I promised my new friends here, an audience with King Thorn. Is he at the palace?" Beric said.

Nix took Beric by the arm and pulled him close so that a passerby could not hear her voice.

"Unfortunately, he is not. That is why I rode down here to greet you, Beric. Thorn is missing," she said her voice filled with worry. "Come to the palace, and I will tell you all that I know."

                              *

Once they arrived at the palace, it took Beric and Luxon an hour to tell the Queen all they had seen in Silenzia and of the quest to seek allies against Danon. Now she was sat, white faced, her hands gripping the wooden arms of her throne tightly.

They were inside the palace's main audience chamber. Tapestries depicting various scenes of the Kingdom's history lined the marble walls, and a large banner with the symbol of a Gryphon hung on the back wall behind the raised dais and thrones of the King and Queen. Nix sat on her throne whilst Luxon, and the others stood around her. Young Alderlade was roaming the room with Eripa for company, his eyes full of wonder at the banners of the realms various Bannerlords that hung from the ceiling.

"The N'Gist in Silenzia? Danon conquering your homeland? By the gods, how have we been so blind to such dangers," the Queen said in disbelief. "Such dire news made worse from the reports coming from Dilar."

"What is the news from Dilar, your majesty? We encountered some Dilar villagers who told us that their Queen has raised her banners."

The Queen sighed and rubbed her eyes tiredly.

"According to the messenger from Dilar who visited us earlier this week, the Nurious are raiding the south of Silas' kingdom. Apparently, the Nurions have a new War Chief, one who seems to have unified the squabbling fiefdoms."

"Why do I have a bad feeling that's got something to do with Danon?" muttered Ferran. Luxon nodded but kept quiet.

The Queen rose from her throne and stepped closer to Luxon and gestured for Ferran and Sophia to approach. Beric was standing at her side.

"I must speak in low tones as only a handful of my most trusted servants know what I am about to tell you. Kastador will do all it can to help you, but I must ask something of you in return," she added, looking at Luxon.

"Whatever we can do to help your grace," he replied.

"My husband, the King, is missing. Six days ago, he led an expedition into the Gryphon Mountains to scout out the passes. We had received reports of strange activity on the border, and as is my husbands' lust for adventure, he insisted on going himself. He was only supposed to be gone for a day, maybe two at the most. I have done all I can to suppress any rumours and gossip amongst the courtiers, but I cannot hide the fact their King is absent for much longer. I trust no other with this mission Beric. I want you to take a handful of your most trusted men and venture into the mountains and find my husband."

The Queen faced Luxon and the others.

"I would like you to go with him. From your story, it sounds as though all of you are very capable, and as you are strangers to this land, no one will ask questions. If you agree to my request, then Kastador will be indebted to you, and I will know that we can trust you."

"I cannot speak for all of us your highness, but I will go with Beric," Luxon said with a bow. "All I ask is that the crew of our ship and my young charge-' he said pointing to Alderlade who was now receiving a piggyback ride from Welsly around the throne room. "-will be looked after and protected. I cannot stress enough how important that boy is."

"You're not going without us," said Sophia with a smile. Ferran nodded at her words.

"Where the wizard goes, I go," the Nightblade added.

"You're not going anywhere without me again!"

They turned to see a sheepish looking Eripa standing close by. She'd obviously been earwigging their hushed conversation.

"C'mon, I'm a bard. I volunteered for this voyage so I can record and write all that I see, what we see. I missed out on hunting the Devourer. I won't miss out on seeing this land," she added, crossing her arms. Her expression dared someone to challenge her. The Queen smirked.

"You remind me of myself when I was younger," she said with a chuckle. "Very well. I have arranged quarters for you and your people here in the palace. I am sure after all your travelling and adventures. A nice rest is in order."

"Thank you, your grace. May I ask about the reports you've received? You said that there was strange activity afoot?" Luxon said.

A frown crossed the Queen's features, and she began to pace in front of her throne.

"All we know is that a week ago we received reports of strange lights having been spotted by the shepherds that frequent the area. According to some of the reports, the lights are - magical in nature. You must understand that in Kastador, magic use is rare as we have very few trained mages in the realm. Those with magical talent must be exceptional to be taken in by the mage schools of Old Kastador. The Bannerlords often recruit those that possess the ability to use magic to act as healers, spies, and emissaries. However, across the border in the Tulin Empire, self-proclaimed Wizard Lords rule and are often probing our borders for weaknesses."

Luxon nodded in understanding.

"We will discover the source of these lights and return your husband to you."

*

The next morning Luxon awoke in a bed so comfortable that he wished that he didn't have to leave it. His room in the palace was small but had all the comforts of his chambers back home in Caldaria. It even had a tiny washroom attached to it. With a groan, he rolled out of bed and staggered into the washroom. He reached the porcelain basin that was full of warm water and dunked his head into it. The water did its job of refreshing him. Next, he got dressed and pulled on his green wizard's cloak. He went over to the chest at the end of the bed and opened it. He took out his staff Dragasdol and the bandolier that he used to strap it to his back. Underneath the staff was Asphodel glinting in its sheath. He reached for it, hesitating as he did so. The voice he'd heard hadn't spoken again. He picked up the weapon, savouring the power that filled him as he did so, before strapping the scabbard to his belt. He looked at himself in the room's solitary mirror. He barely recognized himself anymore. He wasn't the young boy who'd been sent out into the world all those years ago. Now he saw a man, one with eyes far older than the body he possessed, and one dressed like the powerful wizard he had become. He pulled up his hood and exited the room. He stepped out into a hallway lined with arched windows that overlooked a stunningly beautiful and well maintained garden. Marble statues stood among immaculately trimmed trees and bushes that surrounded a large fountain made of obsidian. He turned as a door opened down the hall. It was Eripa. The bard was tying her long hair into a ponytail. She, too, was dressed for travel. A warm looking fur cloak covered her red jacket, and a pair of sturdy leather boots offset her trousers.

"Are you ready?" she asked.

Luxon nodded.

*

Luxon and Eripa arrived at the palace's main courtyard to find Ferran and Sophia already there along with Beric and two of his most trusted Bannermen. Horses had been saddled and were weighed down with supplies.

"Hopefully, we won't need all this stuff, but it always helps to be prepared. The Gryphon Mountains can be a dangerous place," Beric explained. Luxon was directed to a black mare that snorted and stamped its feet as he approached.

"Darkflash there is a very loyal steed, and he has some experience with having magic users ride him," said Beric patting the animal affectionately.

"Oh?"

"Meric, Queen Nix's brother, rides him occasionally. He's a magic wielder too and Thorn's trusted advisor on all things magical."

"Will Meric mind me riding him?" Luxon asked as he strapped Dragasdol to the horse's harness and climbed into the saddle.

"No, I shouldn't think so. Meric is with Thorn, wherever they are, and from what the Queen said he was riding in one of the wagons. Meric dislikes riding, he always complains about getting a sore arse."

Ferran and Sophia were already mounted, but Eripa needed a helping hand from Beric to mount her horse. Hers was as white as snow whilst Ferran's was a pale brown and Sophia's a chestnut in colour.

Beric and his Bannermen formed up in single file while Luxon, and the others fell in behind them. With a gentle nudge of his boots, Luxon spurred his horse on and towards the imposing Gryphon Mountains.

CHAPTER 10.

It was good to be on the road again. Spending too much time on the *Agatha* had made Luxon yearn to be travelling under his own momentum again. The weather was good with only a slight cool breeze betraying that Kastador too was experiencing winter. The palace now lay a dozen miles behind them, and the landscape was now one of woodlands interspersed with farmers' fields.

He chuckled to himself as he remembered how much he'd hated the idea of embarking on such a journey when he was younger. Back then, he'd only wanted to be safe and comfortable behind Caldaria's crystal walls. It was strange how things changed. He looked at his companions. Ferran too was a changed man. When they'd first met, the Nightblade had been barely able to conceal his dislike for him. Now, however, after everything they'd experienced together, he had softened slightly, and Luxon considered him to be one of his greatest friends. Sophia meanwhile had always been like a big protective sister to him, and over the years she had grown ever wiser and a person he could always turn to for advice. In his heart, he knew that without them, he would never have had the courage to achieve all that he had. They had saved his life numerous times and been there for him during his darkest moments. In effect, they were his family. It had been Sophia who had comforted him when his mother had died, and it had been Ferran who had risked his life to save his own when the Void sickness had almost destroyed him. Riding in front of him was Eripa. The bard sat sideways in her saddle and in her hands was a piece of parchment and a quill. She looked deep in thought. She smiled as she noticed him looking at her.

"Can I help you, Master Wizard?" she asked coyly.

Luxon blushed. He was embarrassed at being caught.

"Sorry, I didn't mean to stare. What are you doing?"

She winked at him and then reached down into one of her saddlebags. She pulled out a scroll and tossed it to him. He caught it easily, and curious, pulled the string and unfurled it. Scratched onto its surface were masterfully drawn sketches of some of the sights they had seen in Tulin. This scroll featured a depiction of the wondrous gardens of Zlegend and a detailed drawing of- himself. He'd never seen a picture of himself before, not even the ones that had been painted after his heroics in Eclin and on display in the King's Spire at Sunguard. He found it too embarrassing. Not to mention the fact that he'd been depicted in various heroic poses.

It was Eripa's turn to blush as he showed her the scroll with a raised eyebrow. He smiled. There was certainly an attraction there between them, but his heart was with Hannah, and that would never change.

"These are amazing illustrations," he complimented.

"Thank you. As a bard, I find it useful to draw the things I see. Helps me visualize people, places, and events for the songs I write. I've already started composing a piece about Silenzia, but I think this land too will warrant its own ballad. It's beautiful."

Luxon nodded in agreement. The sprawling mountains now dominated the horizon and beneath the towering peaks were vast lakes of clear turquoise waters shimmering in the sunlight. It made him think of home and a pang of homesickness twisted in his stomach. He longed to see Hannah again.

The scenery changed again as they entered some woods. Tall conifer trees lined the stone paved road and to their left trickled a fast-moving stream.

Beric called for them to stop and the group dismounted.

"We shall camp here tonight. There's a rune stone just off the road," he explained.

"Your Queen said your lands are free of Fell Beasts," Ferran remarked.

"If only that were so. Kastador is far safer than other regions, but devoid of all Fell Beasts? No. I have been a soldier for many years, and from experience, I know not to get careless at night," Beric replied.

They moved off the road a little way and emerged into a small clearing. Standing in the centre was one of the mystical rune stones. They were a common sight in Delfinnia and to see one in Kastador made Luxon yearn for home.

Beric's men took the horses to the nearby stream for a drink whilst Luxon and the others set up the campsite. Each of them had been given a small one person tent and a pack of necessities such as cooking equipment. Before long, they had a fire going, and the tents pitched.

Night came quickly and along with it the cold of winter. They huddled close to the warmth of the fire's flames and ate a meal of venison stew. Eripa played her lute and sang songs of Delfinnia much to the delight of the   Kastardorrians. It wasn't long before they called it a night. They had a long day ahead of them.

                                    *

They awoke just before the sun rose, had a hearty breakfast, and packed up the camp. The night had passed without incident thanks to the safety provided by the runestone. They followed the road for another few hours until finally by early evening, they arrived at the base of the mountains. A solitary inn stood at the roadside called the *'Peaky Climber'*. Beric and Luxon went inside to purchase some more supplies and to gather any news from the mountains. The others meanwhile stayed outside to see to the horses. The interior of the inn was much like any other. A roaring fireplace dominated one wall and was surrounded by comfortable looking armchairs and several dozen tables and stools. The bar was in the centre of the main floor and manned by a burly looking innkeeper.

"How can I help you, sirs?" he asked, looking up from his task of tankard cleaning. The man was taller than Beric and was broader too. A hat made of animal fur was on his head, and a thick brown beard covered much of his face. His clothing too suggested he was a man well versed in the mountain life. He wore a thick coat of furs and trousers made of what looked like sheep's wool.

"We're heading into the mountains and need to top up on our supplies," Beric said.

"I can certainly help you with that," the innkeeper replied. He clapped his hands and a small boy dressed in similar attire appeared from a doorway behind the bar.

"Tomas here can help you. Just tell him what you need, and he'll fetch it from the larder."

Whilst Beric sorted out what they'd need for the journey into the Gryphon Mountains; Luxon approached the innkeeper who was back to cleaning his tankards. He kept a close eye on the boy who was leading Beric to a supply room at the back of the inn.

"Tell me, innkeeper, have you seen or heard anything strange recently?"

The innkeeper stopped his cleaning and paled slightly at the question. The man was obviously afraid.

"Why would you ask me that? N-no I've not seen nor heard anything."

His eyes were wide with fear.

Luxon leaned on the bar and lowered his voice.

"You're an awfully bad liar sir. If you know something, then please tell me. We can help. My companion is a Bannerlord."

The innkeeper regarded him with suspicion.

"I've heard some strange noises from up the mountain passes. Noises that would make your blood run cold. I've run this inn for twenty years and never have I heard the like before. Something evil is in those peaks. A week back, a strange bunch of folks passed through this way. About twenty of them of in all. All hooded and cloaked in mystery they were. I asked them if they wanted to stop for a rest before they headed up into the mountain passes, but they just ignored me and pressed on. They had a sinister feel to them, and this will sound crazy, but I swear to the Gods that some of their number, well, their eyes glowed."

Luxon thanked the innkeeper for the information and headed outside. He walked over to Ferran and Sophia, who were busy helping Beric's men load the supplies onto their horses.

"We have a problem," he said. "I just had a chat with the innkeeper. The Sarpi are here in Kastador."

"Are you certain?"

Luxon nodded.

"I am. According to the innkeeper, twenty of them passed this way a week ago. Right about the time the reports of strange lights reached the Queen and just before King Thorn went heading off to investigate. I think we can assume that N'Gist are with them."

Ferran touched the hilt of his Tourmaline blade.

"This confirms it then. The enemy beat us to Tulin. Who knows how long they've been here?"

"I think we can surmise a few months at least. The way they infiltrated the Silenzians suggests that to be the case," Sophia said.

"The real question is, what are they doing in these mountains?" Luxon replied.

"Whatever it is, it can't be good," Ferran said ominously.

*

The group spent the night in relative comfort at the *'Peaky Climber'*. Each of them had a small room and bed and awoke at the crack of dawn well rested. After a breakfast of hot porridge they were back on the road again. As they rode past the inn, the road they'd been travelling on narrowed into a dirt path that began to climb upwards.

The temperature plummeted making Luxon grateful for the thick furs they'd taken with them. Before long, a gentle snowfall began, and by the middle of the day, they had reached the base of one of the Gryphon Mountains passes. A thick forest of birch and pine trees covered much of the landscape, and an expansive lake filled with clear, clean water reflected the splendour of the magnificent peaks.

Beric raised a hand to slow the group. He dismounted and gestured for the others to do likewise. The carcass of a horse lay in the middle of the path and dried blood covered the surrounding area.

Ferran approached the dead animal and crouched next to it.

"Something big did this. Look at the claw marks on its flanks. Whatever killed this poor creature has immense strength. It ripped its innards out with a single swipe of a razor sharp talon."

"A Fell Beast?" Beric asked his voice full of concern.

"Perhaps, although I've never seen injuries such as these before. A Nightstalker tends to take a few swipes with its claws to kill something this big, and it would've devoured every part of its prey. No, this is something else. It struck suddenly and left it here to rot."

Behind them, Luxon was studying the ground.

"There are footprints in the mud and snow," he said.

"And there's this," Eripa said as she held up a piece of the horse's ravaged bridal. On it and etched into the leather was a symbol of a Gryphon. Beric's eyes widened, and he hurried over to her.

"That's King Thorn's symbol," he exclaimed.

"These tracks lead up the path. I'd say a dozen or so men and horses fled in a hurry," Ferran said as he continued to study the scene. He was an expert tracker having spent much of his life hunting Fell Beasts across Delfinnia.

"There's more blood further up the path suggesting that the rider of this horse was injured in the attack. He must have been alive and rescued by one of his companions."

"Why would they not retreat down the mountainside?" Sophia wondered.

"Perhaps they couldn't. Perhaps the creature that attacked was in pursuit and hunting them."

Beric climbed back into his saddle and squeezed the piece of bridal tightly in his fist.

"Whatever the case, we press on. We must find the King."

*

They continued to follow the tracks but the light snow shower that had begun earlier in the day had now grown heavier. The wind too, had increased in strength to send swirls of snow and ice dancing around them. The horses slipped and struggled on the path, and the cold was biting through the thick furs they all wore.

Luxon looked to his left. They were several hundred feet up the mountainside, and the forests were now far below them.

"We need to find shelter and soon," Ferran shouted over the now howling winds.

A screeching noise pierced the air causing them to freeze.

"What was that?" Eripa asked.

"It's just the wind - right?" Beric answered.

The snow was now falling fast, and a thick mist had begun to roll down the mountainside reducing their visibility. The sound came again, this time closer than before.

"That's not the wind!" Ferran muttered.

Luxon looked up and shouted a warning. Diving from the sky was the shadowy impression of a giant winged creature. With lightning speed, it punched through the swirling snow; its talons held ready for the kill. The Gryphon elicited another screech as it attacked and grabbed one of Beric's men from his saddle. The man screamed, but it was too late. The Gryphon scooped him up in his talons and flew back into the sky. Eripa cried out in terror as the beast raised the screaming man to its monstrous beak and ripped his head from his shoulders.

Sophia drew her bow and shot an arrow at the Gryphon, causing it to shy away with a frustrated scream.

"RUN!" Beric yelled, kicking his spurs into his horse's flanks. The others did the same and fled up the path. The terrain was treacherous, and the snowfall made the horses slip. Ahead, one of Beric's men's horses skidded and tumbled over the mountainside, the rider's screams fading as he plummeted into the abyss below. Luxon spurred his horse to go faster until he was leading the pack. He raised a hand and channelled his magic. Using a fire spell, he melted the ice and snow on the path as they fled. Steam rose from the path, but the horses footing was now much more secure. Behind the Gryphon was in hot pursuit its screeches echoing off the surrounding mountains. It swooped in close once more, its sharp beak snapping savagely. Sophia shot another arrow this time striking the Gryphon in the side of its neck but bounced off due to the creature's thick feathers. The Witch hunter shouted in frustration. Ferran now used his magic to launch a fireball, but the Gryphon saw it coming. With incredible agility, it cartwheeled through the air, dodging it easily. They thundered along the path; the enraged Gryphon hot on their heels.

"I thought you said these things were friendly!" Ferran yelled to Beric over the sounds of horse's hoofs and the screams of the beast pursuing them.

"I don't understand why it's attacking, the Gryphons have never been hostile before," the Bannerlord shouted back. "We must reach the Snowy Pass. It's not far from here. The terrain will provide us with some cover."

Ahead of them, the path widened slightly and curved to the right where it dipped down to run between another mountain to their left. Ferran narrowed his eyes, sure enough, he could see a pass where the two peaks stood close to one another.

"We're almost there!"

A cry came from behind them, causing him to look over his shoulder. The Gryphon had attacked again, and this time it was Eripa's horse that was its target. Its beak snapped, slicing the horse's rear leg clean off and sending it and the bard crashing to the ground. The Gryphon landed on the path with a thud. It stabbed its beak into the dying horse and flung it aside. Its huge eyes were fixed on the now unmoving Eripa. Immediately, Ferran yanked back on the reins of his horse to bring it around. He reached down and drew his Tourmaline Blade and ignited it with magic. The bright blade snapped into life with a snap-hiss.

"Keep going, I'll get Eripa," he yelled to the others. He kicked his heels into his horse's flank and charged back up the path towards the Gryphon.

Beric raced on towards the mountain pass, but Luxon and Sophia skidded to a halt. They watched as Ferran bellowed a challenge to the Gryphon and leapt onto the saddle of his charging mount.

Just as the Gryphon was about to devour the prone Eripa, he launched himself through the air, his sword held in a two-handed grip behind his head. He flew and swung the weapon with all his might, causing the magical sword to slash deeply into the Gryphon's face. The mighty beast reared back, lost its footing, and screeched in agony.

Ferran landed heavily, the ice causing him to fall onto his stomach in a spray of snow and slide towards the now flailing beast. He looked back and using a telekinetic blast shoved Eripa's unconscious form over the ice towards Sophia and Luxon who were running towards them. Luxon reached out with his magic, desperately trying to grab the fallen Nightblade with his magic. Sophia screamed, but it was too late. The Gryphon's talon snared Ferran's ankle, and as it fell over the mountainside, it pulled him along with it. Frantically he tried to grab onto something, but the weight of the Gryphon was too much. He fell over the mountainside. Sophia ran to the edge of the path only to see her husband falling into the thick swirling mists below. Ferran was gone.

CHAPTER II.

Gryphon Mountains, Kastador

Sophia stared into the swirling mists, unable to take her gaze from the spot where Ferran had fallen. The snowstorm had now become a blizzard, but she didn't care. She didn't feel the cold, just a numbness in her heart. She flinched as Luxon placed a hand on her shoulder.

"Sophia, I'm so sorry, but we must seek shelter from this storm. We can search for Ferran when the storm passes," he offered weakly. "Please, Sophia."

She looked at him, her eyes betraying the desolation she felt, it hurt Luxon's heart to see it. Gently, he helped her stand and walked with her down the path. Ahead, Beric was waiting with the wounded Eripa. Blood from the wounds to her leg had turned the snow crimson.

"She's bleeding pretty badly. Come, I spotted a cave a bit further up the path. We can find shelter there."

"Lead the way."

The group fought their way through the swirling snow and ice. Eventually, the cave Beric had spied earlier appeared through the whiteout. The night was quickly approaching, and the temperature would plunge to well below freezing. They reached the cave and gratefully went inside. Immediately the howling winds abated. Luxon cast a light spell so they could hitch their horses and led the way deeper inside. From what he could see, the cave was, in fact, a long tunnel like structure that went on for several hundred meters. He slowed as he spotted a flickering light emanating ahead.

"Someone's already here," he whispered to the others. Beric passed Eripa to Sophia and drew his sword. Luxon held Dragasdol at the ready. Together they crept forward and there they found a group of four men all sat around a campfire. They all wore armour save for a tall skinny man who wore a long grey cloak and a big pointy hat. Beric smiled and gestured for Luxon to lower his staff. He stepped out of the shadows.

"By the Gods King Thorn, you know how to scare the snot out of a man," he laughed. The men jumped up in surprise, but at seeing Beric, they relaxed. The tallest of the bunch pulled the Bannerlord into an embrace.

"Beric, my friend, you found us," the man said in relief.

"Nix sent us, and it looks like it was a good thing she did too. You look like shite," Beric replied, taking in the sorry state of the group. Two of the men were injured, with one wearing a blood-soaked bandage on his head and the other had a splint affixed to his leg.

"Us?" the man asked warily as he noticed Luxon and the others.

"Forgive me, this is Luxon Edioz, Sophia Cunning, and the injured girl is a bard named Eripa. This,' he said, pointing to the bedraggled man, 'is King Thorn of Kastador. It's a long story, but from the sounds of that storm we will have plenty of time to tell it."

Thorn was a tall slim man with a head of neatly trimmed black hair. His face was covered in dark stubble. His eyes radiated with intelligence, and like the others, he looked exhausted.

Luxon stepped forward and bowed.

"Your majesty," he greeted.

"I thank you, stranger, please share our fire," Thorn said, waving them closer to the warm flames.

Luxon helped Sophia get Eripa comfortable.

Sophia reached into her pack and pulled out some bandages which she then expertly wrapped around the wound.

"This should stem the bleeding, but it will require healing magic to get her back on her feet and walking again."

Meanwhile, Beric was telling his countrymen their story. When the tale reached current events, Sophia walked away from the fire and back towards the cave's entrance.

"Leave her be. She needs to grieve," Luxon said his voice full of sorrow. He pushed back tears and focused on helping Eripa.

He placed a fur blanket over her and lifted her leg into his lap to examine the wound. The Gryphon's claw had punched deeply into her calf.

Luxon knelt next to Eripa. He rubbed his hands together and focused on the magic within. The familiar tingling sensation flooded through his body and channelled into his hands. They began to glow, and then he placed them over the wound.

Eripa stirred and groaned as the healing magic did its work. Underneath the bandage, the damaged tissue was fusing itself back together. Sweat broke out on Luxon's brow as he kept up his efforts. Healing was always exhausting, and despite his power, he'd no doubt feel the effects of using such magic for the next day or two.

The skinny man with the pointed hat approached and watched with interest.

"I am Meric,' he greeted 'a magic user like you. I must say it's fascinating to meet a wizard from another land. Tell me, how are you using magic without the need for incantations or spells?"

"I am a Thaumaturgist, I can tap into the magic within me just by thought and concentration," Luxon replied, his concentration fixed on Eripa's wound. He could sense the flesh binding itself under his palms.

Meric's eyes widened.

"I knew it! I knew people, such as yourself, existed. Those old fools at the mage college in Old Kastador would never believe it. I say 'mages' they're more like cheap party magicians, wouldn't know a fireball from their wrinkly asses. Anyway, I digress-"

"Meric. Leave the wizard to his task. You can talk his ear off later," Beric chuckled. Meric held up his hands and mouthed an apology and went back to tending the wounded men.

Satisfied with his handiwork Luxon sat back and wiped his brow. Eripa was now sleeping soundly.

The tiredness was already threatening to overwhelm him, but he fought it off.

"Why did you venture into the mountains sire?" Beric asked.

Thorn exchanged a look with Meric.

"We received reports of strange lights in the sky and of odd behaviour from the local wildlife from the folks that reside at the base of the mountains."

"Naturally, I assumed magic was the cause. And I was right. Someone is using dark magic that has driven the Gryphons and other mountain critters mad," Meric added.

"We were heading for the old watchtower and Imris when Gryphons attacked us. I've never seen them act so aggressively. We set out with thirty good men, we're all that survived," said Thorn sadly.

"The innkeeper at the *Peaky Climber* Inn said that he'd seen Sarpi ascending the mountains," Beric muttered.

"And where the Sarpi goes you can be sure the N'Gist are with them," Luxon added bitterly.

"The N'Gist? Here? Impossible." Thorn exclaimed in disbelief.

Luxon fixed the King with a hard stare.

"Danon and his followers seek to conquer the entire world. They have already made a move against Silenzia, and they will seek to destroy your realm too. Whatever they're doing in these mountains, you can be certain that's their goal," he said more harshly than he meant. He sighed. "Forgive me. It's been a long day. I need to see if my friend is okay. It was her husband who fell."

Without another word, he walked away from the warmth of the fire and back toward the cave entrance. Sure enough, Sophia was standing there looking out into the now howling storm. It was freezing, and he shivered against the chill. Regardless he approached Sophia and placed a hand on her shoulder. She tensed at first and then stepped close, wrapping her arms about him. He held her as she sobbed, her body wrenching with misery.

*

Eventually, Luxon convinced Sophia to come close to the fire, and she quickly fell into a haunted sleep. He watched over her and Eripa for a while before finally, exhaustion took him.

The next morning, he stirred with a pounding headache, and his leg ached. Groggily he sat up and lifted his trouser leg. A wicked bruise had formed. That was the price of healing magic. Magic also required a price. When it came to healing wounds, the caster would pay for it often by manifesting a wound of their own. A skilled healer like Hannah would have been able to negate the effects, but to a relative novice in the art like he was, he took the full brunt of the side effects. He rubbed the bruise, and gingerly got to his feet. It was painful, but he'd live. He'd heard tales of some healers attempting to heal severe wounds that in turn died themselves for their efforts. Beric and his kin were packing up their belongings, and Eripa was sitting up and talking gently to Sophia. Seeing he was awake, she smiled. King Thorn and Beric were having a heated debate.

"We lost all our horses to that Gryphon, but if the N'Gist are here we must discover their plans without delay," Thorn said as he strapped his sword belt around his waist.

"I still advise that we head back to Kastador and gather reinforcements," Beric replied. Thorn looked to Luxon.

"What say you wizard? Do we press on or head back and gather our strength?"

Their group was in a sorry state, but he knew that they had to act quickly if they were to discover and stop the N'Gist's plans.

"We have three horses left. Your wounded men can take Eripa and use one to get back to safety. The rest of us should push on. I've fought the N'Gist for years now, and I've learned that they never do anything without a reason. We have to stop them as soon as we can," he said. Eripa opened her mouth about to protest, but Luxon shook his head.

"We cannot lose another of our company Eripa. It's too dangerous for you."

The bard crossed her arms.

"I may not be a wizard, warrior or witch hunter but I know how to look after myself and- well, you need all the help you can get."

"She's right," Sophia interceded softly. "Without Ferran, we need her."

"It's decided then," Thorn said. "Reese and Galadran will take one of the horses and head home. There they will inform the Queen of what has transpired. Tell her to send my Banners in full force to the mountains as soon as she is able. If we fail, we cannot allow the N'Gist to establish a presence here."

The two wounded bannermen bowed to their King and with help from Luxon and Beric climbed into the saddle of Beric's horse. Outside, the weather had cleared, but the bitterly cold wind continued to blow.

"Ride fast, and if you spot a Gryphon, pray to the Gods."

The two bannermen set off on the path down the mountain. Sophia and Eripa shared one of the remaining horses whilst Luxon insisted on walking to allow King Thorn a mount. The man looked more exhausted than the rest of them. Luxon, Meric and Beric set out on foot to lead the way. The path was covered in several inches of snow, making it slippery to traverse. As before Luxon held Dragasdol before him and using fire magic cleared a safe route. They walked on for several hours, Meric asking questions all the way. The path went ever higher into the mountains until, finally, it levelled out onto a flat plateau. They stopped and took in the view. It was breathtaking. They could see for hundreds of miles in all directions. To the south, they could see Kastador almost in its entirety, to the west the vast mountain range spread on into the horizon and to the north were the lands of the Tulin Empire. They walked on until they found a small cave where they decided to stop to rest.

"Tell me about the Empire. Are its rulers truly wizards?" asked Luxon as he looked out over the mountainside. Far below, the mountain path wound its way down into a deep canyon that led onto a wide plain and the Empire beyond.

"We don't have much to do with them, to be honest,' said Meric. He reached into one of his satchels and pulled out an old dusty book that he handed to Luxon. "Aside from their last invasion attempt a decade ago, we haven't heard much of a peep from them. Of course, there's always the rumours of one wizard lord waging war with another to gain more lands and power for themselves. As for whether they're true wizards, I can't really say, but they certainly do have some ability in the magical arts. That book was written a few decades ago, but it's the latest information we have on the Tulins."

"It's a divided place, not worthy of the title of an Empire. It's a place stuck in the mists of history," Thorn added with disdain. "Once, the Empire ruled this entire continent, but the petty squabbles of the self-proclaimed Wizard Kings led to the peoples of the south driving them out and winning their freedom. After the fall of the Golden Empire, those wizard kings that hadn't been slain retreated to Tulin and then spent the next six centuries trying to restore it.

The Freedom Wars as we in the south call them led to our people, eventually winning their independence and driving the Empire back across the mountains. As Meric said, they sometimes launch invasions against us, usually when one Wizard King gains enough strength to declare themselves Emperor. The last invasion was stopped at the battle of the White River. Many good men died that day."

Luxon flicked through the book Meric had given him and scanned the words within. It was written in a different dialect than he was used too, but he could just about understand the meaning. He frowned and looked out over the plains below.

"Why would the N'Gist come here? There must be a reason for it. You say these Wizard Kings are skilled at magic, could they possess something that could be of use to Danon?"

Meric snorted.

"I'd hardly call them 'skilled', but yes, I guess they could have something of magical value. Much knowledge was lost when the Golden Empire fell to ruin after all," said Meric thoughtfully.

Memories of the strange vision he'd experienced flashed into Luxon's mind. Tentatively he touched Asphodel's hilt.

"Are there any Portal Towers in the Empire?"

Meric frowned at the question. He took the book out of Luxon's hands and thumbed through its pages. He stopped and passed the book back to him. A crude drawing of a tower was sketched onto the page.

"How could I be so dim!" Meric exclaimed. "There are two known to be in Tulin lands. One of which is the most important of them all. The Nexus Tower."

Luxon read the page, and his heart sank.

"What is it?" Eripa asked. The bard had been watching the conversation in fascination. In her hands were a quill and parchment. She'd been writing down as much as she could. Luxon walked over to a patch of undisturbed snow and using his staff drew a crude map.

"This is Esperia or the lands that we know of at any rate,' he explained. "This is Delfinnia, Yundol, Sarpia and Tulin,' he continued pointing to the different shapes he'd drawn.

"It is said that during the Age of Discovery, early in the second age, the first mages travelled the world and, in the lands, they explored, they constructed towers that allowed them to traverse vast distances instantly. The Portal Towers. The one in Delfinnia is located at Tentiv, the former fortress of the Diasect. The others we know of are located on the Isles of Magic and here on Tulin. There's also the tower of Yin Mons on Yundol, and according to ancient texts another was located on Vucrar."

"-But they don't work anymore and haven't done so since the fall of the Golden Empire. All knowledge of how they work was lost," Sophia interjected. As a witch hunter, she too was an avid student of the world's history. After all, it was often the failures of mages and their magical mistakes that she often ended up having to hunt.

"Wrong," Luxon said seriously. "There is one who knows exactly how they work. Danon. During the Age of Darkness, he used the portals to send his armies across the world in the blink of an eye. It was Zahnia the Great who managed to deactivate them in his war with the N'Gist."

"By the Gods," Thorn muttered in horror.

"This must be why the N'Gist is here. Where are the two towers of Tulin located?" Luxon asked.

Meric thought for a moment.

"If I recall, there is one here in the Gryphon Mountains and the other, the Nexus is in the Tulin Empire capital of Ordvine."

Thorn groaned.

"I don't like the sound of that."

"During the days of the Old Tulin Empire in the Second Age, there was a city built high in the mountains, built around the portal tower. The arrogant Emperors ruled from it claiming that because they lived so close to the heavens, they were superior to all others. You see, it didn't matter that it was so remote, the tower allowed people and material to travel to it from all corners of the world instantly. If I recall correctly, it was called Skyrule or something equally as pretentious."

"What happened to it?" Eripa asked, fascinated.

Meric stroked his chin.

"According to legend, it was destroyed by Zahnia during the final days of his war against the N'Gist. The location was lost, but legends speak of the ruins of a city somewhere among these peaks."

"These mountains go on for a thousand miles Meric, it'd take us a century and every warrior in Kastador to find it," Beric moaned.

Luxon shook his head.

"I can find it," he said with determination.

"How?"

"There is a technique called scrying. It allows a magic wielder to detect and find things that possess magic. Something like a Portal Tower should be pulsing with power and easy to find."

"Fascinating," cooed Meric.

He closed his eyes and channelled his magic. He tightened his grip on Dragasdol and placed his hand on Asphodel's hilt, drawing on their power.

"Sophia, hand me a bowl from your pack and fill it with snow," he said. Sophia did as he asked and quickly handed him one of the bowels they used to cook with over a campfire. It was packed with snow, but Luxon used magic to melt it. Now that it was filled with water, he focused his gaze on it. The others watched him in bemusement, but he stood still, his eyes not blinking as he cast the spell.

"You may as well get comfortable. This might take a while," he muttered.

*

Several hours had passed, and still, Luxon was sitting and staring into the bowl of water. The others had started a fire and were eating some of their supplies, a soup of onions and leeks. The temperature had plummeted, but the warmth of the fire kept the worst of the chill and bay.

Suddenly a tingling sensation shot up Luxon's arm causing him to gasp.

Eripa called for the others, a look of concern on her face.

"What is it?" she asked.

He breathed in deeply and focused. There was something of immense magical power nearby.

"The tower is near. Its magic is muted as though someone is trying to block me from seeing it."

"I think we can guess who's doing that," Sophia growled.

"How close is it?" Thorn asked.

Luxon furrowed his brow and concentrated harder. It was close.

"A few miles to our east, ten at the most, I think. The N'Gist are really making me work for this. They must know someone is on to them," he said through gritted teeth. As soon as he got a clear image of the Tower, it was scattered, as though someone had thrown a stone in a pool. The N'gist were trying to confuse him.

"I can see a forest that grows beneath it."

"The Vaden Woods, it must be. It's the only forest for a hundred miles, and strangely, it is the only one to grow at such altitudes," Meric surmised.

Thorn walked over to Luxon and clapped him on the back.

"Well done Wizard. Let's get some sleep. Tomorrow, we head east and find this Portal Tower."

CHAPTER 12.

The journey east took them along narrow trails that wound through the mountains. The edge of the cliff was dangerously close, and more than once, the horses nearly lost their footing. The weather had cleared to reveal spectacular views.

They stood in awe as the great mountains loomed before them, cold grey crevices holding many mysteries. While the lower passes wore a cloak of greenery, the peaks were crowned with ice. Without a word passing between them, their hearts knew it to be a sacred place and stilled their minds. Rivers glinted in the sunlight and a carpet of trees spread for a hundred miles to the north.

The day wore on, and they eventually arrived at the ruins of an ancient looking tower carved into the mountainside.

"The watchtower of Imris," Thorn said. "We need to keep our voices low, for folk say it is haunted."

Luxon looked at the dark doorway at the ruined structure's base and shuddered. He could sense something watching them from within, and it was nothing good. They quickly moved on and travelled through a narrow rocky pass that opened out into a dense forest of oak and ash trees.

"Is there anything magical in these woods?" Luxon asked. Now, he was sure of it. There was something of immense power close by.

"These are the Vaden Woods. There's nothing in here aside from some eccentric woodcutters. In fact, I was about to suggest we pick up the pace. This place is renowned for giving people the creeps," Meric replied.

Luxon stopped and tightened his grip on Dragasdol. Without a word, he walked off into the trees.

"Hey, wait!" Eripa cried. Sophia sighed irritably, unholstered her bow and strapped a quiver of arrows to her back before dismounting and hurrying after them.

"He tends to do this sort of thing," she muttered to Beric.

*

Luxon walked deeper into the woods. As he did so, the trees grew thicker, and the light grew darker.

Upon the forest floor lay the desiccated corpses of trees fallen in storms long forgotten. The seasons in the mountains were harsh, stripping away the bark and outer layers, yet rendering them even more beautiful. The trunks had the appearance of driftwood, twisting in patterns that reminded Luxon of seaside waves; even the colour of the moss that covered every scrap of ground was kelp-like. They were soft, damp, yet his fingers came away dry when touching them. He tilted his head upward; the pines are several houses tall, reaching toward the golden rays only found on a crisp winter's day. Birdsong came in lulls and bursts, the silence and the singing working together as well as any improvised melody.

The sensation grew stronger until finally, he emerged into a clearing. Eripa was right behind him.

"Wow," she exclaimed at the sight.

A stone structure stood in the centre of the clearing. It was covered in moss and thick vines. The building looked like some ancient temple, half buried by the ages and submerged in thick mud. Luxon cautiously approached, looking for a way inside.

The bushes parted, and the others joined them.

"By Niveren, what is this place?" Sophia said in wonder.

"Whatever it is, it's ancient. I'd say by the carvings on the stonework that it dates to the Golden Empire at least," Meric replied as he ran his fingers over the stones. What had once been an ancient doorway was blocked by rubble.

"Fascinating. It's so deep in the woods that it's little surprise no one has discovered it," the magician cooed.

"There's something incredibly powerful inside. This must lead to the Tower," Luxon said. "Help me find a way in."

They walked around the structure, hacking away the vines and moss until they discovered a narrow hole in the stonework.

Luxon reached into the pouch on his belt and took out a firestone. He rubbed it, and the magical item burst into life to cast a bright orange glow. Carefully, he clambered over the stone and squeezed his body through the crack. Cobwebs and thick dust greeted him on the other side. The firestone illuminated the interior to reveal a stone staircase leading downwards. The stones were cracked with many of the steps chipped or broken. Turning, he helped Eripa squeeze through the crack. Sophia and the others were close behind.

"Well, Luxon I see you've discovered another dark dungeon of a place for us to explore," the Witch hunter muttered sarcastically as she brushed dust off her black leather armour.

Luxon held up the firestone, and together they carefully walked down the steps. The descent felt like it went on for hours, but eventually, they emerged into a small antechamber. Eripa gasped in fright and pointed to the corner of the chamber. Luxon cast the firestone's light over it to reveal a skeleton.

"Look at the clothing," Thorn said, kneeling next to the corpse. The tattered remains of ornately decorated cloth covered the bones and jewellery faded and worn by the ravages of time lay scattered at its feet.

"A Wizard Lord, it must be," Meric surmised. "C'mon, let's push on."

Luxon led the way through a triangular shaped doorway and stepped into a vast room. A corridor stretched on for what looked like miles but at its end was a glimmer of daylight. They walked through the eerie darkness, the only sound breaking the silence their footfalls. There was a deep air of oppression as they drew closer to the end of the corridor, and they tensed as they expected some monstrous attacker to strike from the shadows.

"The N'Gist," Luxon muttered. "I'd recognize that presence anywhere. Stay alert."

They reached the end of the corridor, and there discovered a staircase that wound upwards towards the light. Cautiously they ascended, until suddenly, they found themselves standing in a wide plaza. Stood around its edges were ancient stone structures, a city. Meric's eyes widened at the sight.

"This is it! The lost city of Skyrule."

Vines and moss covered every surface, and ruined statues lay like toppled toys around the edge of the plaza. Standing tall over the silent ruins was an imposing tower that reached high into the clouds. Luxon could sense the power throbbing from within.

Together they moved through the derelict streets careful not to make any noise.

"This place must have been abandoned over a thousand years ago. What an archaeological find this is," Meric whispered excitedly.

Beric shushed him.

"I'm sure it's fascinating Meric, but we don't know what could be living in this place-"

"Oh, I think we have an idea," Thorn interrupted. The King stopped and pointed to an open square nestled amongst the narrow stone streets. A pile of branches and twigs filled the space.

"A nest?"

Thorn nodded.

"This must be the place. This must be the Gryphon's nesting site."

Sure enough, they spotted more and more of the huge nests nestled amongst the ruins and weather ravaged towers.

Meric paled and immediately closed his mouth. The last thing he wanted was another encounter with an enraged Gryphon. The group crept through the ruins toward the tower. Beric froze and held up a hand in warning. In the wreckage of what had once been a large three-story structure was a Gryphon. The huge creature was asleep; its loud snoring echoed in the silent city. One by one, they carefully crept past it, careful not to make a sound. Finally, they reached a narrow street that led directly to the base of the broad steps that led to the Portal Tower proper. They ascended them with weapons at the ready, but no N'Gist or Crimson Blades were waiting for them. Luxon took the lead, Dragasdol in his left hand and Asphodel in his right. They moved through the massive stone archway that marked the tower's entrance, where once a mighty door had stood, there was now only splintered oak and large iron hinges that creaked in the breeze.

Inside the tower was a long-curved corridor that led to another big arched doorway and along its edges were other doors, most of which were broken or decayed completely.

As they drew closer to the doorway at the end of the corridor, a strange humming sound could be heard. They picked up the pace and reached the door. Unlike the others, this one was made of iron. It was covered in rust and vines grew through cracks at its sides.

"Someone has been here," Sophia said, pointing to footprints on the dust covered floor.

"We have to get this door open."

They looked for a way to open it, but nothing was visible. Luxon spotted a small hole at the base of the door.

"I can get us in," he said. He faced Thorn, Beric and Meric. "What I'm about to do might seem a little weird to you but know that it's perfectly safe - I think." He shrugged off his cloak and handed it to Sophia and gave his weapons to Eripa.

"Are you going to do what I think you are?" Sophia asked with a raised eyebrow. Luxon shrugged and nodded.

"Time is of the essence, and I don't think there's an alternative. There must be a mechanism on the other side of the door that opens it. Just make sure you look after my clothes," he added with a wink.

He stepped back and rubbed his hands together.

"Okay, Luxon concentrate," he muttered to himself as he remembered the training he'd received at the hands of Master Kvar. Transmutation was one of the trickiest magical abilities there was, and there was a reason those who practised it regularly were more than a little odd. He eyed up the small hole and focused his magic.

"A mouse should do it," he thought. He'd pulled off such a transformation a few times before, but it was never a pleasant experience.

He imagined a tiny field mouse scurrying about his feet and channeled his power into the thought. Weariness flooded his body, and his head ached. A strange sensation filled him as he felt himself get smaller and smaller. The world became muffled until suddenly it became sharper than ever. He could hear the startled gasps of the Kastadorians. If he could, he would have smiled, but his new mouse body couldn't replicate the action. Strange smells filled his nostrils, and his whiskers picked up every vibration in the air. With his mouse ears, the dull humming was now near deafening. He fixed his gaze on the hole and scurried toward it. His hunch had been correct. The hole ran right through the door; he could see light flashing from within the room beyond. He moved through the hole and emerged into a vast chamber.

Strange alcoves lined the walls and in the centre was a massive metallic contraption. Cables made of metal were attached to it, giving it a bizarre squid like appearance. The power emanating from the object was immense. Stood around its base were figures. There were a handful of N'Gist and Sarpi and - his eyes widened. The High Witch was there overseeing proceedings. Four Crimson Blade Assassins acted as her bodyguard. None of them noticed the tiny mouse as he looked around for a way to open the door. Sure enough, on the wall was a lever jutting out of a mechanism. Keeping to the shadows, he moved underneath it. Now was the tricky part. He focused on his human form, and a tingling sensation filled his body as he reverted to his former self. The transmutation occurred quickly. Now he stood as naked as the day he was born defenceless in a chamber filled with enemies. He dared to glance over his shoulder. The N'Gist were focused on the strange device that was now humming louder and louder; then the witch spoke, her voice filled with glee.

"You're very arrogant to think you could escape my notice wizard."

He swore at his foolishness, of course, the High Witch had sensed him. Without waiting for her to strike, he dived for the lever and pulled it down. An invisible fist struck him from behind, smashing him against the wall. Stars exploded in his vision, and the world spun. With a series of clicks and groans, the door began to open.

Just as the High Witch was about to launch a fireball his way, Sophia dived under the door bow in hand. She came up in a roll and shot an arrow striking the witch in the shoulder. Yinnice staggered back and yanked the arrow from her now bloody shoulder.

"Time for some payback, bitch!" Sophia snarled.

Immediately, the Sarpi drew their swords and charged at the Witchhunter. Sophia tossed her bow aside and drew her short swords. She parried the first Sarpi and with incredible skill flicked her other blade upward to slash her attacker across the throat. She ducked a strike aimed at her heart and punched a sword into the groin of another Sarpi.

"I'll kill you all!" Sophia screamed. Her rage was like a physical force, a power of its own. Into which she poured all her pain at Ferran's death. Crossing her swords, she blocked the third attacker before delivering a savage head butt that sent him sprawling to the ground. She leapt on the fallen Sarpi and stabbed a sword into his neck.

Beric and Thorn entered the fray, their swords swinging as they engaged the enemy. Meric followed behind with his magician's staff. A bolt of light flashed from its tip to blind the N'Gist. Eripa dashed over to the dazed Luxon and put his cloak over his naked body.

"Can you stand?" she asked over the noise of the fray and throbbing tones of the strange machinery.

He nodded and groggily got to his feet. Eripa handed him his staff and Asphodel. Meanwhile, the High Witch had turned away from the fight. Her attention was focused on the strange device at the centre of the room. Light began to emanate from it, and the volume of the pulsing grew. Luxon shrugged on his cloak and tapped into Asphodel's magic to clear his still spinning vision. His eyes widened. The witch was now standing in front of a pedestal that had emerged from the stone floor. In her hand was an object; it was the amulet the Shar of Silenzia had worn about his neck!

She placed the metal plate into a slot on the pedestal. A blinding flash lit up the chamber causing the combatants to disengage and shield their eyes from the glare. The light faded as quickly as it had appeared to reveal a shimmering rectangle of light. It was a portal.

"You're too late, wizard," Yinnice cackled.

Luxon took a step toward her, but she edged closer to the portal.

"What have you done?" he shouted.

"Only what my master commands. This land will fall just as Delfinnia will. Kill them all and take the sword," she snarled. She raised her hands and muttered an incantation. Dark smoke emanated from her palms to envelop the Crimson Blades standing protectively in front of her. Then, the light in the chamber faded to cast it into shadow. Ice formed on the walls and floor. Beric cried out as his sword froze in his hand. Unearthly moans and a sickening crunching noise filled the chamber. Then, just as quickly as it had dimmed, the light returned to reveal four salivating monsters. The beasts were the height of a man, and they stood on two muscular legs, but that was where the similarities to humanity ended.

Their arms were long and covered in spines with hands that were talons, with nails like razor blades. The colour of their skin was a dark grey, and their torsos rippled with muscle and were covered in short black hairs. Most disturbing of all, however, were the faces that bore the features of men they once were, but instead of human mouths, they had open maws filled with sharp teeth.

Yinnice cackled and stepped into the portal, vanishing in a flash.

Luxon stepped protectively in front of Eripa.

"Stay behind me," he warned.

"What are they?" she whimpered her voice full of fear.

Sophia settled into a fighting stance at their side.

"Necrist. The foulest and most deadly of the Fell Beasts."

"She turned those Crimson clad chaps into them," Meric cooed in fascination. The N'Gist and Crimson Blades that hadn't been turned backed slowly away from the Necrist. They knew how deadly the monsters were.

"I think we're in trouble," Thorn muttered.

CHAPTER 13.

The crevasse was narrow and filled with snow several feet deep. The first thing Ferran felt as his senses returned was the numbing cold. Every part of his body ached, but to his amazement, nothing was broken. He opened his eyes and gasped. The fall should have killed him. The last thing he remembered was Sophia screaming his name as the Gryphon pulled him over the mountainside. Wincing, he sat up and looked around. He'd fallen into a deep snowdrift that had absorbed the impact of the fall. His clothes were caked in ice and snow. His fingers were frozen even through the thick gloves he was wearing. He reached into one of the pouches on his belt and pulled out a firestone. Rubbing the stone between his hands caused the magical object to flare to life, and he sighed as it radiated much needed heat.

"How am I going to get out of here?" he muttered, looking up at the spot from where he'd fallen. The ledge was hundreds of feet above him and almost obscured by clouds. A scratching sound came from behind him, causing him to pause. Slowly he turned to see a Gryphon lying in the snow. It pawed the ground weakly and let out a pained squawk. Ferran admired the creature. It was a marvel of creation and one alien to him. No such creatures lived in Delfinnia. Its large eye looked at him, pained and scared. Slowly, he approached and held his hands open to show he wasn't a threat.

"I cannot be mad at you. Something caused you to attack us," he said softly. The Gryphon flinched as he placed a hand on its large head. He was careful to avoid its beak. On closer inspection, it was clear that if it wanted, the creature could easily rend him limb from limb. The Gryphon mewled in pain and raised its front leg. There, lodged into its torso was a thick tree branch that had pierced its flesh just beneath the wing.

"Looks nasty," he soothed. He stepped toward the wound, but the Gryphon lashed out with its front paw, vicious claws extended.

"Easy. I can help you. Beric said that you don't normally attack humans. That you're friendly to people. Let me help."

The Gryphon blinked and lowered its paw. Could it understand him? Ferran took a deep breath and stepped carefully over the paw and focused on the branch.

"This is going to hurt. Please don't eat me," he said, gritting his teeth and channelling his magic. Ferran muttered an incantation and raised a hand toward the branch. Telekinetic spells were tricky at the best of times, let alone when a creature more than three times his size could tear his head off. He sensed the branch, and with a jolt of his arm, it ripped free of the Gryphon. It screeched and reared onto its back legs, but Ferran had already backflipped out of the way and to a safer distance. His hand reached for the hilt of his Tourmaline sword, but he did not ignite it. Instead, the Gryphon rose to its full height and emitted a screech that almost deafened him. He tensed, expecting it to strike but instead, it lowered itself to the ground and to his amazement sniffed him, much like a dog would.

It chirped softly and then flexed its wounded wing. It nudged Ferran softly towards the now bleeding injury and chirped again. Ferran looked it in the eye and nodded in understanding.

"I'm not the best when it comes to healing magic, but I might just have the thing in my pouch," he said. He reached into one of the pouches on his belt and took out a vial containing a bluish liquid that glistened in the sunlight. It was a Potion of Sealing, one that every Nightblade carried when on a mission. Due to them often being deep into the countryside and far from civilization and assistance, the Nightblades had to be able to look after themselves and have the tools needed to patch up any wounds. He pulled out the vial's cork with his teeth and stepped close to the wound. Tentatively he stepped onto the Gryphon's front paw, and to his surprise, the creature manoeuvred him so that he was now above the wound.

"Clever girl," he muttered, having no clue as to what sex the animal was.

He tipped the vial's contents on the wound, and within seconds it began to fizz. Steam rose from it, but the potion had done its work. The wound was now sealed and cauterized. He jumped to the ground and stepped back to admire his handy work. The Gryphon opened its wings wide again and flapped them powerfully to create a gust of wind that almost knocked Ferran off his feet. It screeched again and lowered itself to the ground. It stared at Ferran before moving its head to point at its back. It did this several times before it ran out of patience and gently nudged Ferran towards it.

"You want me to climb onto your back?" he asked uncertainly. The Gryphon nudged again, and its big blue eye regarded him for a few seconds. Intelligence radiated from it, then to Ferran's surprise, it nodded its head.

"Alright then," he muttered. Carefully he climbed onto the Gryphon's back, using its feathers as handholds. He tried to remember how Luxon rode Umbaroth and moved into a similar position just behind its head.

"Okay, here goes."

Satisfied that Ferran was sitting comfortably, the Gryphon spread its wings and launched itself into the air. At first, it seemed as though the injury it had suffered would send them crashing back down to the ground, but with a flap of the wing, it corrected its trajectory. Ferran held on for dear life as the Gryphon climbed higher and higher. It soared out of the crevasse and into the frigid sky. The feeling of flying was exhilarating to Ferran. He recalled his experiences of being carried by Umbaroth and Tratos. Unlike riding those mighty beasts, the Gryphon was far smaller and a lot faster. Below, the landscape went by at dizzying speed. Rivers, forests, and plains flashed by in a blur.

"Where are you taking me?" he yelled over the sound of the howling wind. The Gryphon emitted a loud screech like that of an eagle and then, suddenly, it dived. Ferran screamed, something he never did, but this wasn't a typical scenario. Just as it seemed as though they would crash into the mountainside, the Gryphon pulled up and levelled off. Ferran shielded his eyes with a hand. Emerging through the clouds was a wide valley filled with structures. One, a tower dominated the others.

"What is this place-"

His words were cut off as he spotted a bolt of magical lightning lash into the sky. There were figures just outside of the tower. His eyes widened. It was Sophia and the others. They were engaged in battle.

"We have to help them!" he cried.

The Gryphon squawked in response and dove down onto the fight below.

*

Luxon landed heavily. Blood poured from his nose and the slash on his cheek burned. His cloak was in tatters thanks to the Necrist, only his skill with Dragasdol had kept him alive. Thorn hurried to his side and helped him stand. The King of Kastador was bloodied, his tunic was ripped, and the chainmail shirt underneath had been punctured to reveal a bleeding wound.

"Tis but a scratch," he said, noticing the concern on Luxon's face.

Luxon shook his head to clear the stars swimming about his vision. The Necrist were merciless. Sophia leapt out of the reach of one of the monster's snapping jaws and brought down one of her swords onto its neck. It roared in pain, but its thick hide caused the blade to bounce off harmlessly. Beric joined the attack and stabbed viciously with his sword. The blade punched into the Necrist's hide spilling viscous black blood that fizzed and hissed violently onto the snow. With a snarl, the Necrist stuck Beric with a brutal backhanded blow that lifted the Bannerlord off his feet and sent him flying backwards. He crashed to the rocky ground where he lay unmoving. That left Eripa and Meric to face the other Necrist. Neither was a fighter, but still, they held their ground. Meric took off his hat, reached inside and pulled out a wand.

"I may not be able to cast lightning or chuck fireballs about, but I can summon critters," he muttered. Moving the wand in a circular motion, he began to chant in a language that sounded a lot like ancient Nivonian. A light began to form in the middle of the circle, and then, Meric thrust forward. To Luxon's surprise, a small, winged beast emerged from the light. With a high-pitched roar, the Imp flew at the nearest Necrist and began to claw at its face. Luxon drew Asphodel and charged the now distracted Necrist. He ducked the beast's flailing limbs and slashed with all his might. Asphodel sheared through the monster's legs causing it to topple to the ground in a pained snarl. Sophia took her chance. Using both of her swords, she jumped over the downed Necrist and stabbed down into its eyes. It screeched before falling still.

"One down three to go," Thorn said through gritted teeth. The remaining Necrist circled them like a wolf pack waiting to strike. Luxon went back to back with Thorn while Sophia moved to Eripa and Meric. Standing at the top of the stairs at the base of the tower were the N'Gist and Sarpi cheering on the Necrist.

"It cannot end this way," Luxon thought desperately. He was exhausted, too exhausted to call upon more of his magic. The Transmutation spell and his healing of Eripa had taken its toll. Even the power of Asphodel felt muted as he struggled to focus. The Necrist

crouched, ready for the kill. Luxon held Asphodel in a defensive stance. He could perhaps slay one, maybe two but the remainder would overwhelm him. All hope seemed lost.

A screech pierced the air.

He looked to the sky and couldn't believe his eyes. A Gryphon was streaking toward them and on its back-

"Ferran!" he shouted in joy.

Sophia tore her eyes from the Necrist and looked up. She cried out at seeing her husband. The Gryphon swooped onto the Necrist its claws cleaving the head off one and its beak snapping another nearly in two. Ferran leapt from the Gryphon's back; Tourmaline blade ignited and struck down the last of the monsters. His blade cleaved through the Necrist's arm, but still, the monster fought. Ferran dived out of the way of a claw leaving the Necrist exposed. Thorn took his chance and dashed forward. With a roar, he punched his sword into its flank. Luxon followed with a thrust with Asphodel to its midriff and Sophia finished it off with a blow to its throat.

Stunned, the N'Gist turned and fled, but Meric directed his Imp to chase them down. It flew after them, catching one of the cloaked N'Gist by the back of the neck and threw him to the ground. The rest managed to flee, but the Gryphon took to the skies once more to hunt them down. More screeches filled the air as the Gryphons nesting amongst the city's ruins took to the skies to join the hunt.

Ferran stood panting at the scene of carnage. Black, fizzing blood covered the ground. He dispelled his sword and faced the others with a roguish grin. Sophia ran to him and embraced him fiercely.

"Don't ever do that to me again!" she scolded before kissing him passionately with tears of joy in her eyes.

"Knew you were fine," Luxon chuckled as he wiped the sweat from his brow.

"You look awful," Ferran replied coyly.

Luxon introduced Ferran to Thorn, and together they moved the unconscious Beric back inside the tower and out of the snow that had begun to fall. Sophia shoved the terrified N'Gist prisoner up the steps.

Once inside, Thorn made Beric comfortable by taking off his fur cloak and using it as a pillow. Ferran embraced Sophia, and the two dragged the prisoner to the side of the chamber for interrogation. That left Luxon with Meric and Eripa. With the N'Gist out of the way and the witch gone they were now able to study the chamber properly.

"Take a look at this," Eripa said.

Luxon and Meric walked over to her. In front of her and jutting out of the floor, was the circular pedestal the witch had used to make her escape. Strange runes were etched into its surface and in the centre was a small slot. More runes were carved onto it, and it hummed with magic.

"This is where Yinnice used the Shar's medallion, it must have been one of the lost Portal Keys," Luxon exclaimed, recognizing one of the symbols.

"Look,' he said, pointing to one of the runes. He leaned in closer to study it and rubbed his chin.

"It's the symbol of the Diasect. The one in Tentiv."

When we were in Tentiv it never gave off such energy as this place," Luxon wondered. He paced around the central column and placed a hand to its surface.

"So, these symbols represent other portal towers?" Eripa said.

"Yes, yes, that seems logical. How fascinating. I wonder what these other symbols mean. This one for example-' Meric said, pointing to a circular shaped rune with a Y drawn through it, '-looks different to the others. Perhaps it represents a different land entirely? Y for Yundolus maybe?"

Luxon regarded the Tentiv symbol closer, and sure enough, an N was etched underneath.

"N for Nivonia?" he muttered. They studied more of the symbols and discovered that each had a different letter carved on them.

Meric reached into his satchel and pulled out a book and quill. Next, he took one of the ink pots he always carried and dipped the quill's nib into it.

"I think we can assume that N is for Nivonia, which is now Delfinnia. Y is for Yundolis, which is now Yundol and T is for Tulin," Luxon explained as Meric sketched each symbol.

"This one has an S. Sarpia perhaps?" Eripa surmised.

"Seems logical. There's more over here," Luxon said, pointing to another column. These symbols he didn't recognize at all. "A, U and O. Where do those letters represent?"

"Lands we have forgotten most likely. When the Golden Empire fell, much knowledge was lost with the destruction of the Wizard towers and libraries. Including contact with other far flung lands. The mages of the Empire used magic to travel vast distances, but with their defeat in the Magic Wars, the art of teleportation magic was lost. Heck, here in Tulin even the most basic of magic was lost outside of Imperial lands. The wielders of Kastador, well, we pale in comparison to your skills master wizard," Meric explained.

Luxon smiled and clapped the magician on the shoulder.

"Perhaps when all this is over, the mages of Caldaria can come to Kastador and teach you."

"I would love that!" Meric enthused.

"You're going to have to teach me how to summon Imps. I've never seen that sort of magic in use before."

"I hate to break up the magic love, but this N'Gist scum wants to talk," Ferran interrupted from across the chamber as he wiped his blood covered gloves on his tunic. Sophia shoved the battered N'Gist to the middle of the room, and the others gathered around him.

It was rare that a N'Gist was captured alive. Normally they would fight to the end or take their own lives. Many folk thought that they were monsters or some foul abominations from the Void. The truth was far more mundane. They were magic wielders just like the mages were, albeit ones that practised the dark magics taught by Danon. This one was a young man, not much older than Luxon. His eyes were wide with fright. Centuries of oppression against magic wielders had spurred many mages to defect to Danon, who promised them safety and revenge.

"He's just a kid," Thorn scowled.

"Many of them are, sadly. Young fools who allow themselves to be twisted by Danon's cult," Ferran replied.

"LIES! I am Fentis, Master of the Dark Arts. Lord Danon is the truth, the way. We wielders are the rightful masters of this world, servants to the Dark Goddess. The darkness is deliverance from the repression of the light. Your false prophet- argh," the man's head rocked back as Ferran struck him.

"Enough of your deluded nonsense. Tell us why you're here. What was Yinnice doing here?" Ferran growled threateningly.

"Answer him boy, and I might just let you live as a prisoner of Kastador," Thorn interceded.

"You're too late. Her scheme has already been fulfilled, and soon your kingdoms will burn."

"What have you done?"

Ferran struck Fentis again, breaking his nose. He then forced Fentis' hand flat onto the stone floor. He placed the hilt of his Tourmaline blade above it.

"Answer him or lose the hand."

Fentis' eyes widened in fear. The brave façade he'd put up failing in the face of the threat. He looked pleadingly at Ferran, but there was no mercy in the Nightblade's dark eyes.

"She used the portal to send some of our troops to the Tulin Empire's capital. They were dressed in Kastador colours with orders to cause as much chaos as possible. Don't you see? We don't need to invade this land. We will just turn the people against one another just as we did in Delfinnia."

Thorn reached down and grabbed Fentis by the scruff of his tunic.

"When was this? When were your troops sent?" A hint of panic was in his voice.

Fentis smiled cruelly.

"Like I said, you're too late. By now our other agents will have stirred up the Nerios to strike at your allies the Dilar. Your Free Kingdoms are about to be attacked from all sides. The war will weaken you, and by the time lord Danon has finished his conquest of Delfinnia, this continent will be ripe to fall to his dark majesty."

Luxon placed a hand on Thorn's trembling arm and gently pulled him away.

"He's speaking the truth. When we arrived in Kastador, we learned that Nerios had launched raids against your southern allies. This is how the N'Gist operates. They divide and conquer. It's Danon's strategy. It worked too well in Delfinnia to the point where we're barely holding on. The enemy will pray on every weakness, every petty rivalry to divide you."

"We need to get back to the capital and warn them," Meric said.

"It'll take us days to get back there with Beric injured."

Ferran stepped forward.

"Will the Gryphons not help us?"

Thorn nodded.

"Perhaps. The Gryphons can be fickle creatures at times. They tend to choose who they allow to ride them. My Banner Riders were all bonded with their mounts as soon as they hatched from their eggs. I was amazed to see you riding one. It's incredibly rare for them to take up a stranger like that."

Ferran shrugged.

"I did heal a wound it had suffered. Perhaps it will allow me to ride it again and perhaps take Beric with me."

"It's worth a shot. Here-' said Thorn as he took a thin wooden block off his belt. Ferran raised an eyebrow.

"It's a Gryphon whistle. They are used by Banner Riders to summon our mounts. Alas, I tried to use it to calm the one that attacked us in the mountains, but alas the dark magics were too much. Now, however, with the N'Gist silenced it should work."

Ferran took the whistle and with the help of Sophia and Thorn carried Beric back outside the tower. Gently, they placed the injured Bannerlord onto the ground.

Ferran placed the whistle to his lips and blew. A high-pitched tune emanated from it and was answered almost immediately by the now familiar screech of a Gryphon. They looked up to see the Gryphon that had borne Ferran earlier swoop from the clouds. It landed with a thud and approached Ferran. It regarded him with its eagle eyes for a moment, and then it stepped forward and nuzzled him with its beak.

"I guess that means it likes me," he chuckled. He stroked the creature's feathered face.

"Will you help me one more time, my new friend. Will you carry this man too?"

The Gryphon emitted a mewling noise and then lowered itself to the ground and offered its back. Thorn and Ferran carried Beric and placed him on the Gryphon's back. Ferran followed.

"We will get to Kastador and inform the Queen of all that has occurred," he said.

"Tell my Queen to raise the banners. If the N'Gist have started a war, I want my kingdom ready for it," Thorn said darkly. "Cast the N'Gist in chains. He can pay for his crimes in the capital."

CHAPTER 14.

It was worse than they feared. Luxon and the others had started the journey back down the mountains when they heard drums and war horns. From their vantage point on one of the high mountain passes, they could see down into the valley that led south into Kastador. Sophia lowered her spyglass and handed it to Luxon.

"There must be ten thousand of them at least," she muttered.

"May I?" Thorn asked. Luxon passed him the spyglass, and he held it to his eye.

"Incredible, I can see the wretches as clearly I can see you. What sort of magic is this?" Thorn exclaimed.

Meric rolled his eyes and blushed with embarrassment.

"You'll have to forgive, Thorn. He's never been one to grasp technology."

"Are you telling me we have similar devices?" Thorn asked incredulously.

Meric patted his King on the head like someone would a small puppy or child.

"Yes, my King. It's actually straightforward. You see, at the top of the spyglass; an eyepiece is placed towards the end you look into and then-"

"I'm sure it's fascinating, Meric but I don't have time for a lecture right now. We need to reach Kastador before that army does."

"Could we not speak to them?" Eripa said from behind them. They turned to face her and looked at her as though she had gone mad.

"No offence to you King Thorn, but we aren't the Tulin Empire's enemy. Perhaps if we could convince them that the N'Gist has duped them into attacking, they might stop and turn back. And Luxon don't we need to gather allies? The Tulin Empire might make a mighty one."

Thorn handed the spyglass back to Sophia and shook his head.

"It's too late to parley. Trust me. Once the Empire commits such a force to war, it will only stop with bloodshed. You must remember that the Wizard Lords have long sought an excuse to invade my kingdom. The N'gist have given them one."

"But what of the old treaties? Luxon, you said Grandmaster Thanos gave you the treaties of the Old Alliance. Surely they are still bound to it?" Eripa countered.

Luxon reached into his cloak and pressed a hand to the envelope tucked under his shirt. Were the treaties worth anything anymore? It had been centuries since anyone had used them.

Luxon faced Thorn.

"Eripa's right. I think I must try. The Tulin Empire is not my enemy, not yet anyhow," he said. "If I can convince them of the truth, that they've been manipulated by the N'Gist they might call off their attack."

Thorn frowned at his words.

"I cannot command you not to do it. You're right. They are not your enemy, but they are mine. Your idea is a noble one. But for the sake of my realm, I have to get back to Kastador and raise my Banners."

"I understand. If I can stop a war, I will."

"I like the way you think master Wizard. I too would prefer an end to the needless bloodshed between the Empire and my people. Although I fear, they will not be receptive to you without an army opposing them."

The group continued their journey down the mountain. As the day wore on and the sun began to dip in the sky, they spotted four Gryphons flying slowly over the mountains. Sophia raised her spyglass.

"They have riders," she said.

Sure enough, the Gryphons had harnesses and saddles attached to their torsos and over their beaks. On their backs were armoured men with blue capes flapping out behind them.

"They must be looking for us," Meric surmised.

"Ferran must have made it back to the capital safely. Impressive. We need to signal to them; otherwise, they will pass us by," Thorn said.

"Allow me," Luxon said as he conjured a fireball into existence. He thrust his hand upward to send the magical projectile shooting high into the sky where it exploded in a bright orange flash.

The Riders spotted the magical flare and flew towards it. Thorn and Meric waved as the Riders soared overhead.

"Make way," Thorn ordered.

The Gryphons descended to land in the small clearing, their powerful wings kicking up snow as they did so. Once on the ground the lead Rider leapt from his saddle and hurried to Thorn.

"My Lord King, it fills my heart with joy to see you alive."

Thorn pulled the man into a hug.

"Sir Eeren, I am glad to see you. Get me off these blasted mountains."

*

Kastador City

The palace was a hive of activity, and the city itself bustled as the King's orders were obeyed. Supplies of food and water were being carried inside the city walls, and warriors from the nearby regions arrived with every passing hour.

The N'Gist, Fentis, was thrown into the castle dungeons and placed under the careful watch of the city's mages.

Luxon, Sophia and Eripa reunited with Ferran and the others and were now standing at the rear of the large room Thorn was using for his command centre. It was filled with soldiers and Bannerlords all planning battle tactics and strategies. Since their arrival in the city, they had all taken the opportunity to wash, change their clothes and grab something to eat.

On the large table that dominated the centre of the room was a map of Kastador and the other Free Kingdoms. Thorn was now dressed in a newly polished suit of armour and wore a golden circlet on his brow. He looked like a new man and had the appearance of the warrior king he was. He banged on the table to quiet his people. He looked around the room, making sure to catch the eye of all in attendance.

"The news from the Kingdom of Dilar is grim. The Nerios along with a mysterious new ally who can only be the same N'Gist vermin threatening our lands has ravaged the south and is now moving in force towards Dilar's capital. Their aim is clear. To conquer the Free Kingdoms."

Angry shouts and gasps of horror filled the room. Luxon watched the gathered nobility of Kastador closely. He could see the fear on their faces. The mere mention of the N'Gist had instilled a terror that he understood all too well. To the people of this land, Danon and his dark forces were nothing but mere myth and legend. Now, their homes were under threat from those same tales.

"The mastermind of this attack has executed their plan with a skill that is difficult to comprehend.

In a matter of weeks, the Old Enemy has returned to our shores, sown civil strife amongst the Silenzians, has manipulated the Nerios to invade Dilar and has even managed to trick the Tulin Empire to attack us. This enemy has played on our fears and rivalries. If we allow it too, it will destroy us all."

Thorn pointed to a location on the map.

"Our strategy is this. I will lead an army north to Gryphon Pass and meet the Tulin Empire forces where I shall defeat them. Queen Nix shall lead another force south to support Queen Merith and Dilar."

The Queen stood at her husband's side, herself resplendent in armour. Over the steel plate, she bore her husband's sigil of a blue Gryphon. On her hip was a longsword and tucked under her shoulder a gilded helmet.

A Bannerlord wearing a mantle that bore a red Lion raised a hand.

"Forgive me my King, but is it wise to separate our forces? And what news from Vinium surely King Teodric is aware of the danger."

Thorn crossed his arms and nodded slowly.

"I dispatched a messenger with our plan to Vinium as soon as we arrived in the capital. However, they will take time to deliver it, and I fear that it will be too late for King Teodric to respond before our army must meet the foe in battle. We can expect no support from Vinium at this time. As for splitting our forces, yes, I believe it is vital. I believe the BannerLords of Kastador are more than a match for this enemy, even outnumbered."

A growl of approval went around the room at those words.

"If there are no further questions, then my Bannerlords, march to war."

The room emptied of nobles and warriors to leave Luxon and the others alone with King Thorn and Queen Nix.

"Will you march with us?" Thorn asked.

Luxon looked at Ferran, and the two nodded.

"We will. But as I said in the mountains, the Empire is not yet our enemy. We will observe from the sidelines," Ferran said.

"Unless the N'Gist is present. If they fight on the side of the Empire, then we will have all rights to enter the fray," added Luxon.

"So be it. As Beric is still recovering from his injury, he will be your escort and protector. He was never much good in a scrap anyhow," Thorn joked lamely.

With that, Thorn departed the room, his Queen following close behind.

"We should get our horses ready for the journey," Ferran said, taking Sophia's hand and departing.

Luxon faced the other Delfinnians. Captain Whitelaw raised an eyebrow.

"So, the war for the Sundered Crown reaches across the oceans now. I pray there's a world left by the end of all this. Me and the crew will stay on the Agatha and have her ready to sail. I trust if this battle goes ill, we may want to make a hasty escape."

"Good thinking. Captain, I know it's a lot to ask, but please keep Alderlade safe onboard. Tell him that we will return as soon as we can," Luxon said. He felt terrible for having to leave the lad behind again, but he could not risk the young King falling into the wrong hands. Alderlade was Delfinnia's future, after all. Whitelaw shook his hand, and he too left the room. That left Luxon with Eripa and Welsly. The Nightblade had travelled from the docks with Whitelaw, but now he was determined to stay at Luxon's side.

"Do you think there will be a battle?" Eripa asked nervously.

"From what I've ascertained from Beric and Thorn is that it's very likely. There seems to be plenty of bad blood between the Empire and Free Kingdoms," Luxon answered, studying the map laid out on the table.

"Don't worry, I will keep you safe," Welsly said. He flushed slightly as Eripa smiled at him.

"C'mon let's join the others."

***

CHAPTER 15.

Hundreds of banners fluttered in the cold wind sweeping across the flat terrain that comprised the Gryphon Pass. The Bannerlords of Kastador were gathered and ready to defend their homeland. The sigils of many different Lords were flying. Red Lions, the Blue Gryphon of the King and the Yellow Swallow were the most numerous denoting the rank and status of the Bannerlords who possessed them. The Red Lion banners were on the right flank with Yellow Swallows on the left, and King Thorn's troops took up the centre.

The pass itself was a wide plain of snow-covered grass that narrowed into a valley at the far end. Two towering rocks marked the entrance to the pass. An hour earlier, a dozen or so skirmishers had rushed through. Their attempts at harrying the approaching enemy had slowed the Imperial army, but their efforts hadn't been enough to stop them entirely.

From their vantage point on a high hillside overlooking the plain Luxon could see how Thorn had laid out his forces. At his side stood Ferran, Welsly and Beric whose head was wrapped in a bandage. Both Nightblades were keen to see the Bannerlords in action.

The army's front rank consisted of heavy infantry wearing plate armour whilst the second was made up of lightly armoured spearmen. Bringing up the rear and safely protected by the first two ranks were archers wielding deadly looking longbows. On the flanks were masses of heavily armoured cavalry, the bulk of the elite Bannerlord army.

He could see stewards rushing about attending their charges and dashing to dish out supplies of water, food, and ammunition for the archers. Spare weapons and armour were on a baggage train a few hundred meters behind the army. He didn't envy the young men who would be tasked with providing a constant supply of new swords, maces, and bows. He felt tired, just thinking about it.

"They certainly look the part," Ferran said. The Nightblade stood at his side, arms folded across his chest.

"They almost look as well trained and disciplined as the King's Legion back home," Welsly added.

"Perhaps. But even in the face of Danon, the most disciplined and brave of men have faltered."

Warhorns blared in warning, and a Gryphon Rider flew from the direction of the mountains. The rider landed his steed with formidable skill in front of King Thorn.

They couldn't hear what was said but could easily take a guess. The enemy was near. The Gryphon took to the skies once more, but this time flew toward some woods to the east. It was there that the rest of the Riders waited. They were Kastador's most useful weapons, and they were to be used only if the battle began to turn ill.

"A dragon is always handy in scenarios like this," Ferran muttered. Luxon had to nod in agreement. Umbaroth and his kin had swooped to the rescue more times than he liked. Now that they were thousands of leagues from home and out of the dragon's reach, he felt vulnerable.

Like a tide, the Empire of Tulin's army began to emerge onto the plain. Spear points glinted in the winter sun, and the sound of ten thousand marching warriors boomed like thunder across the open space. Luxon took out his spyglass and looked at the army. Banners depicting a golden star on a red background flapped in the breeze. Unlike the Bannerlords, this was an army comprised mostly of lightly armoured men wielding long pikes and crossbows. The cavalry, on the other hand, was covered head to toe in golden plate armour that shone brightly. Taking up position to the rear of the army were men and women dressed in long flowing robes and wielding staffs.

"They have Wielders," Luxon said, his eyes widening.

Ferran swore.

"Thorn won't have a chance against magic."

"Wait - look," said Welsly pointing to the Kastador army. A small contingent of similarly cloaked riders had arrived. Leading them was Meric. The magicians leapt off their steeds and jogged to the front of the army who cheered their arrival.

"I guess we get to see just how powerful the wielders of Tulin are too," the Nightblade added.

Meric and his band of magicians limbered up and even did some stretches before facing the army and urging them to cheer louder. Next, they jogged toward the enemy army. To Luxon's surprise, the Imperial wielders did likewise.

"What is going on?"

"Oh, both sets of wielders will meet in the middle of the field and hurl insults at each other. You didn't think they'd actually use magic against each other?" Beric said aghast at the mere thought.

"There are treaties in place across the continent that restrict the use of magic in warfare. Treaties, that were introduced after the fall of the Golden Empire. Any nation that breaks the treaty, well it's unthinkable."

"Danon and the N'Gist don't care for treaties. There were similar rules in place in Delfinnia too before the War of the Six Claimants. Now, magic has destroyed entire cities and slain thousands," Luxon said bitterly. He had to take a deep calming breath to ease the anger he felt build in his chest. Danon was inflicting so much misery on the world. Now, here on the windswept plains of a foreign land, his machinations would see more blood spilt.

"What sort of things do they say to each other?" Welsly asked in bemusement. On the plain, Meric and the other magicians were now waving them arms about and making gestures that were undoubtedly rude in nature.

"Meric's favourite is to insult their mothers, and then he questions the size of their manhoods," Beric chuckled. Sure enough, Meric was wiggling his little finger at the increasingly enraged looking Tulin Wizard. Welsly laughed. The magician's antics even put a smile on Luxon's face.

A horn sounded, and the wielders separated with some final hand gestures and foul language. Meric and his companions strode back to the army with satisfied expressions. The Bannerlords cheered.

"Now comes the fighting," Beric said, licking his lips in anticipation.

The Imperial army began to pound on drums, and their archers walked through the ranks of infantry. In response, the Bannerlord archers mimicked the move. The infantry of both sides raised their shields and uttered prayers to whatever gods would listen. A tense silence filled the air and then with a shout, the Imperial crossbowmen loosed. Luxon watched the bolts fly with sick fascination. Each of the projectiles promised injury or death, but he couldn't tear his eyes away.

The volley struck the Kastador forces, and a score of warriors fell to the ground. The deadly crossbow bolts had punched through the steel shields like a hot knife through butter.

"Blasted crossbows," Beric growled. Unlike the small crossbows often wielded by the King's Legion of Delfinnia, the Empire was using large contraptions that required a handle and crank to reload. The power of such a weapon was devastating, even against heavily armoured opponents. It was clear that the Empire was well prepared to battle the Bannerlords.

Now it was the turn of the Kastador bowmen. They stepped forward and pulled back their bowstrings. Their longbows were almost the height of a man and required an immense amount of strength to draw, let alone shoot. The bowmen were all large in stature with massive shoulders that suggested they had trained with the weapons since adolescents. King Thorn lowered his sword and the archers loosed. The volley struck with devastating force, and the arrows slammed into the lighter armoured Imperial infantry. Luxon winced. He could hear the screams of the dead and dying from the top of the hill. The two exchanged another volley, and then war horns blared. The Imperial infantry began to move with the gold plated cavalry advancing on the flanks. The Bannerlords held their ground and let them come. The longbowmen loosed volley after volley until a trail of dead Imperial bodies could be seen on the field. The attacking army came within a dozen feet of their opponents and then with a roar charged. The frontline lowered their pikes and used their range to thrust at the Kastador army. Scores of Bannerlords fell to the deadly steel tips, helpless to engage with their shorter swords.

Meanwhile, on the flanks, both forces of cavalry faced each other. The Bannerlords lowered their lances, and the Imperials matched them. The horsemen smashed together; a vicious melee ensued. Armoured riders were unhorsed to lay unmoving in the snow and horses fell to stabbing spears and swords. The once serene field was now filled with battling warriors and death. Beric roared support to his side, but Luxon stood in silence. Ferran and Wesley too watched the butchery with grim expressions.

The battle raged, but it was clear that Thorn had a strategy. Luxon could see the Kastador centre line slowly fall back. To the Imperials, it would seem as though they were gaining the upper hand, but to Luxon, it was clear the movement was intentional. The infantry continued to slowly fall back to suck in more and more of the Imperial troops. Meanwhile, the Kastador flanks held firm and began to push forwards. The cavalry battle was vicious, scores of Bannerlords had fallen in the fighting, but now the Banner Riders entered the fray. The Gryphons burst from the woods in which they had been hiding and dived into the fray. Their mighty beaks brought down enemy horses whilst their talons cleaved through armour. Some Gryphons took to the sky, and their riders used their long lances to impale the enemy below. A horn sounded, and Thorn sprung his trap. The bulk of the Imperial infantry was now surrounded on three sides as the centre had fallen back to trap them between the solid flanks. Luxon could see the panic rippling through the Imperial ranks as they realized, too late, what had happened.

"Impressive," Ferran said.

Luxon nodded in agreement. The discipline of the Kastador army had been stunning. Only with such bravery and training could an army hope to pull off such a tactic so brilliantly. The Imperial army was being cut to pieces, and the Gryphons broke its cavalry. A mournful tone echoed over the valley and Thorn bellowed the order to halt the slaughter. The Empire had been soundly defeated. Its soldiers threw down their weapons in surrender while those who could flee escaped the field.

Kastador had won the day.

CHAPTER 16.

It didn't take long for the Tulin prisoners to be rounded up and bound. Of the ten thousand who'd marched against Kastador, a third had been slain in the quick but decisive battle. Thorn's strategy had been executed perfectly resulting in very few Kastadorian casualties. While the Bannerlords celebrated their victory, the King walked across the field with Luxon, Meric and Ferran at his side. Shambling before them was the Tulin Wizard who'd verbally sparred with Meric before the battle. To Luxon's surprise Meric and the wizard, who was introduced as Torvar, were chatting amicably among themselves. He realized that the relationships between the continent's various factions were far more complicated then he'd first thought. Welsly, Eripa and Sophia meanwhile were helping tend to the wounded of both sides. Torvar was far older than Meric with a bald head, and a thick silver streaked beard that almost reached his stomach. There was a keen intelligence in his pale blue eyes.

Torvar stopped next to the mangled body of one of the Imperial cavalrymen. His armour was dented, and arrows jutted out of the thick plate. A single puncture caused by a charging Bannerlord's lance had been the thing to kill him.

"This,' Torvar said with a hint of disappointment, 'was the Wizard Lord Eretor. It was he that led this army."

Meric stroked his chin.

"And you say he marched upon Kastador without orders from the Emperor?" he asked.

Torvar nodded.

"I warned the young fool not to rush to war, but alas he believed that avenging the 'Kastadorian' attack on the capital would win him honour and rank."

Thorn knelt next to the body and gently closed the young man's eyes.

"I will accord him the burial rights of your people. A fool he may be, but he too was innocent and unaware of the true danger facing us all," he said bitterly.

Torvar nodded.

"If what you say is true, King Thorn, and the Old Enemy is behind the attack on the Imperial capital. The council will want to hear of it. The Empire is in chaos, the Nexus tower captured, and the Emperor rumoured to have been taken hostage. Such a thing has never been allowed to happen in all our history."

Thorn stood and gestured for Luxon to approach.

"Perhaps we can assist with your current predicament. I must now hasten south to join my Queen in dealing with the Nerios incursion in Dilar, but perhaps my new friends here can assist with your N'Gist problems?"

Torvar regarded Luxon with a curious eye and slowly began to pace around the young wizard.

"Your clothing and posture- are you a wizard perchance? That staff looks impressive, and I sense you carry something incredibly powerful," Torvar muttered.

Meric rolled his eyes.

"Torvar, cut the mysterious magic user act. I literally just told you who he is and what he carries. Forgive me, Luxon. The one thing you should know about the Tulin are that they have a knack for the dramatic."

Torvar stopped his pacing and glared at Meric.

"Spoilsport," he grumbled. "Yes, yes, Meric told me who you claim to be. A Wizard from across the sea and one who wields the sacred blade of legend. Tell me, are the wizards of your land as highly respected as they are in the Empire?"

Luxon shook his head.

"No. In fact, before Danon's return, we magic wielders were hunted if we dared set foot outside of Caldaria. Wielders were treated terribly, in fact."

Torvar's face had an expression of disgust upon it.

"Your homeland sounds like a savage place. In the Empire, we wizards are highly respected for our wisdom. People come to us for all sorts of ailments and concerns. We wielders are the pinnacle of humanity. The very visage of what our creators intended us to be. Those who lost their ability to wield magic deserve to be subservient."

"Watch your tongue Torvar. Despite your claims of superiority, we Kastadorians can whip your hides when required, as we demonstrated today," Meric scolded.

"Bah! I was just joking. And besides, that young idiot Eretor was a fool to think he could invade the Free Kingdoms with just ten thousand men," the older man muttered, shaking his head.

"Your ideology sounds similar to the N'Gist," Luxon said unimpressed.

Torvar looked aghast at his words.

"No, my boy, we are nothing like those monsters. We respect magic. We respect the natural laws of it. The N'Gist'- he spat 'corrupt that law. They are our enemy just as much as they are yours. Is it not the laws of nature that dictate that the strongest and fittest dominate others? Magic is that advantage over other men."

Luxon fixed the wizard with a withering stare.

"Magic is a gift and one that should be used to protect the weak and defend mankind."

Torvar spat again and wagged a finger in Luxon's face.

"You speak the words of the false prophet Niveren! He who forsook the Gods and their true desire for wielders to dominate."

Luxon looked to Ferran who shrugged his shoulders. He couldn't exactly argue with Torvar's view of Niveren. He himself had issues with him. Knowing that Grandmaster Thanos was the immortal in disguise was hard to bear. He knotted a hand into a fist and pushed through the anger he felt. What Torvar said was true, it was Niveren who had taught restraint, and that magic was a gift to be used for the betterment of mankind. It was why the mages of Caldaria were nothing like these Tulin wizards. Some of the anger faded. He knew Thanos, Niveren, wasn't the hero the Niveren Cult made him out to be, and he knew that he wasn't a villain. His experiences on the Isle of Magic had revealed his true nature. He was a man cursed by squabbling Gods to live forever; a man cursed to do battle with his brother Danon for all time. He and even Danon were victims of the Gods.

"Perhaps your people should heed the teaching of Niveren, Torvar, you nasty little piece of weasel dung," Meric scolded.

Thorn sighed in exasperation.

"I am leaving for the south. I am trusting you, Torvar to keep my friends alive in your lands. Tell any Wizard Lord who wishes harm upon them that if a hair on their head is harmed I will gather the full might of the Free Kingdoms and I will burn their failing Empire to the ground. The same goes if any other foolish hot-headed Lord decides to attack my Kingdom," Thorn warned darkly.

Torvar paled at the King's words and bowed.

"I will ensure that no harm shall befall them, Lord King."

"May I ask something of you, Lord King?" Luxon asked. Thorn nodded.

"Please send word to Captain Whitelaw that we are heading to the Tulin capital. Tell him to join us when he's able."

"I will. Good luck to you, my friends. May the Gods protect us all."

*

They watched as Thorn and his army departed the battlefield. Thousands of prisoners had been taken and the weapons and armour plundered was now being loaded onto carts. The loot would be sent back to Kastador. That left Luxon, Ferran, Welsly, Eripa and Sophia with Meric, Torvar and Beric who had insisted on travelling with them.

"I'm not much use in a battle at the moment, but I can still wield a sword against this little shit," Beric had quipped gesturing to the Tulin Wizard.

They mounted their horses with Torvar riding with Meric and started north. First, they entered Gryphon Pass and followed its course for a full day until they emerged from the mountains and onto the plains beyond. They were now in the Tulin Empire itself, and it was a land with a landscape that reminded Luxon of the lush farmlands of Robinta. Thick forests spread for as far as the eye could see and standing like monoliths among the trees were tall spires that Torvar explained belonged to the various Wizard Lords that ruled their respective regions.

"Tell me Torvar, is the Empire truly an Empire still?" Ferran asked the old Wizard who was bickering with Meric once more. He spun about on his saddle and fixed Ferran with a foul glare.

"The audacity of such a question! The glorious Empire has stood for millennia and shall stand for eternity as the Gods command!"

Meric rolled his eyes and chuckled.

"Please. The 'Empire' is nothing but a land full of squabbling warlords who call themselves wizards to instil fear and respect from the poor peasants living under their heel. The Emperor changes every other week too. If there were a competition for regicide then this lot would win it hands down," Meric mocked.

Torvar grimaced.

"Perhaps in the past but our current Emperor is a man even I have put my faith in. He serves the Gods and has vowed to restore glory."

"And who is this emperor? We in the Free Kingdoms don't even know his name," Beric added from behind them.

"He is Zeno, and one day you southerners shall shake with fear at his name."

Beric and Meric exchanged a look before bursting into laughter. Torvar grumbled to himself and folded his arms.

"You'll see."

*

It was odd being in a foreign land that no one from home had set foot in for over a thousand years. What little Delfinnia knew of the Empire was from ancient scrolls found in Caldaria's Great Library. As an avid scholar of history, Luxon had read most of them. It was a land stuck in the past, one still thinking that it was the true successor to the now long dead Golden Empire of Zahnia the Great. Luxon wondered if the inhabitants of the Empire either knew or cared that the rest of the world had moved on long ago. It was the third day of their journey, and aside from spotting tracks on the road, they hadn't encountered a living being. They'd passed through ominously deserted villages that looked as though they had been abandoned long ago and were now traversing a road that led to a walled town. As they approached a shiver ran up Luxon's spine. No smoke rose from the stone house s chimneys despite the chill of the day.

"Is there anyone alive in this cursed land?" Meric complained. "I yearn for a good meal and a tavern bed. Three nights we've slept under the stars and in the cold. I'm miserable!"

"Is there something you're not telling us Torvar?" Luxon asked softly. They reached the town's walls to find its portcullis raised and the drawbridge wide open.

Torvar was quiet. He'd stopped making quips and sparring with Meric. He looked at the Bannerlord, his eyes full of concern.

"Something is amiss. This town is Rator. It is the busiest trading settlement of this region, and yet I do not see a soul."

"Be on your guard," Ferran warned, drawing his Tourmaline sword and igniting the blade. Luxon held Dragasdol in a tight grip, and Sophia placed an arrow on her bow's string.

They entered the town and rode slowly down the main street. Houses stood empty with their doors ajar and on the pavement were scattered pieces of broken pottery. It was deathly silent. The road led to the town's main market square, and this too was devoid of life. A trader's stall was broken, its produce of ceramics shattered on stone.

They dismounted their horses and carefully went from building to building searching for a living soul. None were found.

"No bodies. There's no sign of struggle, save for some broken pottery on the paths. What happened here?" Sophia asked, her voice full of concern.

"We shouldn't linger. How much further to the capital?" Welsly said.

Torvar was standing at the edge of the market square with his eyes closed. He hushed the Nightblade.

"Master Wizard. Can you feel that?" he muttered.

Luxon nodded.

"I do. I sense panic in this place. We need to hurry. I fear this land is in terrible danger."

Torvar opened his eyes and nodded.

"The capital is another two days to the north. I advise we avoid the towns and villages from here on if possible," he said.

A sound came from one of the houses behind them. Instantly Ferran and Welsly ignited their Tourmaline blades and quickly moved toward the building. Sophia drew her bow and aimed it at the doorway. On Ferran's command, Welsly kicked open the door and dashed inside. Ferran followed close behind. A panicked shriek came from within, and the two Nightblades returned with a young woman in their grasp.

The woman was struggling, but when she saw Torvar, she let out a cry of relief. She broke free of Ferran and ran to him.

"Wizard please protect me!"

Torvar pulled the woman into a hug and stroked her hair soothingly.

"Calm my child. What has happened here?" he asked softly.

"A band of warriors came through and told us to flee to the sanctuary of Renspar in the hills. They said that the Empire is threatened and that all should seek safety. I stayed behind to protect my wealth, but what can I do if an enemy does come?"

"That solves the mystery of where all the people are," Beric said.

They calmed the woman some more and assured her that she was safe. Torvar scolded her about her greed before telling her to pack whatever she could carry and make for the sanctuary with the others. They watched her flee west while they remounted their horses and hurried out and away from the town. They did as Torvar advised and kept to the roads and avoided settlements when able. Meric moaned until eventually, even he fell quiet as the eerie silence of the empty land sank in.

On the third night, they camped on a small hill that was protected by a steep incline to their rear and a fast flowing river to the west. Ferran didn't say it out loud, but everyone knew he was deliberately choosing locations they could defend if needed. Each of them took turns watching the darkness of the Tulin countryside, but much to their relief, nothing emerged from the oppressive black.

They continued north, but still, they saw no signs of life. The roads were empty; they'd not even encountered a wandering peddler. The road dipped into a wide valley that in turn became a series of canyons that followed the course of the broadest river Luxon had ever seen. It dwarfed the Ridder River in Delfinnia by a considerable margin. The roaring water was a constant hum even when the road ascended onto a hilly expanse. Now they were high up and able to see the scale of the watercourse.

"The Great River Expa," said Torvar as they stopped to take in the view. "It flows from the volcanic lands in the north for a thousand leagues to the sea. It is the lifeblood of the Empire, and yet I see no vessels on her surface. Come, we are near the bridge of Vandar."

They continued until the sun began to dip in the sky once more. On the horizon, they could see the bridge. It was breathtaking. Tall pointed towers engraved with exquisitely carved golden figures stood at both ends and stood in alcoves every twenty feet or so were massive statues made of marble stone and lined with massive intricately carved statues it was a marvel of engineering.

"Built by the Golden Empire. This bridge has stood for a thousand years. Some say the mages of old enchanted it so that it may never age nor fall into disrepair. Every statue that lines its sides is that of an Emperor or Empress," explained Torvar proudly. "In my youth, I studied the statues in an attempt to name them, but alas, the fall of the Empire saw those records destroyed, and many of them remain unnamed."

"Imagine being an Emperor of the most powerful Empire to have ever existed and history forgetting your name," Sophia said sadly.

"Time is a cruel mistress," Beric agreed.

They rode across marvelling as they did so. Golden sculptures of Fell Beasts and warriors were carved into the marble, but the most impressive sight occurred when the sun dipped below the horizon. With the advent of the night, the magical runes engraved on the bridge's surface began to glow a soft white colour. It meant that the bridge could be seen for miles in all directions and lit the way for any travellers crossing its width. Ferran decided that they should set up camp on the bridge as it would be easier to defend then open ground. As with the night before they fell into a restless sleep, but no attack came. When the sun began to rise, they were all relieved, yet none of them could explain why. They ate a breakfast of bread and bacon before resaddling their horses and continuing their way. They made good time, reaching the other side of the bridge before midday.

The further north they went, the colder it became, and now they spotted snow on the ground in the distance. A range of hills ran from west to east and there sat nestled amongst them was another structure. This one, unlike the wizard tower they'd sighted earlier, consisted of three spires that reached high into the grey sky.

"The Temple of Balance," Torvar said, breaking the silence. "It has lain abandoned for a century. A brutal war was waged over these lands between rival Wizard Lords, and the monks that once tended to it were forced to flee. They never returned, and it has stood empty ever since."

"What happened to the monks?" Eripa asked. The bard was once again scribbling notes in her journal.

Torvar shrugged his shoulders.

"Nobody knows for certain. Some folks say they were captured by pirates that used to frequent the waterways; others say the God of Balance himself took them to his realm."

A familiar voice filled Luxon's mind.

'A temple to little old me?'

Luxon tensed in his saddle. He looked at the others. Aside from a curious tilt of the head from Eripa, who was now sketching the temple. Nobody reacted to the voice.

'Don't worry, wizard they cannot hear me. I'm speaking to you via the magic of Asphodel. Pretty neat, huh?'

Luxon moved his hand to Asphodel's hilt and squeezed it.

'I thought you were a figment of my imagination?' Luxon thought, guessing that telepathy was the way to respond to the God.

'How rude! I converse with a mortal for the first time in forever, and he thinks I'm just a dream! Why I-'

'Okay, okay, I'm sorry.'

The others were now talking amongst themselves, unaware that the sword on his hip had a voice of its own.

'You need to go to that temple. Inside you will learn something of great importance. Something that could very well decide the fate of many.'

'What's inside? Do you know what's happening in these lands?' Luxon asked in his head.

No response. He tried again, but frustratingly the God did not speak again. They were now riding past the temple that lay a short distance down a side road. He hesitated. What if he was just imagining the voice? He slowed his horse to halt and glanced nervously down the other road.

"I think we should go this way," he said his voice full of uncertainty. How was he going to explain this? He sighed and waited for the inevitable questions. It was Sophia who asked.

"Why? Luxon, we cannot tarry in this place. You said yourself that you sensed dark magic."

The others had now stopped. Ferran and Welsly were at the front and leaned in closer to hear what was being said.

"You won't believe me," he muttered. "I just have a feeling is all."

Ferran trotted back up the line and stopped beside Luxon. The grim faced Nightblade looked at him for a moment.

"We do what Luxon says. He's never steered us wrong in the past."

"We don't have time to waste!" Torvar sputtered indignantly.

"We turn down this road and go to the temple. There will be no debate," Ferran retorted sternly. He nodded to Luxon and then led the way down the other road. Luxon sighed and hurried to catch up. Once alongside Ferran, he said, "Thank you for trusting me, Ferran. I want to tell you why; I really do, but I'm not sure even you would believe it."

"I have known you for a long time now, Luxon. I trust you."

"You should know what an honour that is for him to say that" chimed in Welsly from behind them, "I doubt the Rogue Blade trusts anyone, except for maybe his wife."

*

The road led them through a small thicket of trees before it bent to the right and into an open field of tall grasses. Weeds and vines had grown through the stone, and as they drew closer to the temple, they discovered a series of abandoned buildings. Most looked like lodgings, but the timber roofs had collapsed long ago, and nature had reclaimed the interiors. The Temple of Balance stood ahead, its three spires dominating the landscape around them. Torvar had got over his annoyance at the detour and was now enthusiastically showing off his country to the Delfinnians.

"The three spires represented the three essences of Man. The Light, The Dark and Balance. Inside each spire is a temple where the monks would pray and plead for the God of Balance to return to the world. Different sects of monks worshipped in each of the spires all locked in a never ending struggle," he said sadly.

'The Spire of Darkness is where you must go.'

Luxon shook his head. Nope, the voice was back again. One time he could have put the voice down to tiredness, the second a trick of the mind, but a third time? Either he truly was going mad, or the God of Light was really talking to him through Asphodel. They reached the temple complex's central courtyard, just like every other place they'd encountered in the Empire, it too was empty.

"Where is everybody? This is seriously starting to creep me out," Eripa said. Luxon nodded in agreement. They tied up their horses and walked deeper into the complex. Passing under a colossal archway, they entered a wide-open space, in the centre of which stood an enormous statue made of solid gold. It was in the shape of a man wearing armour, and in his hand, it held a sword aloft. Luxon's eyes widened as he recognized Asphodel.

"The Statue of the God of Balance and the Sword of Light. Another remnant from the Golden Empire" said Torvar.

"Is there anything you lot have made?" Meric quipped, causing the Tulin wizard to scowl in annoyance.

The detail on the statue was beyond comparison, further illustrating the magnificence of the artisans of the Golden Empire.

"I'm amazed no one has stripped the statue of its gold leaf," Ferran remarked his tone full of suspicion. "We must be on our guard here. It has a very ill feel to it." Luxon yearned to explore the site in detail, but the voice was persisting that he should go to the Spire of Darkness. He asked Torvar which of the spires it was.

"It's that one on the right. Be wary Wizard. They say the Dark spire is a home to evil itself. That some worship and praise the Dark Goddess still."

Luxon chided himself. He should have guessed which spire was the correct one for the spire, Torvar pointed to was made from pitch black obsidian. The tower of Light meanwhile, was constructed from the purest white marble, the Tower of Balance a mishmash of both materials.

"I think I need to do this alone," Luxon said as a chill ran through his body. Now that he was looking at the black tower, he could sense something. It was a dark malevolence the likes of which he'd only encountered once before. "Wait here. All of you."

Sophia was about to argue, but Ferran held up a hand in warning.

"Trust him."

Luxon didn't wait. He walked away from the others, his feet carrying him forward, despite the rising fear in his heart. He walked along the deserted path, the black tower growing larger and larger and then he arrived at a door made of blackened steel. Taking a deep breath, he pushed it open and stepped through into darkness.

CHAPTER 17.

Deep shadows greeted him. The interior of the temple was just as black as the exterior. Not a single light source was visible. He drew Asphodel, and it began to shine, but even its light struggled to drive back the oppressive darkness. Luxon could just make out the shape of objects, and he almost cried out when his foot bumped into a short block of obsidian. He glanced at it and instantly regretted doing so. Dried blood covered its surface and scattered around it on the floor were the bones of countless men and women. It was a place of blood sacrifice and full of horror. The walls were as black as night and smooth to the touch. He yearned to turn back and flee, and his senses were screaming at him to get out, to return to the light of the outside world.

He pushed on. The passageway narrowed into a corridor that was barely wide enough for a single man to walk down. He moved slowly as out of the dark he spotted vicious looking spikes jutting from the walls. One wrong move and he'd been cut to ribbons.

"Why would this place be allowed to exist," he muttered. It was like something out of a nightmare, and his memories flickered back to the haunting dreams he'd once had of a spectre. That had turned out to be Danon himself, communicating with him from the Void. He shuddered at the memories. He'd been chosen by evil itself to fulfil its wishes; now here he was in a temple devoted to it. He held Asphodel before him using its magic light as a torch. Even so, the most powerful artefact of the light seemed overwhelmed. Eventually, the spike filled passage opened out into a vast antechamber. A dais stood at the centre of the room. On top of which was an altar in the shape of a humanoid figure. Cautiously he approached, and as he did so, he could make out that it was the visage of a cloaked woman.

'I am the keeper of night. I am the end. I am the darkness,' a voice whispered from the shadows.

Luxon froze, and his heart raced. The feeling of malevolence grew and grew until he wanted to scream. He forced himself to stay calm. He had faced evil before. He would not flee in the face of this. Gripping Asphodel's hilt tightly, he slowly advanced toward the altar.

'There's nowhere to hide. Your odds are ruined. I am the darkness, and I am your undoing.'

"I've encountered you before," Luxon said, doing his best to stop his voice from cracking with fright.

'Yes. Long ago. You were there, an intruder of time. You saw me. And I saw you.'

Luxon's breathes now formed as a mist as the temperature of the chamber plummeted. Ice began to form on his clothing and skin.

'Long have I watched you—the one who will do my bidding. I have savored your pain, your fear, your despair and been angered by your joy, your love, your hope',' the voice whispered.

"I will not serve you, Esperin," Luxon answered defiantly. He emphasized the Dark Goddess' name. An excited hiss came from behind the altar, as though the use of her name had aroused her somehow.

'You will. You must. For if you do not, then my disciple will win, and the Void shall cover all worlds.'

Luxon frowned.

"And- you don't want that?"

'Danon has grown beyond my influence. He is- something else. A creature of madness, a creature of Vectrix.'

Luxon's eyes widened in surprise at the revelation. He had been to the Void. It had been there that Danon had shown him the corpse of Vectrix, the God of Madness and creator of the Void. Danon had defeated Vectrix, absorbing his power to escape the prison that Zahnia the Great had banished him too so long ago.

"He doesn't know, does he?"

'I yearn for the stars to go out one by one. I yearn for the light to be extinguished. Not for the madness to prevail. For madness is chaos and not the sweet serenity of shadow. No, he does not know that Vectrix has infected him. Danon believes the God dead, no, a God can never truly die. Vectrix allowed himself to be consumed. Like all things trapped in the Void, he needed a soul, a body to possess if he were to walk this world again. He has possessed Danon and now seeks to bring his mad creations here. This I cannot allow.'

"That's how he can control the Fell Beasts. How do I stop him?" Luxon asked. "I have Asphodel."

The voice laughed mockingly.

'Asphodel can harm Danon, but it cannot kill him alone. When I was one with my brother as the God of Balance, we forged the blade not to defeat the darkness but to slay our children should they ever threaten creation. Balance is the heart of all things. It is the only blade that can truly kill an immortal. Only when the avatar of one is slain can the other truly die. One of the Light, the other of the Dark. It is a weapon of balance. It yearns to serve the light, but it also serves the shadow that dwells in the hearts of men. It yearns to take life.'

Luxon stepped back in horror as the meaning of her words sank in.

"You mean Niveren."

To truly kill Danon, Niveren too would have to die, and only Asphodel could bring them death.

Another hiss, this time it sounded like laughter. A shadowy figure moved from behind the altar. Luxon held the sword up defensively. From the way, it moved he could tell it was female in form. Esperin made manifest. It stood just outside of the dimming light cast by Asphodel.

'*The horror in your heart pleases me. For too long, I have waited for a hero to realise what must be done to end Danon for eternity. Another stood where you do now, I told him the solution, but he chose - poorly. For he inadvertently led Danon to Vectrix. You have one advantage over Zahnia; however, you know who and where Niveren is.*'

"There must be another way!" Luxon shouted. Niveren, disguised as Grandmaster Thanos, had mentored him, trained him. The realization struck him like a lightning bolt.

"He knows," he gasped. "Thanos knows."

Even though the chamber was pitch black Luxon could have sworn the shadow smiled.

"*Bring me your soul, bring me your hate. In my name, you will create. Bring me your fear, bring me your pain.*"

Luxon stepped back, and the shadow took a step closer. Terror rose in his chest until with a cry he couldn't take it anymore. He turned and fled the chamber.

'*You will destroy in my name. I am the darkness. Your odds are ruined. I am darkness itself. I'm your undoing. I am death.*'

CHAPTER 18.

Luxon fell to the ground, his chest heaving. He'd never run so fast. Warm blood was on his arms from where he'd cut himself on the spikes of the narrow corridor. He didn't recall his escape but knew that only his longing to reach light had carried him. He blinked against the glare of the outside world and sighed in relief. He dared look back at the looming Black Tower and shuddered. He heard running footsteps. Looking up, he saw Ferran and Welsly hurrying towards him, expressions of concern etched on their faces. He got up slowly, wincing as the cuts on his arms and legs made their presence felt.

Ferran reached his side and helped him stand.

"Welsly get some bandages and bind those wounds. He looks like he's lost a fight with a wild cat."

Welsly did as ordered and took out some white linen bandages from his pack. Ferran helped Luxon away from the tower and to a nearby stone where he gently lowered him into a sitting position. Welsly set about binding the worst of the lacerations.

"What happened in there?" Ferran asked seriously.

"I saw her. I saw the Goddess of Darkness. She told me- I know what must be done to stop Danon. Only, I'm afraid that I cannot do it," Luxon replied, his eyes haunted and close to tears. He touched Asphodel's hilt and shuddered. Everything was wrong about the weapon. Mankind had believed the sword to be the bulwark against the darkness, and yet the truth was terrible. It was a weapon forged to kill the God of Balance's own creation, mankind. He looked at Ferran with pleading eyes.

"Please do not ask me anymore. Not yet, anyway."

Ferran exchanged a worried look with Welsly. He nodded. "Very well, I will not press further. While you were gone, Sophia and Meric went into the Temple of Light. There's something there that I think you'll want to see."

Curious Luxon got to his feet and followed the two Nightblades back to the centre courtyard. There, waiting for them, was the others.

"By the gods, what happened to you?" Beric remarked at his appearance.

"I'd rather not talk about it. Not yet anyhow," Luxon answered softly. "What have you found?" he added, quickly changing the subject.

They walked on towards the Temple of Light and pushed open the heavy oak doors. Unlike the Temple of Darkness, the interior was brightly lit and spacious. Sunlight poured through hundreds of hollows that, Torvar explained, would have housed stained glass windows, but thanks to the passage of time and the elements they had been destroyed long ago. Vines and moss grew on every surface except for the altar that stood in the centre. Meric stood in front of it and had brushed dust from the altar's golden surface.

"The inscription reads, *'Rindar gave light to the universe and the light of righteousness to man. Let they who wield the sacred blade renew its glory'.*

Luxon stepped toward the altar and drew Asphodel from its sheath. He could feel its power, but now it felt diluted as though his encounters with the N'gist and Esperin had drained it somehow.

'I do feel a tad tired' Rindar's voice grumbled in his head. Above the altar was a large circular stone panel that was built into the temple's ceiling. Long rusted chains were connected to it, suggesting that it was intended to be moved. He looked around the room.

"There," he said, pointing to a small section of the wall. An iron lever was visible, but it too looked as though it was rusted beyond repair. Beric walked over to it and gripped it tightly. With a grunt, he tried to move the lever. It wouldn't budge. Ferran and Welsly joined him, and together the three men pulled with all their might. A loud screech of metal sounded, and then, the lever shifted. A rumbling came from the temple's walls and then the chains began to move with a clink clink clink.

The stone panel began to slide aside, causing dazzling sunlight to pour into the chamber. Luxon placed Asphodel on the altar, and the light seemed to be absorbed into the blade. It looked like it was drinking the light. It began to glow until it was so bright that Luxon and the others had to shield their eyes from the glare. A few moments passed, and Luxon feared that they'd all be blinded by the glare.

'So much better!' exclaimed Rindar's voice.

Luxon dashed forward, his eyes still protected by his arm and reached blindly for Asphodel. His fingers touched the pommel, and he pulled it from the altar. Immediately, the light dimmed, allowing them to see once more.

Power coursed through the weapon, Luxon could feel it throbbing through the metal. As he tightened his grip on the hilt that power flooded into him and the weariness he'd felt since healing Eripa and battling Yinnice vanished. The others cried out as he lifted off the stone floor to float several feet above the altar. Light flooded through his body until his very veins shone. He'd never felt so alive. The sudden surge of power eased, and he floated gently back to the ground.

His eyes were wide, and he was panting with exhilaration. The others watched him with mouths agape. Ferran cautiously approached and asked if he was all right. Luxon nodded.

"Just give me a second. That was intense, to say the least."

"What was that?" the Nightblade asked regarding Luxon with concern.

"It felt like Asphodel was recharged somehow. The sunlight must have empowered it,' he said, his voice full of wonder. 'It feels more powerful than it did when I first held it," Luxon replied, looking at the sword in a renewed fascination.

He sheathed Asphodel, and the group left the temple.

*

Once outside, they froze. A platoon of heavily armed warriors was in the central courtyard, their spears all aimed at them. Luxon counted at least forty of them. A fight was not an option. It was Torvar who broke the tense silence first. The old wizard stepped forward, his arms held wide in surrender.

"Hail!' he said 'I am the wizard Torvar. Servant to the - former Lord Eretor."

The spears parted, and a man wearing a helmet adorned with a red plume trotted his white stallion forward. He was young, no older than twenty at most, but his eyes shone with a sharp intellect. His face was clean shaven, and the hair that could be seen poking out from under his tall ornate helmet was the colour of straw. He regarded Torvar for a few moments and then his gaze drifted to Luxon and the others.

"Former Lord Eretor you say?" the man said in a deep voice.

Torvar nodded.

"Ah, yes. Sadly, my Lord Eretor marched his army to Kastador, and I am afraid to report he was slain in battle with King Thorn. May I ask your name?"

The warrior frowned at the news of Eretor's death. Then with a sigh, he took off his helmet and ran a hand through his long hair.

"Eretor was a hot headed fool,' he stated calmly, 'but one that had a lot of men at his command. Men that I could do with right about now. If only he had awaited my command, then he would not be dead."

Torvar's eyes widened as he realized who the mysterious man was. Without another word, he bent the knee and bowed his head.

"Emperor Zeno,' he said in reverence. Luxon and the others looked at each other in confusion before following the wizard's lead. Beric and Meric stayed standing. The Kastadorians would not kneel to an enemy.

"My Lord, Eretor believed he would gain prestige for striking back at Kastador and those who he believed responsible for attacking our capital. When rumours spread that you had been taken prisoner, he felt that war was inevitable."

Zeno dismounted his horse with agile ease, and his long red cloak fell behind him to kiss the ground. His armour was gold with the chest plate carved in the shape of a well-muscled man. His pauldrons were likewise covered in gold leaf, and two faces were hewn into their surface. His pauldrons were polished to perfection, and his boots were decorated in intricate patterns. He looked the epitome of an Emperor.

"He was a fool" Zeno said sternly. "Those rumours of my capture were very much mistaken as you can clearly see. Spread by my rivals for the Imperial throne."

"Tell me, wizard Torvar, what are you and your companions doing here. This place is rarely visited these days," Zeno said eyeing up the Kastadorians with an amused smirk.

"We have grave tidings, my Lord. My companions here believe the Old Enemy is here in our lands. That it was the N'Gist, who attacked the capital under the guise of Kastador."

Zeno's pale blue eyes settled on Luxon, and he ushered him forward. Luxon did as commanded and stepped forward.

"My spies have told me of your presence on Tulin. They say that wherever you go, trouble has followed. They say that shortly after you arrived in Silenzia that chaos engulfed that land. You arrive in Kastador, and that realm falls into war."

"A war one of your Lords started," Beric grumbled. Zeno flashed him a furious look before glaring at Luxon, who held his nerve and matched the Emperor's unflinching gaze.

"Your Empire is in grave danger, as is all of Tulin. Danon and the N'Gist are waging war across the world, and my homeland is in grave peril. It was they who attacked Silenzia, it is they who are threatening Kastador, and it is they who captured the Nexus Tower."

Zeno's eye twitched at the mention of the tower.

"A High Witch of the N'gist is leading the enemy. From what I can surmise, she intends to activate the Nexus tower and hand control of the portal towers to Danon."

"Impossible. All knowledge of portal magic has been lost. The Tower is nothing more than a landmark from a bygone age. An age that I yearn to drag my people away from."

Torvar took a pace forward and dropped to his knees.

"Oh Emperor, what the outlander says is true. If you do not trust his words, then trust these men," he pleaded, gesturing to Meric and Beric.

Zeno crossed his arms.

"A Bannerlord of Kastador and a Magician only good at party tricks, you expect me to believe their lies?"

Meric bristled at the insult, but Beric placed a hand to his chest to restrain him.

Luxon closed his eyes and tapped into his magic. He had to show the Emperor the truth. As he had done in Silenzia, he muttered an incantation and conjured a projection. As before, he pushed all his memories of the war into it. Panicked cries came from the Tulin warriors, and swords were drawn from their scabbards. Luxon could hear Ferran shout a warning and he could vaguely see the Nightblades standing in front of him, their blades ignited and ready to defend him if needed.

The projection ended and Zeno staggered back a step. His face was pale, and a gleam of sweat was on his forehead. To his credit, he composed himself quickly. Luxon drew Asphodel, and again the warriors gasped. Some fell to their knees and wept, others stood forlorn. Only two of the men reacted negatively to the sword's presence, and they threw down their spears and fled, screaming into the undergrowth.

"The sword of light,' Zeno muttered with tears in his eyes. To Luxon's surprise, the Emperor of the Tulin Empire fell to his knees and bowed his head in reverence.

"You wield the sacred blade. I will assist you in stopping the N'Gist. First, I have something to ask of you Master Wizard. Help me take back the Nexus Tower and rid my Empire of my enemies. The capture of the tower has emboldened my rivals to declare me unfit to rule. They must be shown what you have shown me. If you do this, I will commit the Empire to your war against Danon. My ships and armies will be yours to command."

Luxon offered Zeno his hand and helped the Emperor to his feet.

"We will help you," he said solemnly.

Zeno spun on his heel and barked orders at his men to reform and prepare to march. He faced Luxon and the others.

"Ride with us to the capital. I will show these N'Gist that the Tulin Empire still has the strength to defy them."

Luxon and the others joined the Tulin warriors, and together they set off on the road.

CHAPTER 19.

The capital of the Tulin Empire made Sunguard look like a backwater village in comparison. It spread like a carpet of masonry for dozens of miles in all directions. They had approached from the southwest, using a wide flat stone paved road that allowed them to make the journey in double time. From their vantage point on a low hill, they could take in the entire magnificence of the place. The landward side of the city was protected by a massive stone wall, the likes of which Luxon and the others had never seen before. Large defensive towers stood every mile along its length. Beyond the walls, the city itself was laid out in a grid pattern with various quadrants designated for different purposes. On the far side, the city met the sea. An artificial bay carved out of the limestone cliffs provided the city with a vast seaport and harbour for a fleet of over fifty tall and lean warships. At the heart of it all, however, stood the Nexus tower. The structure was enormous and made the Portal Tower they had discovered in the mountains look tiny in comparison. Even the mighty Arch Tower in Caldaria paled against it. Zeno and his troops led the way toward the city walls where a full regiment of armoured riders challenged them. At recognizing their Emperor, the men dismounted and bowed.

"What is the situation commander?" Zeno asked the stern looking wiry built soldier who had identified himself as commander Vitus. The commander clapped a hand against his chest in salute.

"Emperor, the Kastadorian invaders remain contained in the Nexus Tower. All attempts at breaching it has been met with heavy resistance. Several Wizard Lords have sent scouts to probe the city defences but have yet to make a move to attack."

Vitus spotted Beric and Meric and scowled.

"My Lord, you ride with the enemy."

Zeno shook his head.

"No, Vitus. Kastador is not behind all this, and those Wizard Lords seeking to usurp my throne must be dealt with. Do you know who challenges me?"

Vitus nodded.

"The Wizard Lords, Hador, Grindar and Wexeliian sir. They seem to have allied against you. An envoy arrived yesterday with a message demanding that you abdicate or else they will besiege the capital."

Zeno rubbed his eyes tiredly.

"I have been fighting nonstop to keep this Empire intact, and now these fools think they can usurp me?"

"They believe that since you were away on campaign against the mountain tribes, it is your fault that a hostile force captured the Nexus Tower," Vitus answered uncertainly.

Zeno's face flushed red with anger.

"Tell me, commander, do you agree with that assessment?" he growled.

Vitus paled.

"No sire. I am loyal to you. The city guard is at your disposal. I took the liberty of moving the citizenry to the citadel for their protection."

Zeno's stern expression softened at that.

"You did well Vitus. Forgive me for my anger. I am tired from travelling. You did the right thing moving the citizens to safety. We do not know what these villains are capable of, after all."

Zeno gestured for the guards to open the city gates. With a sound of grinding metal, the massive steel gate swung open, and the mighty portcullis was raised. Vitus and his men escorted them through.

Once through the gate, Zeno marched towards the Nexus Tower. The wide paved streets echoed with the clip clop of horse's hooves. Like the town they had encountered earlier, the capital was deathly quiet.

They rode on until they reached a long squat structure that was surrounded by masterfully manicured gardens. Fountains made of pyrite and marble gurgled, and birds tweeted from the trees. Encamped in the garden grounds were several thousand Tulin warriors.

Vitus barked an order and squires ran from the interior of the structure to tend to the horses. Luxon and the others dismounted and joined the Emperor inside a large tent that stood in the heart of a well-tended lawn.

"We set up in the Gardens of Aniron and have established a defensive cordon in the streets surrounding the tower," explained Vitus. In the centre of the tent was a squat wooden table. A map of the city and its surrounding lands lay on top. He traced a line with his finger to point out various checkpoints he'd established.

"We still do not know how the Kastardorians -" he paused glancing at Beric and Meric before correcting himself, "- the enemy, got inside the Tower but after their initial assault they halted here, at the central Agora," he said pointing to a square on the map.

Zeno studied the map for a few moments.

"I must tell you that this enemy is the N'Gist. The Old Enemy is here in this city and is a grave threat to the Empire," Zeno said quietly.

Vitus' was horrified by his words but quickly regained his composure.

"What is their objective?" Torvar asked, looking at Luxon and the Delfinnians.

"Well,' Luxon began, 'we know that Yinnice the High Witch of the N'Gist has the means to activate the portals within the tower and then that via the Nexus Tower she will be able to travel to anywhere in the world within the blink of an eye. She cannot lose the tower now that she has it."

"It also means that she can bring others here," Ferran added.

"That is most concerning,' Luxon agreed. 'I think we can assume that the N'Gist intend to use the Tower to launch an invasion of the Empire to secure it."

"We have seen no sign of such an invasion force. However, whenever we have approached the tower, we have encountered a magical barrier. Our wizards have been unable to penetrate it."

"Amateurs," Meric scoffed.

"A shield spell no doubt," Luxon said, stroking his chin in thought.

"Perhaps the witch is betting that the shield spell will hold. Danon's forces aren't limitless, maybe he doesn't have the manpower to spare to attack the Empire yet," said Welsly.

"You're hoping that Kaiden is giving him a fight. I hope so too."

"Yinnice doesn't know that we survived her Necrist," chimed in Eripa. "What if she believes that Luxon is dead, maybe that's why she thinks the tower is safe from attack."

"If you can breach that shield spell and get us inside, we can handle the rest," Vitus said confidently. Ferran shook his head.

"No. I doubt you will. The Tower is important to the enemies plans, which means it will be protected by N'gist wielders, Crimson Blades assassins and who knows what else."

"You have a plan?" asked Zeno who'd been listening to the conversation closely.

"I do. We will get inside. A small team can infiltrate the tower far easier than an army. We will find Yinnice and kill her," Ferran said simply. "Meanwhile, your forces will assault the shield. Hopefully, that will draw out some of the enemies. Your men will fare far better in more open ground."

Zeno nodded in agreement and offered Ferran his hand.

"If you can do this. You will earn my support," he said seriously.

*

Vitus led them closer to the tower. As they drew nearer, the streets became more chaotic and maze like. It was the old part of the city he explained, and some of the buildings dated all the way back to the Golden Empire. From the diversity of the architecture on display, it was clear that the city had seen much through its long history. Stone structures stood side by side with wooden ones and various styles of masonry.

After traversing the warren of narrow streets, they reached a vast square of open ground located beneath the gigantic Nexus Tower. Vitus gestured for them to stop. He bent down and picked up a small stone. Arching his arm, he hurled the stone towards the square. It never reached its destination. Instead, it struck an invisible barrier that vaporized it into dust.

"That's a nasty shield spell," Luxon muttered. Usually, such magic just prevented something from passing through, not destroying it as well. He raised Dragasdol and channelled his magic through the staff. It crackled and fizzed as the power flooded through it. He stepped forward and thrust the tip of the staff at the shield. It struck with a blinding flash and tendrils of magical energy shot over the shield's surface. Luxon gritted his teeth and pushed more of his power into the dispelling spell. A loud crackling sound filled the air, and for a heartbeat, it looked as though the shield was wavering. Ferran shouted a warning across the courtyard and from the tower's huge doors emerged a dozen cloaked figures.

"N'Gist," he snarled.

The enemy had given up its guise of pretending to be from Kastador and now revealed themselves. Behind the N'Gist came Crimson Blade assassins who took up defensive positions in front of the wielders. Luxon doubled his efforts, and his arms began to tremble with exertion. The shield began to flicker, but then the N'Gist raised their staffs. A loud bang and Luxon staggered backwards.

"It's no use. They're reinforcing the shield. I can't break it alone," he gasped. He drew Asphodel and tried again, but this time the N'Gist were joined by the High Witch herself. Yinnice strode out into the square a mocking smirk on her face and her one good eye glinting with malice. She added her power to the N'Gist, and the shield held. Luxon fell back but was caught by Welsly before he could strike the stone path.

"By the Gods," Vitus said. The tower doors were now wide open to reveal at least a hundred shambling figures. The moans carried on the breeze, and as they emerged from the tower, the dead were revealed in all their horror.

"Undead. She's brought undead here via the portal tower," Luxon exclaimed.

The undead moved into the square; their dead eyes fixated on Luxon and the others.

Vitus called the retreat, and they hurried back through the streets and back to the Emperor's hastily erected camp. They rushed to Zeno's tent and there found him standing at the map table with Torvar and three other Tulin wizards.

*

"The shield is impenetrable. It'd take many more magic wielders than what are gathered here to break it," Luxon explained, pointing to the map. "We need to find another way in."

"Even if we could break the shield the undead will be unleashed upon the city," Sophia pointed out.

Vitus folded his arms and frowned.

"Walking dead do not frighten the warriors of Tulin, my lady. We have battled their ilk for centuries. Many are left over from the Magic Wars and regularly plagued the northern lands."

"Undead alone are dangerous enough, but with N'gist commanding them they are far more lethal," Ferran said.

Zeno sighed and rubbed his forehead.

"It seems to me that we are at an impasse. If we wait, the enemy will continue to be reinforced via the portals. If we somehow neutralize the shield, the undead will be unleashed into the city, and I fear that we do not have enough warriors to stop them.' He slammed a hand on the table in frustration. 'Damn those rebellious Wizard Lords, Hador, Grindar and Wexeliian. Only with their armies can we stand a chance."

Torvar cleared his throat noisily.

"If I may suggest my Emperor, allow us to ride to the Wizard Lords camps and tell them of what is occurring here. Surely, even they will be loathed to hear that the Old Enemy is in the Imperial capital."

Zeno stroked his chin in thought as he considered the old wizard's words. Finally, he nodded and called for a scribe. Within moments a flustered man wearing white robes entered the already crowded tent with a quill, parchment, and ink in hand.

"Write this down, scribe. I, Zeno Emperor of all Tulin and Archon of the Dinium Isles request your presence inside the city under terms of peace. Although you defy me, there is a greater struggle that must be dealt with. The N'Gist are in the city and seek to destroy our homeland. I implore you to come and see this terror for yourselves, and I hope that you will be convinced to aid me."

Satisfied with his words, Zeno commanded the scribe to copy the note in triplicate. Once that was done, he used a wax seal on each and handed them to Torvar and the other wizards.

"Under Tulin law a wizard cannot be harmed so you will be safe. Give these to the rebels and convince them to come to the city."

Torvar and the others bowed before hurriedly exiting the tent and heading toward their horses.

Luxon and the others had watched in silence, but now Zeno faced them, his piercing eyes drilling into his own.

"You failed to break the shield spell."

"I did," Luxon replied coolly despite the exhaustion he felt.

"Then I suggest you try another strategy. Remember, you owe me that witch's head in return for the Empire's support. You will try again in the morning. In the meantime, lodgings have been provided for you and your companions."

Luxon and the others bowed and left the tent. A servant led them through the camp and towards a stone structure a few streets away. Just like many of the other buildings, Zeno's soldiers had occupied it. Judging from the interior décor, the place was a vacant tavern. Large barrels of ale lined one wall, and a wide oak bar dominated the heart of the ground floor. The servant led them up to the third floor where rooms had been prepared. On a table on the wide landing was a variety of meats, cheeses, and wine.

"The Emperor wishes for you all to be treated well," the servant explained.

Meric was overjoyed by the prospect of a hot bath and meal. After they consumed their fill, they went to their assigned rooms. All of them were tired and longed for sleep. Luxon staggered into the small cosy bedroom where he slid Dragasdol, and its sheathe from his back and placed it against the comfortable looking bed. A small fireplace crackled in the corner to cast warmth and an orange glow. He sat tiredly on the bed and unsnapped his sword belt.

"What a day," he said before lying back and closing his eyes. Sleep quickly took him.

*

A gentle knocking on the room's door brought him back to consciousness. The fire was now just embers casting just enough light for him to see. Outside it was pitch black, and stars could be seen twinkling in the sky. A light snow had fallen over the city to cover the tiled rooftops in a dusting of white. Luxon rubbed his eyes and groaned. The knocking came again, this time more persistent. He threw back the warm fur blanket and put on his shirt and boots. Groggily he walked to the door and opened it a crack. Standing in the hallway was Zeno. The emperor wore a thick cloak and a hood that cast his features in shadow.

"Walk with me," he said quietly.

Luxon unlocked the door and quickly put on his cloak and strapped Asphodel to his waist. He decided to leave Dragasdol where it was. Stepping out into the hallway, he could see that Zeno was alone save for a bleary eyed child who was holding a lantern. Without a word, the Emperor turned on his heel and walked downstairs and through the silent alehouse. They exited via a side door and stepped out into a narrow alleyway. The boy stayed close to the Emperor and lit the way. Still in silence, they travelled through the city being careful to avoid the patrols of soldiers tasked with keeping an eye on the Nexus Tower. In the distance, Luxon could see other soldiers patrolling the city's vast walls, their torches nothing but tiny points of light moving horizontally in the dark. After a few more turns through the warren of streets, they entered a small walled courtyard. Stood in the centre was a small squat stone structure with a domed roof that glinted gold in the boy's torchlight.

"You walk in the steps of a great hero Luxon," Zeno said suddenly.

Luxon nodded.

"It hasn't been lost on me that I am following in the steps of Zahnia the Great," he replied. "Whether I can repeat what he did and defeat Danon, I do not know."

"No," Zeno said sharply, "you are not merely following in Zahnia's footsteps. You must do what he could not. Come."

Without a word, the Emperor walked on, and the boy pushed open the small buildings' ancient looking doors. The hinges squealed in protest, but the heavy doors parted.

"Leave us," Zeno commanded, taking the lantern from the lad. The boy bowed before scurrying off into the night.

The lantern barely illuminated the building's interior, but in the flickering light, Luxon could see incredibly colourful images daubed on the walls and on the floor was a mosaic of such intricate detail it took his breath away. The image was of a bearded man wearing a suit of shining armour. In his right hand was the unmistakable image of Asphodel, in his left, he held a staff, Erdasol.

"This is Zahnia's tomb,' Zeno explained as he walked deeper inside the building. He lit candles as they went until they reached the rear of the main chamber. There lay a solid gold platform with a rectangular block of marble on top. Carved onto its surface was a sculpted figure depicting in effigy the deceased that lay within. It was a figure of the man on the mosaic and next to him was the visage of a woman resplendent in a white dress and holding in her delicate hands a red rose. Luxon gasped at the sight.

"The Saviour and founder of the Golden Empire himself in all his glory. Lying in eternal rest with his beloved Empress Eudoxica," Zeno said.

"I- I can't believe it. Scholars in Delfinnia have always believed that he was buried somewhere in Sunguard, that during the Magic Wars his tomb was lost when the city was sacked."

Luxon ran a hand reverently over the effigy's surface.

"His capital was in Sunguard, but his Empire was vast, and his love for his Tulin wife was far greater than his love for that city."

Luxon nodded in understanding. He was learning and discovering so much about the wider world. The histories and books in Caldaria were proving to be wrong about a great many things.

"I brought you here Luxon because I wanted you to see the man you must emulate and surpass."

"Surpass?"

"Yes. Zahnia may have bested Danon and his N'Gist, but he failed to save the world. All he did was buy it time until now, once again the enemy threatens us all. It is you whom the gods have deemed to follow in Zahnia's footsteps. You wield Asphodel!"

Luxon touched the sword's hilt absently, remembering what the Dark Goddess had told him inside the temple.

"You are following the same journey those other heroes before you have tread. All of them failed to do what must be done. You must not." Zeno walked over to a small, curtained alcove in the wall behind Zahnia's tomb. He pulled a string, and the curtain fell to one side to reveal a hidden doorway.

"Come."

Luxon followed the Emperor through the door and down a narrow corridor. At its end was a staircase that spiralled downward. They went down the steps and emerged into a cavern underneath. A stone altar stood in the centre and behind that was a rack on which hung a cuirass.

"This is the armour worn by Zahnia during his final confrontation with Danon.' Zeno said as he lit a brazier on the wall. The fire illuminated the cavern to reveal that the rack was also displaying pauldrons and greaves. Each glinted in the light.

"My wizards tell me that it is enchanted with all sorts of magical wards and that the armour is made of a material known as White Steel, a rare metal from some distant corner of the world. It is virtually impervious to damage. I want you to have it."

Luxon blinked.

"I cannot accept this. This armour must be very important to your people."

Zeno nodded in agreement at his words and crossed his arms.

"To us, Tulins, Zahnia is a saint, our greatest hero. The founder of our Empire that we are tasked with preserving, and perhaps one day restoring." He held up a hand to forestall any argument. "As long as the N'Gist exists, that goal is under threat. It is clear to me that the gods have chosen you and that it is right for you to wear the armour of our beloved champion. Go on, take it. If it does not fit, then I will get my armourers to adjust it."

Luxon was lost for words, but he stepped toward the cuirass and lifted it off the rack. To his surprise, it wasn't heavy; it felt as light as a feather. He shrugged off his cloak and with Zeno's help put it on. To both of their amazement, it fit perfectly.

"Try on the rest," Zeno persisted.

Luxon strapped on the pauldrons, greaves, and gauntlets. Stretching his arms, he took a few paces. It felt like a second skin. It didn't impede his movements at all, nor did it restrict his ability to raise his hands. He drew Asphodel and to his surprise, the power coursed from the blade and into the suit of armour.

"The epitome of a warrior wizard," Zeno remarked.

The runes engraved on its surface glowed, and he gasped as all the tiredness he'd felt evaporated to be replaced with vibrant energy.

"Wear the armour of Zahnia and tomorrow destroy the N'gist," Zeno said with a satisfied smile. "Oh, and before I forget, a messenger told me that a ship had been sighted sailing towards the city flying a flag of a seven-pointed star. I trust this is your vessel?"

"Yes, it is. The *Agatha*."

"Very well. Go and get some rest."

CHAPTER 20.

The next morning a tense calm had fallen over the city. A thick mist had rolled in from the Dividing Sea to blanket the buildings in a veil of eeriness. Luxon and the others had awoken early and made their way back to the Nexus Tower. The shield protecting it flickered as moisture carried in by the mist struck. Behind the shield, the square was now filled with the undead that stood as still as statues.

"They're dormant," Ferran whispered.

After his time with Zeno, Luxon had paid Ferran and Sophia a visit back at their lodgings. The *Agatha* had slipped into port in the early hours of the morning, and Captain Whitelaw had joined them at the lodgings. The voyage north had been an eventful one with the vessel sighting an enormous tentacled sea monster far off the coast. They had also spotted a small force of Tulin warships in pursuit of one of the many pirates that plagued the northern shores of the continent. After a hearty meal, they had spent the rest of the night deep in discussion. It had been Sophia who had come up with the daring scheme they were now trying to pull off. She pointed to the small side alley she'd spotted on their previous attempt, and they crept their way down it. At the end of the alley was a small circular grate atop a short stone structure. On regular days, the well would have been used by the city's citizens for their source of water. Now it would be used to get underneath the enemy. Ferran and Welsly prised the grate off as quietly as they could and carefully placed it on the muddy cobbles beside it. Ferran looked down the well and tilted his head. The sound of running water greeted him. He unfurled the rope they'd brought with them and secured it to an iron rung at the well's top. Next, he climbed over the side and tested it. Satisfied that it would hold their weight, he took a firestone from one of the pouches on his belt, activated it and tossed it. The orange glow illuminated the well's lichen covered walls as it fell into the icy cold water below. Sophia followed and then Welsly. Luxon faced Eripa.

"Remember the plan. When the shield drops, you get to safety. Zeno's men should be in position by now. They will hold the undead for as long as they can. Hopefully long enough for us to put an end to Yinnice."

"Don't worry about me. I'll head to the docks with Meric and Beric and get to the *Agatha*. If all goes ill, we will sail back to Kastador."

Eripa pulled Luxon into a hug. He flushed slightly as her perfume filled his nostrils. She stepped back, and he began the descent into the black cold. The armour of Zahnia was under his green cloak, and it felt like a second skin. It didn't impede his movements whatsoever. He resisted the urge to gasp as he slipped into the cold water. Ferran held a firestone in his hand and led the way. A narrow gap was in the side of the well's wall, and together they squeezed through. Once on the other side, they discovered an ancient tunnel.

"This must be part of the city's old sewer system I guess," Ferran said, his voice echoing through the tunnel. The sewer was a maze, and the lack of light made every shadow appear as though it were alive. It was a place where the imagination could quickly run riot if they let it. The air stank of damp and mould, but even after centuries of disuse, they could make out the master craftsmanship of the ancient builders. They had no clue where they were headed, but Ferran surmised that the tunnels would contain similar markings to the ones found underneath the old cities of Delfinnia. Sunguard was the most ancient city of them all, but it had been rebuilt numerous times over the millennia. The old sewer network created by the Golden Empire had never been topped, however. Ferran held up a hand to signal them to stop. He raised the firestone closer to one of the walls.

"Similar markings as those found in Sunguard's tunnels."

"They probably would have used a similar system too. I recognize this one. It's like the one that represented the King's Spire back home," Sophia added, pointing to a faded image of a triangle with a diagonal line drawn through it.

"It does point north," Welsly added, checking the pocket compass in his palm.

"We follow this tunnel," Ferran agreed after a few moments of thought.

They pressed on until they began to hear the moans of undead coming from above. Down in the tunnels, the groans of the damned were even more terrifying as they bounced off the walls.

"Zeno must have launched his attack on the shield to get them all riled up like that," Welsly said hopefully.

"Or they've caught our scent," Sophia replied with a wink. Welsly paled at the thought. Fighting undead in the daylight was scary enough; he couldn't imagine the horror of battling them in the pitch black sewers. They waded on, the sounds of battle growing louder with every step until finally, they reached a section of tunnel that split into three. The chamber had opened so that the roof was now a lot higher. From the right hand tunnel, they could hear fast flowing water.

"That must be the main sewer artery to the sea," Ferran surmised. "Which means the left hand tunnel leads deeper into the city and the centre one towards our destination."

He pushed on, and before long, he was proven right. The tunnel narrowed at first and then widened to reveal a vast subterranean space. A wide river of water flowed down the centre but before that was a ladder made of iron rings that led back to the surface. They began the treacherous climb and reached the base of a heavy metallic manhole cover. Ferran tapped into magic to enhance his strength and with a grunt shoved upwards. The cover lifted, and he pushed it to one side. They quickly clambered out of the hole and found themselves in what looked like a crypt. Tombs complete with effigies filled every spot of spare space, and grave markers were carved into the walls.

"Must be where the Wizard Lords are buried," Luxon said.

Welsly placed a hand on his chest in warning. He pointed to one of the tombs.

"I think the N'Gist may have recruited some of the local residents to their cause."

Sure enough, several of the tombs were broken, as though someone had burst their way out from within.

"Keep quiet and keep your wits about you," Ferran warned.

Luxon drew Asphodel, and the Nightblades ignited their Tourmaline blades. Sophia had her bow held at the ready, an arrow ready to fly from its string. They moved quickly and quietly through the undercroft until they reached a narrow staircase that spiralled upwards. At the top was a landing area that opened into several different corridors. Luxon closed his eyes and focused. He could sense the power of the Nexus coming from ahead. He pointed, and they moved up the central corridor. From inside the tower, they could no longer hear the battle raging outside; instead, they were greeted by an eerie hum that seemed to throb through the walls. The passage opened into a much larger one that was similar in appearance to the one they encountered at the portal tower in the Gryphon Mountains.

"Where are the N'Gist?" Sophia whispered.

So far, they had encountered no one, and that was making them all nervous.

"Watch the shadows," Ferran replied. Cautiously they made their way up the corridor. Ahead was a set of large doors that were wide open. In the chamber beyond a portal was active and glowing brightly. Luxon tried to detect whether any N'Gist were in the portal chamber, but he sensed nothing.

"Either someone is masking their presence, or there genuinely isn't anyone within," he said, gripping Asphodel's hilt tighter.

Ferran jogged forward while Sophia covered him with her bow. He crept inside the chamber. There was nobody there.

"What is this? I don't like it one bit," Wesley muttered.

The others joined Ferran. Luxon hurried to the central dias. Sure enough, the amulet stolen from the Silenzian Shar was slotted into the small hollow in its centre. He reached for it.

"Watch out!" Sophia shouted in warning.

The portal flickered and through it stepped a figure. Without warning it raised a hand and using magic blasted Ferran and the others off their feet. They flew backwards, landing heavily on the polished obsidian floor. Luxon planted Dragasdol into the ground and stayed standing. The High Witch, Yinnice stood in front of the portal, a sneer was on her ravaged face. Her one good eye glared at Luxon; he could feel her anger like a physical force.

"I've waited a long time for this Wizard," she spat. "You're too late by the way. In the time we have had control of this place, we have sent tens of thousands more Sarpi warriors to Delfinnia. What's left of your precious Kingdom shall fall, including Caldaria."

Ferran tried to get back onto his feet, but the witch lashed out with her magic again pinning him to the ground.

"Leave him alone. You want to fight? Then let's fight," Luxon snarled. A rage burst forth in his chest. Had she spoken the truth? He thrust Dragasdol forward, a bright flash of lightning erupted from the tip to lance out toward the witch. It struck her in the arm, causing her to cry out in agony. Luxon advanced. He felt more powerful than he had ever before. With the revitalized Asphodel on his hip and the armour of Zahnia, magic surged through him. He raised his free hand and together with the staff unleashed a combination of fire and lightning. Yinnice tried to summon a shield spell, but even the High Witch was no match for his assault. The shield glowed brightly before collapsing. The fire and lightning struck her in the torso to set her cloak ablaze. She screamed and managed to rip the flaming material from her body. She lashed out with a fire spell, forcing Luxon to deflect it with his staff. The intense heat blistered his fingers, forcing him to toss the now smoking Dragasdol aside and drew Asphodel from its sheath. Its blade shone brightly, and Yinnice flinched at its blinding majesty. She staggered back, her hands covering her eye to protect it from the sword's glare.

Luxon moved with an unnatural speed and swung the sword. Just as it looked as though its tip would slash Yinnice's throat, she blasted herself backwards with a telekinetic spell. She flew back to land in front of the portal. Luxon brought Asphodel up in a two handed grip and charged. Yinnice retaliated with lightning and fire, but with a skill, he didn't realise he possessed, he parried and deflected every attack. Yinnice screamed in frustration.

"You may have won this round, but we will meet again. Very soon!" she snarled before jumping through the portal. It shimmered briefly, and Luxon looked to charge after her.

"Luxon! Stop, we have no idea what's on the other side," Sophia called from behind him.

He shouted in frustration and threw Asphodel aside as he skidded to a halt. Slowly he turned to face Sophia, a look of anger on his face.

"I could have finished her."

"We cannot afford to lose you. At least we have this," Sophia said, walking over to the central dais and pulled the amulet from the slot. The portal flickered for a few seconds before dissolving into nothingness. Luxon walked over to the discarded Asphodel, and hesitantly reached for it. His hand was shaking, and a feeling of dread filled his chest. Finally, his fingers wrapped about the hilt, and he sheathed it as quickly as he was able. Welsly tossed Dragasdol to him, and he caught it easily.

"Well, I guess that settles that," Ferran said, rubbing the back of his bruised head.

"Let's help the Tulins rid their city of the undead, then it will be over," said Sophia.

CHAPTER 21.

The sun was kissing the horizon when the battle ended. The fighting had been brutal with many lives lost, but they had won the day. Smoke drifted over the city, and the cries of the wounded filled the air. Luxon sat heavily on the ground and wiped sweat from his brow. Even with Asphodel, the fighting had been hard work. Finally, the last of the zombies had been put to the sword. He looked up at the sound of approaching footsteps. It was Ferran. The Nightblade offered him a waterskin which he took gratefully.

"A long day," he said.

Luxon nodded.

Ferran sat next to him, drank from his own waterskin, and wiped his lips with the back of his hand.

"That was a good fight. With Yinnice, I mean. I've never seen you fight with a blade like that before."

"I had a good teacher," Luxon replied.

Ferran chuckled.

"I taught you what I could, but you never displayed such skill as you did against the witch. It looked as though that sword took control of you somehow."

Luxon shrugged. He didn't know what to say.

"In fact, I think there's more to that sword than you're letting on."

Luxon closed his eyes. The words Esperin had said echoed in his mind. *'It yearns to serve the light, but it also serves the shadow in all men's hearts. It yearns to take life.'* He shuddered. What the Goddess had said was true. When he drew the sword in anger, he felt as though he was no longer in control, it was as though the sword had seized control of his body, it was as though the blade itself had felt excitement, hunger at the prospect at killing.

"You're right," he said softly. "It's more dangerous than any of us realize. In fact, I'm not sure I should wield it at all."

Ferran raised an eyebrow.

"Do you remember the prophecy when we were seeking it? That only those with the blood of Kings shall wield it."

Ferran nodded. "I do."

"I understand that prophecy now. It is a sword meant for Kings as Kings take lives. Whether for good or ill, a King at some point must kill. Either to defend his crown or to protect his realm. Both light and dark purposes. I have the blood of my father, but my mother was not of royal blood. Perhaps I am not strong enough to wield it. When I fought Yinnice, it was as though the sword was hungry. It possessed me. There's more-"

"Oh?"

"Don't think me mad for what I am about to tell you."

"I will not."

Luxon told him of the God of Light being imprisoned within the sword. Of how Esperin had spoken to him within the Temple of Darkness and of what she had revealed to him. When he was finished, Ferran was pale.

"The Gods are real? As in they're here and now?"

Luxon nodded. He knew the Nightblade would find it hard to believe. He was a Delfinnian, and the worship of the Gods had ended a long time ago to be replaced with the Niveren Cult.

"It's a lot to take in, I know. When I first saw them, I too was shocked. All the legends are true Ferran. I saw it on the Isle of Magic, and they've spoken to me since. I've kept all this to myself, so you all wouldn't think I'd lost the plot."

Ferran clapped him on the shoulder and laughed.

"After all the things that we have seen and experienced together, the existence of legendary Gods isn't all that unbelievable."

Luxon smiled back. He wanted to tell his friend all he knew. That Thanos, the man who all wielders in Delfinnia respected as their leader, was none other than Niveren. He kept quiet. Learning that the Gods were still intervening in the affairs of men was enough of a revelation for now.

"Luxon!" cried a high pitched voice.

Luxon looked down the street and smiled. Alderlade ran through the crowd of soldiers and threw himself into his arms.

"My King," Ferran said with a bow.

"I am so glad that you're safe," the boy said happily. "The trip up the coast was awfully dull, only the stories Captain Whitelaw told me kept me from going crazy from boredom."

"I'm glad you're okay," Luxon replied, rubbing the lad's hair affectionately. He knelt so that he was eye level with the boy. "The witch is dead, Alderlade."

Tears formed in Alderlade's eyes, but he brushed them away. He hugged Luxon tightly. Seeing his beloved nanny die in front of him had haunted the child immensely, more than once had Luxon found him sobbing Elena's name.

"Thank you. Elena is avenged," Alderlade said softly.

"She is, my King. We have also retaken control of the Nexus tower. Danon's plans for this land have been bested, and we now have a strong ally in the form of the Tulin Empire."

"Speaking of," Ferran said, pointing to Emperor Zeno who was striding with purpose down the street. At his side were a dozen heavily armed bodyguards. Luxon took Alderlade's hand in his, and together they followed Zeno's entourage. After a short walk, they were back in the square where the Emperor's command tent was erected. Soldiers were hastily pulling down the makeshift camp. With the enemy cleared from the city, the civilians who had taken refuge in the city's citadel were moving back to their homes. At the centre of the square, Zeno had arrayed a few hundred of his warriors. Before them, were three men in chains. Luxon and Ferran spotted Beric in the crowd and joined him. The Bannerlord, along with the Agatha's crew, had returned to the city following the end of the battle. Captain Whitelaw was in the market square haggling loudly with one of the merchants while Meric stood nearby watching the scene with an amused smile.

"What's going on?" Ferran asked.

Beric gestured to the three men. Each was stripped and shivering in the cold winter chill.

"They are the Wizard Lords, Hador, Grindar and Wexeliian. Zeno invited them and their warriors into the city under the premise of a truce. They arrived shortly before the battle and fought well from what I saw. Then as soon as the battle was over, they were cast in chains."

Ferran stroked his chin.

"Zeno is more ruthless than I suspected. With the N'Gist threat removed, he can now get his own house in order."

The Emperor walked behind the three chained men and made a gesture with his hands. A trumpet blew, and the crowd fell silent, including the now red faced Whitelaw and smug looking merchant. Obviously, the captain had been fleeced.

Zeno raised his arms high.

"Citizens of the Empire I present to you three traitors. Men who sought to usurp their rightful Emperor."

The men cried out in denial and protest, but Zeno pressed on.

"For too long, this Empire has been fractured. For too long have the nobility bickered among itself and sought to undermine the Emperor's will. Well, today that ends. Messages have been dispatched to all corners of the Empire to inform the other Wizard Lords to come here and bend the knee to me. If they do not, they will suffer the same fate as these three traitors."

"No! Our men fought for you. You cannot do this!" whimpered one of the bound Lords.

Zeno was immune to the man's pleas. He drew his sword, and with a mighty blow, struck his head from his shoulders. The watching army roared as he went down the line to finish his grizzly work.

Zeno faced the cheering crowd and lifted one of the decapitated heads high.

"Today, the Tulin Empire rises anew! Today we embrace our destiny. As the events of the past few days have shown, the Old Enemy has returned. Danon and the N'gist once more threaten this world. Will the Empire sit idly by and let his darkness consume this world?"

Roars of no came from the crowd.

"I am glad to hear it. Brave warriors of Tulin. You fought well, but our war with the N'gist is just beginning. We must set aside our animosity with the other powers of this continent and aid them to drive back the darkness. That is why I now march south with our new allies from across the sea. We shall secure the continent, and then we will show the world our might. For our fleets shall sail east and liberate the lands of Nivonia now called Delfinnia."

The crowd cheered at the Emperor's words. The Empire was going to war.

*

The city bustled with activity as the army gathered supplies and prepared to make the long march south to Kastador. Beric had departed with haste back to the Kingdom with the news that the Empire would fight with them against the N'Gist. Luxon stood before Zeno in his still erected command tent. Ferran and the others had returned to their lodgings for some much needed rest. The Emperor regarded Luxon for a few moments before presenting a scroll of parchment.

"I had my scribes search the Tentra Library for this. I'm amazed it's still preserved, but I guess that's the sort of power the old wizards possessed."

"What is it? Luxon asked.

"A treaty that was signed aeons ago by the rulers of the three great empires of man. I wanted to make our alliance official."

Luxon unfurled the scroll and read its contents.

'It is cordially agreed that if in times to come, should one of the kings or his heir shall need the support of the other or his help, and to get such assistance applies to his ally legally, the ally shall be bound to give aid and succour to the other, so far as he is able (without any deceit, fraud, or pretence) to the extent required by the danger to his ally's realms, lands, domains, and subjects; and he shall be firmly bound by these present alliances to do this.'

Luxon smiled and reached into a pouch attached to his belt. He pulled out a scroll.

"This scroll was written by the ancient rulers of the Nivonian Empire of the Second Age. I was given this to present to any allies we might find on this quest," he explained before handing it over to Zeno.

"The wording is the same. Marvellous that our ancestors foresaw the need for such cooperation. Together we will defeat Danon and his N'Gist forever."

Zeno handed back the scroll, and Luxon did likewise.

"I have given orders to Vitus that he is to command the Empire's forces in this campaign. I, as much as I wish too, cannot join the march south and the battles to come. Not yet, anyhow. I must ensure that my rule here is safe and the Empire secure. To that end, you will have two legions of my best fighters as well as the entire eastern fleet. I believe those ships will be sufficient to transport the men and suppliers across the ocean to your Delfinnia when the time comes. I have told Vitus that you will have overall command of our forces to do as you see fit to destroy the enemy."

Luxon bowed.

"Thank you, Zeno. I trust that means you are happy for us to aid the Free Kingdoms who themselves are under assault from the N'Gist. And the Silenzians."

Zeno gestured dismissively.

"Do what must be done. If our 'friends' to the south are in jeopardy, then that danger will make its way here in due course. Good luck and may the Gods watch over you."

Luxon bowed again and turned to leave.

"Oh, there is one more thing," said Zeno. "The amulet that controls the Nexus Tower. Give it to me."

The flap to the tent opened and in walked five Tulin warriors. Their swords were drawn. Zeno pushed back his stool and stood, placing his fists on his desk.

"That was not part of the deal, Zeno," Luxon replied, trying to keep his cool. He cursed himself for being so stupid. Of course, a man like Zeno would want the power of the Nexus Tower for himself.

"I am changing the deal. Pray that I do not change it further. You disrupted my plans by coming here, Wizard. I had an arrangement with the N'Gist. In exchange for granting them access to the tower, they would assist me with restoring glory to my Empire. It was my idea that they pose as Kastardorians when they arrived in this city. I needed my Lords to believe our common enemy had dared attack us. It made for the perfect cause for war. Of course, I did not foresee that foolish Lord Eretor rushing off to seek glory, but even that worked to my advantage. One less enemy and all that. And then when I was returning to the capital to ensure all was going to plan, I ran into you and your friends. Yinnice told me of you, of course, and when I saw that you did indeed carry Asphodel, I saw an opportunity to rid myself of the witch and take the tower for myself. With it, I can restore the Golden Empire. My legions will march across the world and restore its glory."

Luxon turned to face the Emperor.

"You're mad," he snarled.

Zeno chuckled humorlessly.

"I'm not mad, Luxon I am just a man who sees an opportunity. My primary enemies at home have been dealt with. My N'Gist partners are destroyed thanks to you, and now I know that Kastador is vulnerable to attack. I ask this of you, Luxon. Will you hand me the amulet in exchange for all the ships and warriors I promised you or will you defy me and lose any hope of saving your homeland."

Outside the tent came shouts, and the flap parted again. Eripa, Alderlade and Welsly were shoved roughly inside. The Nighblade was bruised, and Eripa had a cut beneath her eye where an armoured fist had struck her. Alderlade glared defiantly at the Emperor.

"Let us go, or I swear you will make an enemy of Delfinnia this day," the young King declared.

Zeno laughed and ruffled the boy's hair.

"You have spirit little King, but I don't think I have anything to fear from you. Command the Wizard to hand over the amulet, and I shall let you go and spare your lives."

"A second ago you said we'd still receive the support of your army and fleet," Luxon snarled.

"Did I? Well, consider that promise broken. Oops."

Luxon clenched his fists and channelled the magic within.

"You're a fool to think you can do this Zeno. I am Luxon. The first Wizard of Delfinnia and Hero of Eclin. You will not get away with this. Cover your eyes!" he shouted to the others. With his left hand, he cast a shield spell over Welsly, Alderlade and Eripa. With his right, he thrust it skyward and summoned lightning. With a blinding flash of searing heat and a deafening boom of thunder, it struck the tent. The magical shield absorbed the impact, protecting Alderlade and the others. Zeno and his men weren't so lucky. The lightning blast vaporized the soldiers and blasted the Emperor out of the back of his tent where he crashed heavily into one of the stone buildings.

"Run!" Luxon shouted, scooping Alderlade up in his arms.

The others didn't need to be told twice. They got to their feet and fled. Luxon led the way. Behind them, alarm bells sounded, and Zeno, who had staggered back to his feet, screamed at his men to stop them. The Emperor's clothing was smouldering, and his face was now severely burnt.

Luxon urged the others onward, and as they ran through the streets, they shouted out to the others to flee. Ferran and Sophia, spotting the commotion, shouted at the Agatha's crew who were enjoying their time in the city to get back to the ship. Some of the sailors drew their swords and were forced to fight their way through some of Zeno's soldiers. A twang sounded close to Luxon's head as a crossbow bolt clattered into the stonework next to it. They kept running. Welsly tossed a fireball at a market stall, causing it to erupt in flame, the smoke helped obscure their escape. Sophia shouted a warning as ahead some of Zeno's men rushed to block the road with a wagon. Luxon unleashed a telekinetic blast that shattered into fragments. By now the entire city was riled, and more and more Tulin warriors joined the pursuit. They rounded a corner and there found Meric who was perusing a peddler's exotic wares. Luxon grabbed him by the shoulder and pulled him after them.

"What by the Gods big blue balls?" the magician cried in surprise.

"We're getting out of here!" Luxon yelled back.

Meric's eyes widened, and he cried out in alarm as angry soldiers poured into the market square. He grabbed his tall hat to ensure it stayed on his head as he fled. Eripa shouted a warning as a volley of Tulin arrows arced high into the sky and began to fall.

Luxon hastily cast a shield spell to envelope them all as they ran causing the projectiles to shatter harmlessly against the magical barrier. They ran around a corner and could now see the docks ahead. The tall mast of the Agatha peaked over the waterside warehouses and administration buildings. A group of Tulin warriors barreled out of a side street to cut off their escape, but Ferran and Welsly ignited their Tourmaline blades and hacked them down without pause. Luxon kept running, doing his best to prevent Alderlade from witnessing the bloodshed. Angry shouts came from all around them as more and more of the Emperor's men joined in the pursuit. They sped toward the docks, and once in range Captain Whitelaw bellowed for the crew on board to weigh anchor and get the ship ready to flee. The gangplank was lowered, and they clambered aboard. Luxon put down Alderlade and told him to get below decks.

"Whatever happens, you stay there," he said, pushing the lad toward the deck hatch. All around him, the Agatha's crew set to their task with Whitelaw cursing and using all manner of threats to make them work faster.

Luxon hurried to the deck rail. A whole battalion of Zeno's soldiers were rushing to the docks. One unit had already arrived with a horse and cart.

"I don't like the looks of that," Meric muttered. The soldiers leapt onto the back of the wagon and began to assemble a catapult hastily. Arrows slammed into the Agatha's hull as Tulin archers moved into range. Sophia and some of the crew returned fire with bows and crossbows.

"A direct hit with that and even this ship will sink," Meric continued, his hands gripping the rail in a white knuckled grip. "The little bastard," he said, suddenly pointing at the visage of Torvan . The elderly wizard was walking at Zeno's side. Meric cupped his hands about his mouth and yelled; "If we ever meet again Torvan I'm going to insult you so much you'll have a bloody heart attack, you old wretch."

Some of the Agatha's crew had deployed the mainsail and raised the anchor in record time, now they rushed to the side of the ship, and using long wooden poles to pushed the vessel away from the quayside. Whitelaw took the wheel and turned her about so that she faced the open sea.

"There are catapults and ballista on the harbour walls, a Tulin warship is moving to block our escape!" shouted the barrel man from the crow's nest.

"Master Wizard, is there anything you can do about them? They will rip us apart," Whitelaw said, fear evident in his tone.

Luxon rushed to the front of the ship. He rubbed his hands together and focused every bit of magic he had. He channelled Asphodel's power and that of Dragasdol. Even the magic within Zahnia's armour. Over the city, dark clouds suddenly formed as Luxon summoned the energy within the atmosphere. The very air crackled and fizzed until with a roar the lightning bolts lanced from the sky to strike the harbour's defences. With a flash of light and a loud boom of thunder, the catapults and ballista exploded into a million fragments cutting down and vaporizing the soldiers manning them. Luxon changed his focus to the Tulin warship that was moving to block their escape. Again, the sky flashed, and this time, a massive bolt of lightning struck the ship. The tall mast shattered into flaming splinters and the vessel split in two from the force of the strike. Luxon closed his eyes and leaned heavily against the rail. Eripa rushed to his side and caught him before he fell from exhaustion. He didn't want to watch the deaths of so many men. The two halves of the warship quickly sank beneath the waves, and the Agatha sailed over the wreckage and out to the open sea. They had escaped.

CHAPTER 22.

Luxon opened his eyes and groaned. He was in his bunk aboard the gently rocking Agatha. It was dark outside suggesting that he'd been asleep for at least a few hours. With a groan, he sat up and rubbed his eyes tiredly. His gear had been stripped from him and was placed neatly in the corner of the cabin or in the trunk at the bottom of the bed. Tucked under the trunk was a piece of paper. He walked over to it and picked it up.

'Meet us in Whitelaw's cabin when you wake' – F.

He put on his trousers and shirt before pulling on his boots and cloak. He opened the trunk. Hesitantly he reached for Asphodel and then stopped, his hand was shaking.

"What am I to do with you?" he whispered before stepping back and closing the trunk. Instead, he took the steel dagger he often carried and tucked it into his belt. He felt weary after using such powerful magic, and it would likely take another day at the least before he was back to his full strength. He exited the cabin and made his way through the bowels of the ship. As he walked through the lower decks, the *Agatha's* crew greeted him, and some even took his hand and thanked him for his actions in the harbour. He reached Whitelaw's cabin and knocked on the door.

"Come in," came the captain's voice. "Ah, Luxon, you're awake at last," Whitelaw greeted. "come take a seat; you must be famished."

Luxon nodded, and his stomach growled. He was certainly hungry. He took a seat at the captain's long dining table next to Alderlade. The young King smiled at him before returning to regaling Sophia with a tale of his adventures chasing rats in the bowels of the ship. The Witch Hunter smiled at him and feigned interest. Sitting on his other side was Meric. The Kastadorian magician looked pale.

"I never realized until now that travelling by sea is not for me," he moaned.

"You'll get your sea legs soon enough lad," Whitelaw cackled.

Ferran was sat further down the table with Welsly and Eripa. He stood and gently tapped on the table to get everyone's attention.

"Now that Luxon is here I think it's time to discuss our next course of action. We succeeded in stopping Danon's schemes for the Nexus Tower and slew the Witch Yinnice," the others cheered at that, "but" Ferran added thoughtfully, "we have made a powerful new enemy in the process. Emperor Zeno betrayed us and is now threatening Kastador. The army and fleet he promised Luxon is now being sent against them."

"And King Thorn is busy fighting in Dilar! Kastador cannot fight on two fronts, not against such a force," Meric said glumly.

"This all our fault," Luxon said quietly. "Danon predicted our plan, and now we have imperilled the entire Tulin continent. We should never have left Delfinnia."

They all flinched as suddenly Alderlade slammed his small fists onto the table.

"No! You are wrong, Luxon. We *had* no choice. We *have* no choice. Delfinnia cannot defeat Danon alone. The plan was the correct course of action. I say we give the free peoples of this land more credit. We know King Thorn can fight and we have allies in Yazid and the Morvan. Do not despair. I am the King of Delfinnia. I may just be a boy, but I will not sit here and listen to those who my subjects are depending on to wallow in despair and remorse."

A silence fell over the cabin before Luxon finally nodded.

"You are right sire, forgive my despair. You're certainly wiser than your years," he said with a bow.

"The King is right," said Ferran with respect in his tone, 'The situation may appear grim, but Kastador will not be taken by surprise. Beric has a head start on Zeno, so the capital will know an Imperial army is approaching."

Welsly raised a hand.

"Except, he doesn't know that Zeno has betrayed us."

Ferran nodded.

"That is true, but we will beat the Imperial fleet by some days, especially after Luxon's actions at the harbour. They will have a warning. Whether King Thorn can return north in time is another matter, but at least they will have a chance."

"What about Silenzia?" asked Sophia. "When I was in the market in the Imperial capital, I overheard a merchant say that the fighting there has been fierce. It sounded as though Yazid and the Morvan have not made it easy for the Sarpi."

Luxon tapped his chin in thought.

"We need to destroy the enemy so that it will smash Danon's grip in these lands for good, or at least long enough to free them so they can send aid to Delfinnia," he said.

"How can we do that? The fighting is spread across so many fronts. The Empire will attack Kastador from the north. The Sarpi and N'Gist from the south."

"Three battles. First, we must defeat Zeno."

Meric shook his head and laughed in disbelief.

"How can we defeat the might of the Empire when the bulk of Kastador's army is in the south?"

Luxon smiled as a plan formed in his head.

"We use the terrain of the Gryphon Mountains. His armies must march through the mountains if they are to attack Kastador, correct?"

Meric nodded.

"We use the mountains and narrow passes to our advantage. Trust me. We can defeat his armies."

"Then what?" asked Eripa excitedly. She was enjoying this brainstorming.

"We defeat the Empire then we ride hard with every warrior we can muster to Dilar and aid King Thorn in defeating the Sarpi and Nerios."

"Then push on to Silenzia? It's a long march to those lands." said Ferran.

"And then there's the problem of convincing King Thorn and the others to go along with this mad plan," Meric added.

*

Kastador

The *Agatha* took just three days to reach Kastador. The winds had been in their favour, and during the times when it had faded, Luxon had used his wind magic to power the vessel on. There had been no sign of the Empire's ships in pursuit, and they had rounded the cape without incident. Meric disembarked at the first Kastadorian settlement they had sighted and was now riding from settlement to settlement to raise the Kingdom's citizenry and any mercenaries he could find to battle. The ship slipped into the capital city's harbour at midday to a fanfare of trumpets, but the celebrations were soon cut short when Beric saw the severe expressions on her crew's faces. Now they were in the palace with Beric railing against the treacherous Emperor. An emergency council of the city's nobles had been hastily called with more rushing in from the surrounding countryside by the hour.

"Never trust the Tulins!" Beric bellowed as he paced the throne room. Luxon and Ferran stood calmly as they watched the Bannerlord vent his fury. Finally, Beric calmed down enough to begin the emergency council meeting.

"Messengers have been dispatched to the King and Queen informing them of the approaching danger, but I fear they will not be able to reach us in time."

Luxon then explained his plans causing an uproar among the nobles. Many said he was mad, others that a foreigner had no right to assert their authority. It was Beric who silenced those voices by slamming a gauntleted fist onto the arm of his chair.

"We have enough men to make this work. We must make this work. We do as the Wizard says and use the Gryphon Mountains as our shield. Now, muster your men and bring them to the city. We march in two days."

The room emptied of disgruntled and petrified nobles. When the last of the nobles had departed, Beric walked over to a table close to the empty thrones and poured himself a large glass of wine.

"They're terrified," he said to Luxon and the others who had watched the debate from the sidelines. "and with good reason. The last time the Empire came in such force, Thorn wasn't even King yet. We won that battle by the skin of our teeth then and that was with the full might of our Banners."

"Your people are brave, Beric. They will fight harder because of what is at stake. Your one comfort is that the N'Gist are lost to them. Luxon's defeat of the witch and escape with the Portal key means that they will not have any wielders on their side," offered Ferran.

Beric downed his wine and reached for the bottle.

"And we have the Wizard. Do not underestimate him," Eripa added. Beric raised his glass to that.

"Using magic in war goes against all the rules, but these are dark times, and we will need every advantage we can get." He rubbed his eyes tiredly and downed his wine. "Get some rest. Tomorrow is going to be a busy day."

*

The next morning, Meric arrived at the capital with a contingent of mages from Old Kastador. He was flustered and moaning about how sore his arse was from all the riding he'd done.

"The word is being been spread, and every sword in the land who didn't march with King Thorn has been summoned here. I also found a company of Red Lion Bannerlords who were returning from a job in Silenzia. It sounds like the Morvan is giving the Sarpi one hell of a fight."

The city was a hive of activity as the citizenry set about the grim task of preparing their home for a possible siege. The city walls were being reinforced, and extra food was brought in from the surrounding countryside. The roads into the city were packed with hundreds of mules, oxen, and horses. On the river, several of the small Kastadorian ships were arriving at the docks. Most carried border guards who had heeded the capitals call whilst others brought in the militias from the nearest towns and villages. Every man and woman who could wield a sword would be needed.

Luxon walked through the narrow streets towards his destination. He could smell the place long before he arrived at the long building. The structure had three chimneys that were all spewing out thick black acrid smoke. He went inside and found Meric and a group of other mages hard at work.

"Ah, Luxon there you are. We have followed your instructions exactly, and the powder should be ready within the next few hours. I've tasked some of the city watch to fill barrels with the stuff. You will really have to teach me the recipe."

Luxon checked the barrels and ran a finger through the powder. It was of the correct consistency, Meric and his mages had done their job well.

"I read about it in a book back in Caldaria's Great Library. The mage who discovered it claimed to have encountered it in a land beyond Aniron's Spine. He called it Boom Powder after he blew up his laboratory and from his descriptions of its effects, it's just what we need. The main ingredient is saltpetre, a nitrate salt of potassium. Potassium nitrate, sulfur, and carbon react together to form nitrogen and carbon dioxide gases and potassium sulfide. The hot expanding gases, nitrogen and carbon dioxide, provide the propelling action."

"Fascinating. Boom powder, eh? I've heard that the Sarpi have weapons that use something similar." Meric shuddered. "Can you imagine such weapons?"

*

At midday, alarm bells tolled as an army was sighted advancing from the west. Beric summoned Luxon and the others, and together they hurried to the walls. A single rider forced his way through the throng and entered the city where he leapt from the saddle and rushed to meet them. Escorted by two guards, he was brought to Beric.

"My Lord," the man panted. It took him a few moments to catch his breath. "Good news, my lord. King Teodoric is here! The Kingdom of Vinium has come at last."

Beric cheered the news, and within the hour the army of the Kingdom of Vinium crossed the Gryphon river and arrived at the city walls. The gates were left open, but the army began to set up camp in the fields surrounding the city. Beric and the others were back in the throne room and waited for Teodoric to enter. The double doors swung open and in strode the King of Vinium. He was taller than any man Luxon had seen before and built like a bear with muscles that rippled on his bare arms. His knotted beard was a light brown and reached to his waist, and his head was covered in a long mane of hair the same colour. His eyes were large and green. He looked like no King they had encountered before, even more rough around than the edges than Faramond the King of the Tribes back in Delfinnia. His torso was protected by a shirt of scale armour and his legs by a pair of steel greaves and heavy iron boots. At his hip was a savage looking war axe and strapped to his back was a long two handed Warhammer.

"Beric! You ugly turd, how long has it been?" Teodoric exclaimed. He opened his arms and pulled Beric into a bear hug.

"Too long Lord King. Twenty years at least. I am so glad you are here," Beric replied, relief evident in his tone. He then proceeded to tell the King of the dire situation they now found themselves in and told him that King Thorn and the rest of the army was too far away to help. Once he was done, Teodoric stood silently and swirled the wine in his glass.

"If I knew things were this shite I would have stayed at home. You say this Emperor Zeno seeks to conquer the Free Kingdoms? I say let the bastard try. You-" he said, pointing to Luxon. "Is what Beric says true. You are a powerful wielder?"

Luxon nodded.

"I am sire, and I am deeply sorry for what we have brought upon you."

Teodoric waved dismissively.

"None of that talk lad. The Empire has always been a pain in our collective arses. It was only a matter of time before some upstart like this Zeno tried to conquer us all again. You did good stopping him gaining control of that - what did you call it again?"

"Portal tower, sire," Luxon answered.

"Portal tower. Imagine the mischief a bastard could do with one of them buggers eh!" The King cackled. "Your plan to meet them in the mountains is a sound one. With our support, we will send them packing have no fear."

"I wish I shared your confidence, sire," Beric muttered. Teodoric slapped him on the back and laughed heartily.

"For too long, I have had to satisfy my blood lust on those cowardly little buggers from Nerva. It's no fun lobbing off the heads of raiders like that. Hardly a challenge at all. No, my men yearn to face the Empire in battle once more."

*

As the day wore on more and more fighting men and women arrived in the city. Many were just farmers armed with pitchforks and slings, but there were also some mercenary groups comprised of men with swords and bows. Just as Beric had commanded, the gathered ragtag force gathered outside the city walls. Along with the *Agatha's* crew, the army that would face Zeno numbered just over six thousand with the bulk of it being comprised of Teodoric's troops.

"It's not enough," Beric panicked.

He, Luxon and the others were standing on the city walls and looking the army over. Ferran and Welsly exchanged a worried glance.

"It will be enough, trust me," Luxon said with more confidence than he felt. He faced the others. "Right, you all know the plan. Let's get to it."

The Delfinnians would depart before the army and head to the Gryphon Mountains with all haste. Ferran took the Gryphon whistle Thorn had given him and blew it. A high-pitched screech sounded from above signalling the arrival of a Gryphon. It dropped from the sky to land in a spray of dust and snow in the courtyard below. Soldiers rolled barrels of the Boom Powder out to the courtyard and began to load them onto the Gryphon's back.

Meanwhile, other Gryphons, already loaded with similar barrels were being led out from their stables and joined the wild one that had grown attached to Ferran. Their riders helped them onto the backs of their steeds with Luxon and Eripa sharing one and Sophia and Welsly sharing another. Meric and Beric meanwhile would march with the army. The Gryphons took to the skies and shot off towards the distant, frigid peaks. It would be there, among them that the fate of the Free Kingdoms would be decided.

It took them a few hours of flying to reach their destination. Luxon pointed to the narrow pass they had used to spy on the previous Imperial army that had threatened Kastador. They descended at a dizzying speed and landed at the top of the narrow path that led down to valley floor. Luxon slid to the ground and joined Ferran at the path's edge.

"This is the place all right. Can you do it?" the Nightblade asked seriously.

"I can. I will," Luxon replied.

"Very well. Let's get everything ready."

Luxon jogged over to the Gryphon he had arrived on and helped the rider unstrapped the barrels of Boom Powder from its back. Meanwhile, Ferran, Welsly and Sophia took off to their own locations. The Nightblades headed towards the far end of the valley while Sophia flew to the opposite side. Once their tasks were achieved, Ferran and Welsly used magic to send a fireball skyward to let him know they were ready. Sophia, on the other hand, simply lit a torch and waved it.

"Now, we wait."

*

The hastily assembled army of Kastador and its Vinum allies arrived the next day and quickly moved to take up a position in the woods that lined the narrow path through the valley. The rest of the force assembled a few hundred meters behind the end of the valley and waited for the enemy to arrive. Scouts riding Gryphons had sighted Zeno's army not far away and reported that his army was moving like a great inkblot through the snowy terrain.

From his vantage point on the mountainside, Luxon watched as Beric moved his forces into the nearby woods. Concealment and timing were key to his plan. On the far end of the valley, he could just make out Ferran and Welsly moving into position. On the valley floor, Zeno's army began to enter the valley. First rode a small contingent of scouts who spread out as much as they were able to detect any ambushes. Luxon tensed and ducked behind a rock as one of the scouts looked up. They rode on, and one of the horsemen blew his horn to signal the rest of the army that the way ahead was clear. So far, the Vinium forces hiding in the woods had remained undetected. He risked a peek over the edge of the rock and could see the first battalions of infantry enter the pass. He licked his lips nervously.

Too soon and Zeno's forces would be able to escape the trap, too late and Beric's forces would be engaged and destroyed. He waited as more and more enemy troops filed into the valley. He tensed as he spotted Zeno himself riding at the head of a column of cavalry. He was halfway along the valley when Luxon stood and launched a fireball skyward. Next, he ran over to the barrels of Boom Powder and lit the fuse. He wouldn't have long to get clear. Using magic, he leapt off the ledge and floated gently to the ground. Imperial horns blared as they spotted the fireball flying skyward.

Then all hell broke loose. The powder barrels set up at the ends of the valley exploded with a deafening boom. Tons of rock and debris rained down onto the Imperial army crushing entire companies of warriors. At the same time, Teodoric attacked from the woods. Volleys of arrows lanced out from the trees to strike downs scores of enemy soldiers. Zeno bellowed orders to his men, but then a loud rumbling from the far end of the valley drowned out the din of battle. With a crack and crash, the far end of the valley collapsed, turning into a devastating landslide that buried the rear of Zeno's army. Luxon watched in horror as thousands of warriors were buried alive.

Meanwhile, those who hadn't been trapped or killed by the landslide were hacked to pieces by the Vinium forces, their axes cleaving men and horses alike. A horn blared from the valley entrance, and the forces of Kastador surged into the fray. Arrows flew, swords slashed, and spears stabbed. It was a massacre. The Imperial forces could not form up due to the confining terrain, and the relentless Vinium attacks spread chaos throughout the ranks. The devastating landslide cut off any chance of retreat and Kastadorian archers shot down those that tried to flee. Luxon sank to the ground and sat staring wide eyed at the butchery. Across the valley, he could see Sophia shooting down into the throng, and in the thick of the fighting, he spotted the Tourmaline blades of Ferran and Welsly flashing. It was over quickly. A horn sounded a mournful tone, and the stunned and bloodied Imperial army threw down their weapons. Kastador had won the day, and the power of the Emperor Zeno was destroyed.

*

Luxon walked through the valley, his heart heavy as he stepped over the countless broken bodies that covered every patch of ground. The few Imperial survivors were herded to the far end of the valley and there held under the guard of a contingent of Vinium Knights. He stopped at the base of the landslide. Broken limbs poked through the rubble and discarded weapons lay everywhere. He felt sick.

"A stunning victory that will go down in the annuals of this land!" cackled King Teodoric who was moving through the battlefield with Beric and Meric. At seeing Luxon, they cheered but soon stopped when they saw his desolated expression.

"Why are you so down lad? Your plan was a masterstroke that has saved Kastador and ensured that the Empire will never threaten us again," the King said confusion in his tone.

Luxon didn't respond. Instead, he just walked away.

*

Zeno's body was found shortly afterwards. The young Emperor had been riddled with arrows, and his face smashed to a bloody pulp by a Vinium Warhammer. The threat from the Empire was over. For now.

Ferran found Luxon sitting next to the stream that ran through the nearby woods.

"I am responsible for all that death," Luxon said softly with tears in his eyes.

"You have killed before, and you will have to kill again before the end," Ferran replied bluntly. "Now, is not the time to linger on that. Beric is eager to depart as soon as possible and march south to join up with King Thorn. He wants to be on the road within the hour, and I agree with him."

Luxon wiped tears from his eyes and nodded. He stood and brushed the dirt from his greaves.

"Forgive me, Ferran. Sometimes it all gets too much."

Ferran's expression eased, and he pulled Luxon into a hug. Luxon tensed but then buried his head into the Nightblade's shoulder where he sobbed.

"I know lad, I know."

CHAPTER 23.

The army marched south to Kastador and there embarked what ships remained in the city's harbour. Not all the troops could be carried, and those that couldn't fit began the long march to the borders of Dilar. As they arrived in the city, there hadn't been time to celebrate the stunning victory over the Empire. Only the temple bells tolled as a sign that any battle had been fought and won at all. Luxon and the others boarded the Agatha and Beric, and Meric joined them. The ship slipped the dock and set off at full sail down the river systems that would take them to Dilar. Lipur took the helm as he knew the waterways well and Captain Whitelaw was happy to let him. Behind them, a small fleet of the much shorter and leaner Kastadorian ships followed. Each was packed with warriors, horses, and supplies.

It took them two days to cross into Dilar, and as soon as they had entered the southern Kingdom, they saw the telltale marks of war. On the horizon, smoke trails drifted skyward and, on the riverbanks, they had passed several burnt settlements. Fell Beasts had taken advantage of the conflict, and at night they had spotted a swarm of Pucks devouring the corpses of slain villagers in the smouldering ruins of a village.

On the third day, they encountered a horseman riding hard along the riverbank. At seeing the ships, he skidded to a halt and shouted a greeting. The Agatha steered closer to the bank and lowered her anchor.

"Hail!" the man said. From his attire, he was a Bannerlord. The dirt covered Red Lion on his chest gave him away as one of that sigils number.

"What news of the war?" Beric asked.

"The enemy are relentless Sir. The Nerios and their Sarpi allies have driven our forces back across the Duin River a few miles to the west. They are using magic in battle!" the man spat in disgust. "King Thorn is hoping to regroup, but we have lost many men in the fighting. Thank the Gods; you have arrived. I will ride on to the encampment and notify him of your arrival."

Beric thanked the rider, and the *Agatha* raised anchor and continued on her way. They reached a fork in the river, and Lipur took the rightmost route. Within an hour they sighted a camp comprised of hundreds of tents and cooking fires on the north bank. To the south, more smoke rose lazily into the air, more homesteads and settlements destroyed by the enemy. The Agatha dropped anchor in a bend on the river, and the other ships did likewise where they could. Before disembarking Luxon put on Zahnia's armour, strapped Dragasdol to his back and tentatively attached Asphodel's sheathe to his belt. He gasped as the energy from the blade surged through him, and all weariness vanished. He feared the power of the blade and he could feel its hunger to take life. Luxon joined Beric and the others on the rowboat to the shore, and there they were greeted by an exhausted Thorn. He embraced Beric and greeted the rest.

"Thank the Gods you are here," Thorn said tiredly when they had all gathered in his tent. Queen Nix was there too, and like her husband, she looked drained. Both were covered in mud and dust from their hasty retreat.

Beric told the King and Queen of their victory over the Empire, and Thorn again praised the Gods for their good fortune.

"Teodoric and the rest of the army is hurrying south, but it will take them another two days at the most to reach us. Scouts have been sent to find him and lead him here."

"The old cad had best hurry. He owes me," Queen Merith said bitterly. The Queen of Dilar was much older than Luxon had expected, but the fire in her eyes made it clear that she was a woman not to be trifled with. Like Thorn, she had dark rings of exhaustion under her eyes and dirt covered her armour. She was a warrior Queen and one with a fearsome reputation, according to Beric.

Thorn clapped Beric on the shoulder.

"You have done well, my friend. I have sent Lord Raron and his Bannermen to harass and slow the enemy as much as he is able, but I fear they will reach the river soon."

Luxon raised a hand.

"The Bannerlord we encountered on the riverbank said that the enemy is using magic?"

Thorn sighed and rubbed his tired eyes.

"Yes. N'Gist wielders used fire and elemental magic to decimate Dilar's forces. What is left of their army is here with us," he said gesturing to the forlorn soldiers mooching around outside the tent. They looked beaten and dejected. Queen Merith pointed to the map.

"There is one place where we have a chance of halting their advance. A mile to the west is Votrill Bridge, the only one for at least one hundred leagues. The rest we destroyed. It is there that we will do battle and-"

A trumpet blared a warning cutting off the King. They rushed outside as a rider barreled into the camp.

"My Lord King, the enemy comes! Lord Raron has fallen back to the bridge and will hold it as long as he is able, but he beseeches that you come at all speed."

Thorn swore loudly.

"So much for laying a trap! Beric get the army on their feet and ready to march, it seems the enemy has forced our hand."

The encampment descended into a flurry of activity as the soldiers rushed to and fro to prepare for battle. Horses were hastily watered, and armoured, quivers were restocked with arrows, and once more, the men of Kastador marched to battle. Luxon and the others joined them as they hastily advanced through the flat grasslands of Dilar. The weather was turning with thick black clouds rolling across the sky. A light shower of rain sprinkled the land making the dirt path slippery. Within an hour they sighted the Votrill Bridge and began to form up on the riverbanks. Ahead they could see Lord Raron's Bannerlords retreating under a barrage of missile fire. Luxon spurred his horse forward and galloped towards the bridge. As he drew nearer, he raised Dragasdol high and summoned a magical shield that covered the retreating Bannerlords. Arrows struck it only to bounce off harmlessly. At seeing Luxon, the army cheered and roared their approval.

The army hastily took up position with the Bannerlords forming a shield wall on the bridge, and the archers lined the banks. Thanks to the river, the enemy would not be able to outflank their position, but Luxon shuddered at the slaughter that would occur on the bridge itself. He dismounted and joined Ferran and Welsly in the ranks of armoured warriors. Sophia meanwhile joined the archers and held her bow at the ready. The rest of the *Agatha's* crew had also joined the ranks whilst Eripa and Alderlade stayed back from the river with Queen Nix and her bodyguards.

Across the river was a thick line of trees and it was from there that the enemy emerged.

There was a dull hammer blow that shuddered across the river. It was the sound of a drum, a large war drum, and on the third stroke, the enemy began to crash their weapons against their shields. The Nerios standards fluttered in the strengthening wind, a long line of flags depicting all manner of bizarre and exotic creatures. Luxon could recognize the image of one of the elephants they had seen in Silenzia.

The Nerios forces wore long leather coats over shirts of mail, and their helmets were tall and topped with the feathers of some exotic bird. The front line wielded vicious looking axes the length of a man while the second carried long pikes and swords. On their right flank was the unmistakable Sarpi forces. They wore black cloaks and plate armour, their eyes shining in the dull afternoon light.

The horns sounded. Luxon drew Asphodel, and as one the army advanced towards the bridge. As they marched, he noticed the enemy forming a shield wall of their own. A warning shout from the front ranks made him look to the centre of the bridge. A few Sarpi warriors had crossed the bridge.

"They're sending out a vanguard to slow us down!" shouted Thorn.

The lightly armoured Sarpi charged screaming at the approaching Kastadorians. Thorn's men were following behind Beric's contingent; the honour of reaching the bridge first was to be theirs. Adrenaline pumped through his body; he took in the situation ahead of him. Beric's men were only feet away from the bridge when a hail of arrows slammed into the leading men like a fist. A dozen Bannerlords fell screaming, arrow shafts sticking out of their bodies.

"SHIELDS!" bellowed Thorn. Luxon raised Dragasdol and cast a shield spell just in time; he almost staggered as a volley of fireballs slammed into it to dissipate harmlessly.

"N'Gist bastards!" Welsly cried.

Sure enough, the cloaked figures of N'Gist wielders appeared in the treeline. They began to launch fireball after fireball at the Kastadorian army, but Luxon planted Dragasdol into the earth and increased his efforts with the shield spell. With the magical staff and Asphodel, it would take more than fireballs to breach his spell.

Luxon looked up to see Beric's men engage the Sarpi vanguard. Swords and axes clashed, men from both sides fell, and some fell into the flowing river Votrill with a scream.

Luxon fell into step with Ferran and Welsly and reached the bridge. King Thorn's men were just behind them and using their shields to protect their flank from the enemy archers who were shooting their arrows with increasing desperation.

The Bannerlords had formed a shield wall to protect themselves from the hail of missiles raining down upon them. The wall was proving effective as few men were falling to the deadly maelstrom. Kastadorian longbowmen unleashed their own volley, the arrows arching overhead and slamming down into the magical shield cast by the N'Gist. Javelins were thrown by Bannerlords at the Nerios archers, impaling a score on their lethal points. The screams of battle rang out over the previously serene landscape.

The bridge battle had now turned into a pushing match between Beric's men and the Sarpi vanguard.

Thorn swore, the longer they were held on the bridge the likelihood that enemy reinforcements would arrive grew. Luxon shouted a warning as he saw a behemoth of a Sarpi in full black plate armour and armed with a massive two-handed axe cleave his way through Beric's men. A half dozen fell in a single mighty blow, Beric among them. Thorn cried out as he saw his friend fall into the river, a massive gaping wound almost splitting him in two.

"Who is that monster!" muttered Ferran in disbelief.

The giant Sarpi decapitated two more Bannerlords and viciously hacked his way through another's torso. Blood and gore covered Luxon and the other warriors.

"A Sarpi Berserker, I've not seen one like him before, I thought they were only stories!" Ferran snarled. Tales of such savage warriors had come from the survivors of the battles of Balnor and Bison, but Luxon had not believed them. Now, he was witnessing first hand such a brute.

"Fall back!" screamed the lead Bannerlords. The Berserker cut down another handful of men as he menacingly advanced on the panic-stricken front ranks.

"Niveren save us," Ferran shouted in frustration. The Bannerlords retreated across the bridge, the berserker laughing mockingly at their backs.

The Kastadorian army regrouped on the north side of the river and waited; no-one was willing to face the Sarpi monster. Thorn rode to the head of the army and appraised the situation. He wheeled his horse to face his men.

"One man holds you all at bay!" he cried. "One Bannerlord of Kastador is worth more than one wretched Sarpi, which of you has the courage to kill that bastard!" he shouted pointing at the Berserker who was picking dirt from under his fingernails with a bored expression. The man was covered in blood and gore; his black armoured   darkened red with blood.

"Why not put an arrow through him, sire!" shouted one of the Bannerlords.

Thorn glared at the man.

"Shoot him like a coward? Never! Sir Beric would never do something so dishonourable. We are Kastador. We have honour. He has slain forty of us, will no man avenge their comrades' deaths!"

Ferran frowned in annoyance.

"Sod the King's sense of honour. The longer that big bastard holds us here, the longer the Sarpi have to reinforce their end of the bridge and push us off entirely," he muttered.

He turned to face Luxon and his Welsly. "We have to get that berserker out of the way."

"I will not allow the use of magic," Thorn shouted as he moved his horse behind them. "This is a matter of honour, and if Beric is to be avenged, then this must be done our way." Ferran was about to argue, but Luxon shook his head in warning. A tense moment past and

none of the Bannerlords volunteered to fight the Berserker. Ferran tightened his grip on his sword and then stepped forward from amongst the ranks.

*

"I accept the challenge," shouted Ferran raising his sword into the air. The Bannerlords stood next to him, clapped him on the back in respect.

"Let the honour of the kill be yours, Ferran of BlackMoor," Thorn said irritably, as he watched from his horse.

Ferran walked onto the bridge. His breathing was echoing in his ears in the confines of his hood. The Berserker filled his vision. His thoughts drifted to Sophia; her beautiful face drifted through his thoughts like a spectre. He glanced to where she stood on the bank. She looked scared. All he could do was offer her a weak smile and a shrug.

'No doubt you'll kill me yourself if this bastard fails too,' he whispered to himself.

He held his sword in front of him and cautiously advanced. The Berserker stood with a keen expression on his blood-soaked features. The man was eager to kill. Ferran would not give him the chance.

He roared a challenge and darted forwards with a speed that took the Berserker off guard. His Tourmaline sword flashed upwards slicing into the Berserkers leather armour and bit into the flesh beneath. Blood spurted from the wound, but the big man was quick too, throwing his body forwards and forcing the blade of the sword to skim off his body. Ferran spun, raising a fist and delivered a savage punch to the Sarpi's face.

The Berserker quickly regained his footing and grabbed Ferran's sword arm, wrenching it with all his might. Ferran bellowed out in pain as he felt his shoulder pop and tendons snap under the force.

The Berserker barked a laugh as Ferran stumbled backwards. His arm throbbed with pain, but he quickly tapped into his magic and healed the injury. He winced when his shoulder popped back into place, and the damaged tendons began to heal. A warm tingling sensation flooded up the wounded limb. Now he would have to focus on both the healing spell and the enemy.

The Berserker brought his mighty axe over his head and swung it down at Ferran's head. The Kastadorian army watched the two skilled warriors in intense silence, praying that their man would win the day.

Desperately, Ferran dodged, deflecting the axe head with his sword, and parrying a series of blows that rained down upon him. Sweat poured into his eyes, and his arm ached in pain, he couldn't maintain his concentration. He couldn't take much more before the berserker added him to the pile of the dead.

Ferran countered savagely, knocking the axe aside and butted the Sarpi in the face with his head. The Berserker roared in pain staggering backwards.

Ferran tossed his sword into his left hand and rained a series of frantic blows with his sword forcing the big man back several steps. He overreached one of his attacks, and the

Berserker deflected the sword causing Ferran to stagger forwards and crash to the deck. The berserker brought the hilt of his axe smashing down onto FerranFerran's back, his armour the only thing saving him from suffering a broken spine. He collapsed to the floor of the bridge. The Sarpi forced his head down onto the surface of the bridge with his foot; axe held high to deliver the killer blow. He could hear the stunned cries of Welsly and Luxon from the mass of warriors. He had been soundly beaten. He desperately sought out Sophia, but he couldn't see her.

"Forgive me, my love," he whispered. He closed his eyes and waited for his doom, but the axe never fell. A whoosh and then a choking noise caused him to look up. The Berserker stood stunned, his axe held high and sticking out of his throat was a silver tipped arrow. At seeing their champion fall, the enemy army roared and charged across the bridge. Welsly dashed forward and helped the wounded Ferran to his feet.

"Sophia," he said. She had shot the arrow and saved his life. The two Nightblades rushed back across the bridge, the enemy horde hot on their heels. Welsly shoved Ferran forward, and the Kastadorian warriors pulled him to safety. Then, Welsly cried out and went rigid as a Sarpi arrow struck him in the back. He stumbled and then another arrow, and another hit him. Luxon tried to reach him and using telekinesis blasted the first ranks of the enemy back. The force of the spell sent dozens of Nerios flying over the sides of the bridge and into the fast-flowing river. Their panicked screams faded as they were swept to their doom. Luxon reached Welsly and dragged him off the bridge. Bannerlord shields protecting them from another arrow storm. Luxon pulled Welsly through the ranks until they reached the rear of the army. On the bridge, the front ranks of both sides clashed with brutal savagery. The Bannerlord shield wall held, but it was clear that the press of enemy troops would force them back in time. Luxon rolled Welsly onto his back. The Nightblade was deathly pale, and blood pooled on his lips. He was gasping, and his eyes were wide with fear.

"Luxon, I-"

Luxon rubbed his hands together and channelled his magic. Desperately he tried to heal his friend, but the damage was done. With one last breath, Welsly died. Luxon shouted in pain. How many more of his friends would pay the price? He looked up to see Eripa and Meric rushing towards him. Meric knelt next to Welsly and reached into his bag, but at seeing him, he sighed, knowing that there was no way to revive him.

Eripa fell to her knees and sobbed over Welsly's body.

Luxon wiped the tears from his eyes angrily.

"Get her out of here," he snapped at Meric. The Magician nodded.

"I will."

Luxon drew Asphodel, and its power surged through him. Fury was in his heart, and he could feel the sword's hunger. This time, instead of fearing it, he embraced it, and with a roar, he charged into the heart of the battle.

*

He was like a God of War. Asphodel took souls with wild abandon as he hacked and slashed his way through the Nerios and Sarpi troops. The sword sliced through armour, shields and flesh like a hot knife through butter and the savagery of his charge had shattered the enemy's front line. Luxon fought with magic and blade alike. With his free hand, he blasted men to pieces with lightning and burned entire regiments to ash with flame. When his foes got close enough, Asphodel would sing and send more to their doom. He hadn't fought with such fury since the Battle of the Watchers. The enemy fell back under his assault, and many threw down their weapons and fled back across the bridge. Inspired by Luxon's charge, the Kastadorian army surged forward, butchering all in their path. Above, the Gryphon Riders who Thorn had kept in reserve were unleashed, and they swooped on the fleeing foe. Luxon stopped once he reached the other side of the river and stepped aside to allow the Kastadorian cavalry to charge. The N'Gist wielders tried to hold their ground, but against Luxon's magical might and the speeding lances and steeds of the Bannerlords, they were quickly dispatched. The battle continued on the opposite bank, but it was clear the enemy were done. Luxon stood panting, sweat beading into his eyes. To him, the battle had felt like mere moments, but as he looked up, he could the sun was on the verge of dipping below the horizon. Hours had passed. His armour was covered in scratches where enemy blades had struck only to be repelled by Zahnia's white steel armour. Weariness flooded over him, only his planting of Asphodel into the muddy ground preventing him from falling.

A horn blew in the distance, the battle of Votrill Bridge was over.

Chapter 24.

Shortly after the battle, the night came quickly, but there was little join in the Delfinnian and Kastadorian ranks. The warriors of Dilar, on the other hand, were jubilant. A delegation from the defeated Nerios arrived in the camp and threw themselves at Queen Merith's feet begging for mercy. They pleaded that their leaders had been manipulated by the N'Gist and on advice from Luxon, Merith accepted their surrender.

After speaking with Merith, he left Thorn's tent and walked aimlessly through the camp. Fires had been lit, and the smell of cooking meat and ale wafted on the cool breeze. Eventually, he found his way to where Sophia and the others had set up a tent of their own. Inside Ferran was being nursed by his wife and a desolated Eripa said quietly in the corner.   's death was a huge blow to them all. As he entered, Sophia looked up and offered him a bowl of soup. He took it and slumped to the floor.

"Ferran will live, but his arm will take time to heal," she said softly. Luxon nodded.

"You saved the day, Luxon. I have never seen anyone fight the way you did today. It will go down in legend."

"It wasn't enough to save Welsly or Beric and all the others killed by the Sarpi," he replied bitterly.

Eripa gave him a hard look, her eyes filled with tears.

"You saved us all. They died heroes worthy of verse and remembrance," the bard said.

They fell quiet, and Luxon lay down and closed his eyes. He could the celebrating Dilar troops and the songs of mourning from the Kastadorians. It wasn't long before exhaustion took him.

*

Early the next morning, the army broke camp. The site was bustling with activity, but already many of the Dilar troops had departed for home or continued the hunt for the surviving Sarpi. Queen Merith thanked Thorn and Nix before approaching Luxon who was packing his things. He had taken off the armour and had loaded it onto his horse.

"Thorn has explained your plight, Master Wizard. We in Dilar will be eternally grateful for what you did for us. But, we are in no fit state to send you assistance. The Sarpi and N'Gist devastated my army, and it will take many months for my Marshalls to return it to strength. To that end, I have agreed with King Thorn that the forces of Dilar will be tasked with overseeing the defence of the Free Kingdoms while he and Teodoric pledge their forces to you."

"You don't need to thank me, your majesty. The N'Gist are the enemy of us all, and I hope that this victory will lead to a new era of peace between you and the Nerios."

The Queen hesitantly placed a hand on his shoulder. Her eyes were filled with sympathy.

"I am sorry for your loss. May the Gods protect you."

With that, she lowered her hand and walked away. Luxon turned back to his horse and wiped tears from his eyes.

"Welsly wouldn't want us to mourn him," a voice said from behind him. He turned and saw a pale Ferran limping over to him. His arm was in a sling, and he winced with every movement.

"You should be resting," Luxon scolded.

Ferran waved his good arm dismissively.

"Pah, I'll live,' he said before his expression softened. 'We Nightblades rarely make it to old age. Welsly died a hero, just as he would have wanted. I owe him my life and the only way I can repay that debt is to free our homeland and plunge my sword through Danon's black heart. We carry on with our mission."

Luxon took a deep breath and pushed down the sadness he felt.

"What's our next move?" he asked.

"We convince King Thorn and Teodoric to sail south and assist Yazid and the Morvan to drive the Sarpi out of Silenzia. One more decisive battle and this continent will be purged of the N'Gists foul taint."

*

Thorn agreed with Ferran's plan and sent Queen Nix and a small contingent of his men back to Kastador. The rulers had an emotional farewell, but it was one that filled Luxon with renewed hope. Late in the afternoon, Teodoric's army arrived, and the King did not hide his disappointment at missing the battle. Thorn and he embraced like brothers and Teodoric's mood greatly improved when he was told that fighting still lay ahead. Thorn dispatched his Gryphon riders to Silenzia and to seek out Yazid. It would take them another five days to reach Silenzia by sea. Captain Whitelaw had moved the *Agatha* closer to the camp, and her crew were now loading the ship with supplies. The crew gathered on the main deck as Welsly's body was wrapped in cloth and carried aboard the ship where Whitelaw said a sombre prayer of Niveren. Luxon and the others watched. Eripa sobbed, and Alderlade needed comforting. After the service, the body was taken below decks where Luxon cast a preservation spell that would freeze it and allow them to return it to Delfinnia.

By mid afternoon the rest of the Kastador ships had arrived, and within the hour they were fully loaded with warriors from both Vinium and Kastador. The small fleet sailed back along the riverways for another two days before they sighted the sea on the horizon. During the journey, Luxon slept throughout, and Ferran continued to be treated by Sophia. It was the night of the third day that Luxon was stirred from his slumber by a knocking on his cabin door. He stirred and sat up, feeling refreshed for the first time in weeks. The use of such powerful magics and the traumatic events of the last few days had drained him. Now, however, he felt revitalised, and he quickly put on his clothes and cloak. He opened the door to see Alderlade waiting on the other side. He smiled at the boy. How long had they been away? He was surprised to realise that they'd been in Tulin for almost a year and the time had seen Alderlade grow. He was several inches taller, and his daily sword lessons with the crew had seen his arms grow strong and his body lean.

"Captain Whitelaw told me to fetch you. There are ships at the mouth of the river. Imperial ones by the looks of them," Alderlade said worriedly. Luxon frowned and followed the lad up to the main deck of the ship. As he emerged from the hatch, his eyes widened at the sight before him. There were dozens of warships at anchor at the river mouth. He hurried over to Captain Whitelaw, who was in a heated discussion with Ferran and Sophia.

"-We can't fight our way through that even with magic on our side. The Kastadorian ships aren't built for war," Whitelaw was saying.

"They're still at anchor can we not try to sail through them? It'll take them time to pursue," Sophia countered.

Luxon walked to the rail and frowned. A rowboat was being lowered into the water by the largest of the Imperial vessels. Stood at the prow with his cloak flapping in the wind was Torvar. The old man was waving his arms and in his right hand was a piece of white cloth.

"He wishes to parley?" Ferran said, his voice full of suspicion.

The rowboat pulled up alongside the *Agatha* and Whitelaw ordered for a rope ladder to be thrown over the side. They waited a few minutes for the old man and two of his accompanying warriors to clamber on board. Torvan   slumped, his breathing heavy but he waved away one of his warriors who tried to help him. Eventually, he caught his breath and righted himself. He bowed to Luxon taking them all by surprise.

"I had hoped to catch up with you Wizard as we have much to discuss. Is King Thorn aboard?"

Luxon crossed his arms.

"He's on his flagship behind us, but we can summon him here. Are your intentions hostile Torvar?"

Torvar looked aghast at the question.

"No, you must believe me. Please summon King Thorn, and we can talk some more. I promise you that you are safe. We do not seek battle."

Luxon glanced at Ferran who shrugged.

"Very well. We will meet in Captain Whitelaw's cabin."

Torvar bowed again, and he and his men were escorted to Whitelaw's cabin.

"Well, this is certainly unexpected," the captain mumbled.

*

The cabin was hot, and a tense feeling was in the air. Sat at the head of the long table was Whitelaw and at his side was Luxon and Ferran. The Kings Thorn and Teodoric sat further down and at the end was a nervous looking Torvar. He cleared his throat before speaking.

"I am here on behalf of the Imperial Council. With the death of Emperor Zeno and many of the Wizard Lords it has fallen on the surviving members of the Council to take charge of the Empire. They ask your forgiveness for Zeno's actions. The Council had no idea that he had made a deal with the Old Enemy. If they had known they would have deposed him and executed him as a traitor."

Teodoric snorted, "What cowards they are. We wiped out your Emperor and his goons, and now you have the audacity-"

Thorn had placed a hand on Teodoric's arm.

"Let him speak," he said softly.

Torvar frowned but bowed his head.

"What King Teodoric says is true. Much of the nobility of the Empire perished in that mountain pass. Those that remain have condemned Zeno publicly, and the citizens have expressed their outrage at his dealings with the N'Gist. To that end the Council wishes me to tell you that they will honour Zeno's pledge to you."

A gasp filled the room. Luxon leaned forward in his chair.

"Is this true?"

Torvar reached into his cloak and slid a piece of parchment across the table. Luxon picked it up and read its contents.

"This is the treaty I agreed with Zeno alright. And these signatures?"

"They belong to the Council members."

Luxon passed the parchment around the table.

"Just three signatures?" Teodoric chuckled "We certainly did a number of you lot didn't we?"

Torvar scowled but carried on, ignoring the Vinium King.

"The ships here in this bay have been ordered to assist you. I had a feeling that you would head this way which is why we are here. Will you accept the apologies of the Council and our help in the fight against Danon?"

Luxon stood, unable to hide the joy in his heart. He reached across the table and shook Torvar's hand.

"We do, and you are most welcome," he said enthusiastically.

Thorn stood too and likewise shook Torvar's hand. He held onto it and leaned in close to the elderly wizard.

"The Free Kingdoms accept this offer, but know that if you betray this treaty, we will show no mercy to the Empire. Today marks a new dawn for our peoples. One where peace will reign."

Torvar paled at the threat.

"The Council wants peace and the enemy driven from these shores, neigh not just these shores, but from the face of Esperia."

CHAPTER 24.

The fleet sailed south sticking close to the shore. Unlike the larger Tulin ships, the Kastadorian vessels were not designed to sail on the open seas. A squall had struck as they entered the warmer climate of the south but before disaster struck Eripa sang her song to calm to the howling winds and raging seas. No ships were lost, and they pressed on. With the coast in sight, they kept a close eye on the shore for any sign of the Silenzians or the enemy. It was on the second day that the lookout called from the crow's nest. In the sky and approaching quickly, was one of the Gryphons that had been sent ahead by Thorn. The beast descended, and the deck of the Agatha was cleared to make room for it and its rider. With deft skill, the rider brought the Gryphon down safely onto the swaying deck and slid from the saddle. Luxon and Ferran greeted the tired looking rider.

"Am I glad to have found you,' the rider said as he gratefully took the wineskin offered to him. He took a large gulp and wiped his lips. "I found the Morvan's forces. They're encamped about six miles inland and about twenty to the south from here. Their forces are gathering at an old desert fortress, and I was informed me that your support is most welcome."

"Did you meet a man called Yazid?" Luxon asked.

The rider nodded. "I did. He has been leading attacks against the Sarpi the past few weeks."

"What's the situation with the military?" enquired Ferran. The Nightblade's arm remained in a sling, but with every passing day, it was improving. The healing spell Luxon treated it with every few hours had accelerated the process, but his efforts were clumsy in comparison what to an expert healer could do. The rider wiped his brow before answering.

"The Morvan has held the desert and interior lands, but every attempt at assaulting the capital has been thwarted. Magic wielders defend the walls and the Sarpi fleet controls the seas so they cannot be starved out."

They thanked the rider for his report and sent word throughout the fleet that contact with the Silenzians had been made. The ships pressed on until they spotted a natural harbour where over a dozen Silenzian ships were docked.

"Must be survivors of the Silenzian navy," Lipur said from his spot at the *Agatha's* wheel. The man had come a long way since they had found him floating adrift at sea. His sailing expertise had proven invaluable, so much so that Captain Whitelaw had promoted him to his first mate and the two men were now firm friends. The fleet dropped anchor off the coast. Luxon and the others boarded one of the *Agatha's* rowboats and joined another boat coming from King Thorn's ship to the shore.

Waiting for them on the beach was Yazid. The dark skinned man opened his arms wide and smiled broadly.

"My friends! It is so good to see you and what allies you bring!" he laughed.

"It's good to see you Yazid. It's been a while," Luxon replied.

"Where is my good friend, Beric?" Yazid asked looking at Thorn and the small contingent he'd brought with him. Meric was with them, and he stepped forward, taking off his tall pointy hat.

"I am afraid that Beric was killed in battle," Meric said softly.

Yazid's smile faded, and he nodded in understanding. He cleared his throat, but it was clear the news had saddened him greatly. He gestured for them to follow and they walked up the beach towards a stone tower built into the cliffside. Thousands of Silenzian warriors were in the camp, and the sound of blacksmiths forging weapons filled the air. The banners of the Silenzian Great Houses flapped in the breeze. Guarding the entrance to the tower were two warriors clad head to toe in yellow cloth. Only their eyes could be seen. Each held a spear and tall oval shield. At seeing Yazid, they stepped aside and allowed them entry. The interior of the tower was sparse of any decoration, and every scrap of space was filled with crates and weapons. They followed Yazid up a spiral staircase and stepped out onto the tower's upper level. From this height, they could see for a hundred miles in all directions. The vast desert stretched to the horizon, making a surprise approach by the enemy impossible. Looking at the view was a person wearing similar garb to the yellow clad warriors. They were small in stature and almost as short as Alderlade. Yazid stepped forward.

"Morvan, these are the friends I told you of," he said.

The figure pulled down their turban to reveal a head of long black hair that fell to their waist. Then they turned around to reveal that the Morvan was a young woman. Her small nose was offset by large brown eyes that regarded Luxon and the others with interest. Luxon was unable to hide his surprise, causing her to chuckle.

"You are surprised the mighty Morvan is a girl?" she said in a broad Silenzian accent.

"Forgive me. Yes, I am a bit, but I know some very fierce women, so it is not a complete surprise," Luxon replied with a smile.

"Yazid tells me you are from far across the sea and that you are here to seek aid in your war against Danon and the N'Gist."

"We are."

"This I vow to you Master Wizard. Help me drive them from my lands and I, as my first task as Shar will be to honour the promises made to you. As much as I despised him, he did not deserve to be slain by assassins. Come, we have much to plan."

The Morvan walked to the stairs, and the others followed. Once at the bottom of the tower, they crossed the inner courtyard and entered a stone structure being used as a base of operations. On the floor was a huge cloth map of the lands of Silenzia. Most of the cities and major towns were located on the coast whilst the interior had only a smattering of settlements. All of those had a circle drawn around them, indicating they were under the Morvan's control. Only a handful of the coastal areas were.

"We have managed to hold the N'Gist in the desert using hit and fade tactics, but their wielders have prevented us from doing too much damage. They seem more interested in the coastal regions as they are far easier to attack and supply. My plan-" she said using a stick to jab at the map. "-is to use our combined fleets to recapture the coastal cities one by one. Then we will make for Zlegend and win my throne. To succeed, we must defeat the Sarpi navy. Its destruction will leave the enemy cut off from reinforcements from Sarpia, and the N'Gist will soon surrender."

"A sound strategy, but one that will cost time that our foreign friends here cannot afford." said Thorn who'd been studying the map intently.

"Oh? And what do you propose   ?" snapped the Morvan.

"I meant no offence, but the way I see it the enemy's stratagem here depends on the Sarpi navy. They know they cannot fight you in the desert so they will have stuck close to the cities. That allows us room to manoeuvre."

"Ha! You mean to go straight for the heart," laughed Teodoric. "I love it."

Thorn pointed at the map,

"The Tulin and Silenzian fleet should seek out and engage the Sarpi fleet. Meanwhile, our armies march on the capital. If that falls and the Sarpi fleet is defeated, then the rest will soon surrender."

"Crossing the desert will not be easy, not with such a large army," Ferran said.

"We are experts at surviving in these deserts. It can be done." the Morvan said stroking her chin in thought. "There are oases that our merchants use when they traverse the Salt Roads. It will be hard going but I think we can do it."

*

They waited until the sun began to dip in the sky before breaking camp. Travelling at night would be much cooler and allow the horses an easier journey. Luxon found Ferran and Sophia preparing their mounts for travel.

"Are you sure you won't come with us?" asked Sophia.

It had been decided that Luxon, Alderlade and Eripa would travel with the fleet. Defeating the Sarpi fleet was vital for their plan to succeed and Luxon's magic would prove most useful at sea. Ferran and Sophia meanwhile would travel with the Morvan, Thorn and the combined armies of Tulin. Throughout the day the Imperial ships had disgorged their complements of warriors on the shore and they would make the perilous march across the desert.

"I think I'll be of more use to Captain Whitelaw, and I need to ensure that Alderlade is safe. After all we're taking him into the heart of a war."

Sophia pulled him into a hug and kissed him on the cheek.

"Be safe, Luxon."

"Likewise. I think I've had my fair share of sand to last me a lifetime," he joked recalling his brief time in the desert of Yundol and the battle against the Devourer. "Just make sure that you're in position. I don't know how the Morvan expects to cross such a distance in just six days."

"She's a fiery one, make no mistake," Ferran said. "I guess we will see you in a few days. Good luck."

The two embraced, and Luxon stepped back as they climbed into their respective saddles. A horn blew nearby, and the army moved out in a thunder of hooves and marching boots. Luxon watched them go and made his way to the *Agatha*.

*

The seas were choppy as the fleet departed and the ships stuck close to the coastline. At night lanterns were lit to ensure that no ship would get lost. The Agatha led the way with Lipur using his knowledge of the jagged coastline to guide them to safety. Luxon stood on the aft deck, his cloak flapping in the wind. He looked to the sky and marvelled at the stunning view of stars twinkling in the black sky.

"Do you remember the promise you made me, Wizard?"

Luxon blinked and looked at Lipur. The man's gaze was fixed ahead, but his words were aimed at him.

"You promised that you would help me free my people from the Sarpi."

"I did."

"I just want you to know that I am grateful to you for saving my life. I never thanked you before. This ship, this crew has become my home, and I am happy here."

Luxon smiled.

"I am glad."

"But..." Lipur interrupted, "my people are still enslaved by the Sarpi. Do you know what they do with their slaves?"

"No," Luxon answered, shaking his head.

"Mostly they use them on their ships as labour or rowers. The rest, the ones they deem too weak, old or young, will be forced to work in the mines of Sarpia in the fading light. It is a brutal fate and one that has befallen many of them. When the fighting starts, I know many of them will die."

"I don't know what to say," Luxon said.

"There is a saying amongst the Vastar. *You can do two things about this fate. Accept it or defy the Gods with every fibre of your being.* Defiance is what I intend to do. I will not be enslaved, and I will not die at the   hands, I will live on, and perhaps one day the Vastar will rise anew."

Luxon fixed Lipur with a hard stare and squeezed his shoulder.

"No. I promised you that we would save your people and that is exactly what we are going to do."

CHAPTER 26.

The fleet rounded a headland that marked the beginning of the stretch of coastline that would lead them to Zlegend. A lone watchtower stood on the cliffside and at seeing the ships a beacon was lit. Thick black smoke that would be visible for miles around rose into the sky. As they travelled on, they spotted more plumes suggesting that more beacons had been lit.

"They know we're coming," Whitelaw muttered. He lowered his spyglass and handed it to Luxon. "We need to be cautious from here on. If I were in command of the Sarpi fleet, I'd use the coastal inlets as ambush points."

Sailing onward Whitelaw was proven right. The Agatha's watchman blew his horn in warning as out of one of the natural inlets appeared a large black sailed ship. Whitelaw rang the ship's bell, and the crew rushed to their battle stations. The Agatha was not built for war, but it was more than capable of defending itself. The magical runes carved into its hull provided it with protection not just from the towering waves of the oceans but weapons too. Behind the *Agatha*, the Imperial navy beat to quarters and the much larger vessels began to fan out.

"Look!" shouted Eripa, who was standing at the bow of the ship. Another Sarpi ship emerged from the inlet and further down the shore more, and more ships appeared. Whitelaw swore loudly.

"We won't have much room to manoeuvre being so close to the shore, clever buggers."

Lipur spun the *Agatha's* wheel, and the ship lurched to the left and headed out into deeper waters and away from the rocks that the Sarpi planned to dash them against. One of the sailors shouted a warning as from the sky fell arrows. The deadly projectiles slammed onto the deck, and several crewmen screamed in pain. The nearest Sarpi ship had matched the *Agatha's* course and was now in bow shot. Luxon ran to the front of the ship and cast a shield over the deck. Another volley fell, but this time the arrows shattered against the barrier. Luxon flinched as an invisible fist pounded on the shield. He looked over to the enemy ship and spotted three N'Gist wielders standing at the ship's rail, their hands held open and pointed at the *Agatha*. One of their powers was nothing to his own, but the trio working together was enough to force him to his knees. Luxon gritted his teeth and sweat formed on his forehead.

"Luxon! Here," shouted Alderlade, who had run onto the main deck with Dragasdol in his hands. Luxon winced as he maintained the shield with one hand and reached for the staff with the other. Using magic, Dragasdol flew from Alderlade's arms and into his hand. At once, the extra power of the staff surged into his tiring arms, and he regained his footing.

"Get back below decks now!" he snapped at Alderlade. The boy, realising the predicament they were in didn't argue and fled back towards the hatch. Luxon could feel the N'Gist redouble their efforts, but then an Imperial warship smashed into the Sarpi vessel, it's huge iron battering ram smashing it in two. Screams came from the now stricken ship and as it split in two Luxon could see the dozens of men and women chained to banks of oars in the lower decks. Many tumbled into the sea. Others were trapped by their chains and sank beneath the waves. More Sarpi ships entered the fray until the sky was filled with arrows and harpoons whistling through the air. Several Sarpi ships unleashed pots of flammable material from catapults that struck the Imperial fleet which was now engaging the enemy. Quickly, the sea filled with blood and the air filled with the smell of burning wood and the screams of the dying. Luxon staggered as the Agatha was rammed from the side. A sickening crash vibrated through the ship. A huge iron platform with an evil looking spike built into its tip had slammed down onto the deck, and now Sarpi warriors were pouring across it.

"We've been boarded! Fight you bastards, fight until you can fight no more!" bellowed Captain Whitelaw.

Luxon dropped the shield and focused on the bridge. Fire erupted from Dragasdol the first of the attackers and then with a flourish of telekinesis he ripped the boarding platform from the Agatha's deck. Sarpi tumbled into the now thrashing waves only to be crushed between the two ships. The Agatha's crew, seeing the fight turn in their favour, cheered and hurled grappling hooks at the Sarpi ship. The sailors armed with cutlasses, some carrying them in their teeth swung across to bring the fight to the enemy. A brutal skirmish began, and Luxon using levitation leapt across to join them. He blasted more Sarpi overboard and unleashed fire and lightning at those foolish enough to attack him. He hurried to the main deck's hatch and using magic ripped the heavy iron grate from its hinges. He hurried down the ladder and found himself on one of the rowing decks. At seeing him, the chained oarsmen pleaded to be set free. He looked for the end of the chain and using his staff shattered the lock.

"Go, you're free now. Take up arms against the Sarpi and help us put an end to them!"

The now freed slaves rushed to help their comrades whilst others clambered onto the decks and threw themselves into the fray. The deck of the Sarpi ship was filled with struggling figures and blood soaked the wooden boards. A crack of thunder made him spin around and look at the rest of the scene. The sea was filled with ships. Some had been smashed in two by the rams of their foes, the rest were locked in deadly battle. The Imperial navy ships were larger than the Sarpi's and the Imperial sailors used that to their advantage. Arrows fell like rain and deadly fire pots smashed to send oil and blinding flame in all directions. The sound of thunder came again and this time Luxon saw the bolt of lightning lance down from the sky to split a   ship in two. He looked desperately for where the wielder who had cast it was, and then his eyes fixed on a huge Sarpi warship. It was different from the others. This one had similar magical runes carved on its hull that now shined brightly. A fearsome figurehead of a snarling dragon was on its mast and standing at the prow was the Witch Yinnice. Luxon ran back to the side of the Sarpi vessel's rail and leapt back onto the Agatha.

"Get the men back on board now! Yinnice is here," he yelled to Whitelaw, who was shouting encouragement to his men from the relative safety of the aft deck. The captain placed a horn to his lips and blew the signal to fall back. Luxon kept his eyes fixed on the witch. She was wreaking havoc on the fleet. Eripa hurried to his side, her blonde hair was a mess, and a cut was on her face. In her hand she held her short sword, its blade was covered in Sarpi blood.

"How can she be here," she cried.

"The portal she escaped through must have taken her to Sarpia. It's only a short voyage from these shores," Luxon reasoned.

The sky boomed again, and another Imperial ship was blown to smithereens. Fire ripped across the deck engulfing the sailors on board.

"Get us closer!" he shouted to Lipur, who was doing his best to keep the Agatha steady while the crew leapt back on board. Of the ship they had attacked the deck was now full of dead Sarpi and jubilant freed slaves who were now busy taking it over. At seeing them, Lipur cheered and praised the gods. With expert skill, he manoeuvred the Agatha through the raging battle. Luxon cast another shield allowing it to push on unimpeded. All around them, the battle raged. A Sarpi ship exploded as two Kastadorian ships unleashed a salvo of pitch filled jars via their catapults. The Agatha sped on, shoving more ships out of its path. It was impossible to tell who was winning. As they drew nearer, Luxon raised Dragasdol into the sky and unleashed a lightning blast of his own at Yinnice's ship. The bolt struck, but the runes carved into the ship's hull absorbed the magical attack with ease. Yinnice staggered to her feet dazed, and her eyes settled onto the Agatha and Luxon. She sneered and thrust her hands into the air. A dark cloud arose from the surface of the sea, and the light of the sun dimmed. Then, a deafening roar so loud that it drowned out the carnage of battle exploded into the air.

Panicked cries came from the Agatha's crow's nest and then six huge tentacles burst from beneath the sea. They writhed and pulsated before one slammed down onto a nearby Imperial ship, smashing it into splinters. Luxon dived to the right, pushing Eripa down with him as deadly shrapnel spun wildly through the spot where they had been standing.

"What is that thing?" Eripa gasped.

The tentacles slammed down onto another Imperial ship snapping its mast and causing it to capsize. The monster summoned by Yinnice lifted itself out of the water to reveal its hideous form. The six huge tentacles were attached to an enormous fish like body that was covered in spines. Its head was like that of a dragon, but its eyes were feral and wild. A quivering mouth filled with razor sharp teeth snapped and growled. It was something from a nightmare.

"By Niveren it's a Lusca! A monster of the ancient world, an Elemental," Whitelaw cowered.

Luxon got back onto his feet and gripped Dragasdol tightly.

"An Elemental?" he whispered to himself, his mind racing. The Devourer had been an Elemental, one of Fire. He looked around, and his eyes fell on the flaming husks of dying ships. The Luska took a deep breath. The sea poured into its cavernous mouth with such strength that it began to swirl. The Agatha lurched forward violently, and the monster's tentacles swept the deck, taking screaming sailors with them. Luxon watched in horror as a Kastadorian ship was suddenly yanked under the surface.

"We don't stand a chance against that thing!" Lipur yelled.

Luxon dashed to the deck's rail and fixed his eyes on one of the pitch filled barrels. Using telekinesis, he lifted one into the air and hurled it at the beast. To his surprise, the Luska moved with incredible speed, easily evading the projectile.

It was then Eripa ran to the prow of the Agatha, opened her mouth and began to sing. Her beautiful voice carried clearly despite the battle raging all about them. She was using Song Magic, Luxon realised. He could make out the words of the song. She was singing a lullaby. The Luska flinched violently, and then its tentacles began to wilt as Eripa's song took effect. She was singing it to sleep. Now was his chance. Luxon reached for another pitch barrel and again launched it at the monster. This time, thanks to Eripa's song, its senses were dulled, and the barrel struck and exploded into flame. The Luska roared in pain. Luxon ran to the aft deck.

"Signal to the fleet to unleash every fire pot and barrel of pitch they have at that thing. It's a water elemental. Only fire can kill it!" he commanded.

Whitelaw gave the order, and one of his lieutenants raised a flag to signal the rest of the fleet of their intent. The ships that had managed to either defeat their opponents or were able to push their way through the carnage did as commanded. Dozens more of the fire pots were launched, and volleys of fire arrows lanced through the sky. As they struck the Luska emitted an ear-piercing squeal. Its flesh began to cook, and the air filled with the smell of roasting flesh. With one last roar, the Luska disappeared beneath the waves leaving Yinnice's ship exposed. From the rocking deck, Luxon could see the witch shouting at her Sarpi crew. The ship swung about and struck further out to sea before veering back towards Zlegend. Luxon glared at it and spotted Yinnice staring back. Tiredly he raised Dragasdol, intent on sending her to a watery grave but exhaustion made it hard to concentrate.

"Let her go lad," said Whitelaw breathlessly from behind him. The captain was covered in soot and blood from a gash on his head. "Look, the Sarpi fleet is in retreat. Niveren knows how, but we've won the day."

Luxon leaned against the rail.

"We cannot allow her to escape. Follow that ship."

*

The march through the desert had been long and arduous, but finally, on the sixth day, the coalition army sighted the city of Zlegend on the horizon. Ferran rode with Sophia at his side and ahead of them was Meric, Thorn and the Morvan. They had moved at blistering speed, using the cooler nights to travel and the Morvan's expert knowledge of the terrain had ensured they'd all had enough water and food for the journey. It was an incredible feat, and one that Ferran was sure would go into the history books of the land. In record time they'd crossed the vast Silenzian desert, bypassing the Sarpi forces on the coast. The Morvan spurred her horse forward and shouted for her captains to get her warriors into formation. Thorn and Teodoric did likewise with their own troops. Anyone watching from the walls of Zlegend would no doubt be shocked to see such a vast force appear like a mirage on the near horizon.

"Hear me Sons and daughters of Silenzia!" the Morvan shouted. "Today we reclaim our realm's capital from the foul wickedness of Danon. Today, I claim my throne and today we win a new future for all the peoples of Tulin!"

The army roared at her words.

"Zlegend's walls are tall and strong but do not fear, for the Sarpi underestimate our cunning. By day's end, they shall fall, and the streets will flow with our enemies blood!"

Ferran looked at Sophia in confusion.

"How by Niveren does she think we can take the walls? We don't have any siege equipment."

Sophia shrugged.

"She seems very certain of herself. I get the feeling she has a trick or two up her sleeve."

As in on cue, the Morvan placed a horn to her lips and blew it until her face flushed red.

"I don't hear anything," Ferran muttered.

The Morvan blew again, and then the ground began to shake. A panicked murmuring arose from the army, and the horses neighed and whinnied in fright. The rumbling grew stronger and stronger, and then one of the sand dunes exploded outwards to reveal one of the massive Sand Whales. All around the army, the gigantic creatures appeared, their enormous bodies swimming through the vast dunes like a shark in the ocean. The Morvan galloped forward, keeping pace with the Whales. At seeing her reckless charge, the Silenzian army surged forward, Yazid at their head. Thorn looked at Ferran in bemusement.

"I guess we follow the crazy woman!" he shouted as he cracked his reins and charged after them. The Bannerlords roared, and they too broke into a charge.

Ferran and Sophia followed.

Meanwhile, the Morvan was rapidly closing in on the city. Alarm bells tolled, and she could see the black clad figures of Sarpi warriors hastily taking up positions on the walls. Arrows began to fall, but she sped on, the Sand Whales barreling on behind her. Just as she reached the walls, she reached down and lifted her spear and raised it. She muttered an incantation and then hurled it with all her might. The spear tip began to shine brightly, and then it struck. There was a blinding flash, and then the wall blew apart to leave a hole wide enough for a man to pass through. With terrifying bellows, the Sand Whales struck the walls, and the damage they inflicted was devastating. The mighty creatures acted as massive battering rams to punch huge holes in the stonework. Some of the creatures died as they struck, but others punched on through to wreak havoc in the city beyond. Clouds of dust and sand swept out in all directions blinding both armies, but it was the Silenzians who were the children of the desert. The clouds masked their attack, and the Sarpi were forced to shoot blindly. Silenzian warriors poured through the breaches, and the fighting began. What N'Gist there were in the city used magic to slay the surviving sand whales, and then the Bannerlords of Kastador and the army of Vinium entered the fray. From the sky attacked the Gryphon Riders. They swept down on the Sarpi archers, and Ferran watched in awe as they ripped a catapult from the top of one of the defence towers. Its crew fell from the sky; their screams silenced as they struck the ground.

Ferran and Sophia rode through one of the breaches in the wall and drew their weapons, but it was clear that the Morvan's stunning assault had shocked the Sarpi to such an extent that most were fleeing back towards the harbour. The Bannerlords rode through the city's streets cutting down any foe they encountered, and the Silenzians took their vengeance with savage glee.

"We have them beat," Thorn cried happily as he galloped alongside Ferran. "Look how they flee."

Suddenly a powerful wind swept through the city knocking men off their feet. Panicked shouts came from further ahead and then warriors began fleeing.

"The witch!" yelled one.

Ferran glanced and Sophia, and together they spurred on their mounts towards the screams. The wind grew in strength, and as they slowly advanced, they could see warriors being forced to cower in doorways or take cover behind walls. Ferran leapt from his saddle and pushed Sophia off hers. They landed heavily, but he dragged her off the street and behind a low building. More screams sounded, and then deadly pieces of metal and wood shot past them to impale anyone too slow to seek cover.

"It's Yinnice. It must be," Sophia shouted over the now howling wind. Together they moved toward the harbour, using whatever cover they could to avoid being impaled by the deadly debris. Ferran dashed across a street, narrowly avoiding being impaled by a large splinter of wood that was cartwheeling wildly and reached the safety of an alleyway. He crouched at the corner and waved Sophia across when it was clear. She sprinted, but a warning shout from Ferran caused her to dive to the ground. A jagged piece of metal whizzed by just above her head. Scrambling, she made it the rest of the way and to safety. Following the alleyway, they reached the harbour and there saw what remained of the Sarpi fleet. Several ships had managed to limp back to safety. Some had huge chunks missing from their hulls or had been scorched by flame. One vessel larger than all the others had crashed into the quayside spilling its crew and slaves into the sea.

Sophia tapped Ferran on the shoulder and pointed towards the end of the dock. There stood Yinnice, her arms held wide and her hair billowing from the vortex of howling winds she had unleashed. They crept closer, and Sophia placed an arrow on her bowstring. She placed the edge of her bow against the stonework of a low wall to steady her aim and drew back the cord.

"You only get one shot at this," Ferran whispered.

Sophia threw him an annoyed look and slowed her breathing. Narrowing her left eye, she took aim and released the cord with a twang. The arrow shot out, but just as it was about to strike, Yinnice lashed out and snatched it out of the sky. She snarled and snapped it in two.

"Witch Hunter, you will have to do better than that to kill me," Yinnice spat with anger. She turned and faced them. She raised her arms again, and lightning poured from her fingertips. Ferran and Sophia dived for cover as the wall exploded, showering them in debris. Ferran got to his feet and ignited his Tourmaline blade with a *snap hiss*. Yinnice was striding towards them with death in her one good eye. He charged and launched himself at her with his blade held in a two handed grip. Just as he swung, she dodged with blurring speed, and he flew past before landing in a skid. She spun and blasted him backwards with a telekinetic spell. He crashed to the ground but leapt to his feet, using his own magic to enhance his body. He lowered his blade, and the two circled one another.

"A Nightblade thinks that he can kill a High Witch of the N'Gist. How quaint," Yinnice mocked. "I could kill you like a bug, but instead I think I'll make you suffer." She reached out with a hand, and a pained gasped came from where Sophia lay. An invisible hand grabbed her by the hair. Sophia screamed in pain as she was lifted off the ground.

"You may have thwarted our plans in these lands but know that this is only a temporary setback. Delfinnia is doomed, and once my master is finished with it, he will come here with his full glorious power. Esperia will be his."

"Let her go," Ferran snarled. His heart was racing. Fear of losing Sophia threatened to overwhelm him.

A shout came from behind, and he dared a glance over his shoulder. Some of Thorn's Bannerlords had reached the harbour and were battling some Sarpi. His eyes widened. Out at sea and speeding toward the dock was the Agatha. He faced Yinnice once more. He had to buy Sophia time.

"You will never win Witch. We have defeated you at every turn and destroyed your armies. The world is uniting against you and your master. Your defeat is nigh," he said with more conviction than he felt.

Yinnice cackled at his words.

"You put your faith into this bunch of squabbling fools? How long do you think this alliance will last? The Darkness will take everything. Already it stirs in the hearts of those you have put your hopes in. Danon will show you all the truth."

The Agatha was rapidly approaching, but Ferran had to keep her talking and distracted.

"What truth?"

"That even the one you believe to be the champion of the light can fall into darkness. Before the end, your faith will be shattered, and Danon will have his revenge," Yinnice said, her eye glinting with madness.

A figure shot into the sky from the *Agatha's* deck.

*

The Agatha had pursued Yinnice's ship to the harbour and Luxon watched in horror as the witch unleashed her power onto the city and the army liberating it. Alderlade was at his side, safe now that the sea battle was over.

"Look over there!" the boy shouted, pointing to the quayside and two figures who were creeping up on the witch. Luxon narrowed his eyes. It was Ferran and Sophia. He watched as Sophia shot her arrow with no effect. His heart sank as Yinnice used lightning and then captured Sophia. He could see her struggling body hanging in the witch's magical grasp. Anger surged through him.

"You have to help them!" Alderlade cried.

Luxon nodded and drew Asphodel. Immediately its power surged through him.

"Stay here," he said.

He channelled every bit of magic he had, and his body crackled and fizzed with energy. His eyes glowed blue, and he launched himself high into the air. He would not let his friends die.

*

Ferran charged with a roar, as from the sky, fell Luxon with Asphodel shining in his hand. Yinnice tossed Sophia over the harbour wall and into the water and unleashed another blast of lightning at Ferran. He caught it on his blade, but the impact sent him staggering. Electricity surged through his body, and his agonized screams filled the air. Luxon meanwhile landed in a crouch, his magic slowing his descent just in time. He was on the brink of collapse, the magic he'd channelled failing him. Gritting his teeth, he stood and pushed through the tiredness and pain. He would not let them die. At seeing him, Yinnice smiled wickedly. She ceased her attack on Ferran who collapsed smouldering to the ground and faced him.

"Even the sword of light will not save you," she snarled. She strode over to him, and he swung Asphodel, but her reserves of magic had not been spent, and she easily swatted it out of his hands to send it spinning to the ground. She darted forward and her bony hands wrapped around Luxon's throat.

"I will squeeze the life from you with my bare hands. So much trouble you have caused my master. You were meant to be nothing more than the tool he needed to escape the Void, yet here you are still defying him."

Luxon clawed at her arm, feebly. He looked desperately at Ferran but the Nightblade lay unmoving. The Agatha pulled alongside the quay, and the ramp was dropped. In the distance, the Bannerlords were being kept at bay. Yinnice squeezed tighter. He didn't want to die. Not here in a foreign land. His vision began to fade, and his thoughts drifted to Hannah and home.

Suddenly, Yinnice's grip eased, and he fell to his knees. He looked up, gasping to see her staring at her chest. Sticking through it was Asphodel's tip.

"For Elena!" came a cry from behind her. Yinnice stumbled to the side, clutching the wound to reveal Alderlade wielding the sword. Light spread through the Witch's body as the sword purged her of evil. For a heartbeat, her black eye changed colour to green, and for a moment, Luxon could see the woman she had once been before she had fallen to darkness. Like Accadus, when the sword had affected him, she let out a cry of utter despair at the horrors she had committed.

"Niveren forgive me," she croaked before crashing to the ground, dead.

Luxon stumbled to his feet and hurried to the quayside. He ruffled Alderlade's hair affectionately as he went and sighed in relief to see Lipur emerging from the water with Sophia in his arms. She coughed up water, but she was safe. The sailor brought her to a ladder on the quayside. Luxon reached down and with Alderlade's help hauled her up onto dry land.

"I leapt in as soon as I saw her fall," Lipur said.

The rest of the *Agatha's* crew had disembarked and were hurrying into the city to offer support where it was needed. Eripa rushed to Ferran's side. With a cough the Nightblade sat up, his armour still steaming from Yinnice's attacks.

Alderlade tugged on Luxon's sleeve.

"Here," the boy said, offering him Asphodel.

Luxon regarded Alderlade for a few moments and knelt so that he was at eye level with him.

"Keep it. This sword was meant for a King, and you have proven your valour."

A great cheer came from the city, signalling that the Morvan was victorious. The few Sarpi still fighting on the harborside threw down their weapons in surrender.

Luxon limped over to Ferran and helped Eripa stand him up.

"It's over. The N'Gist have been purged from Tulin. We did it," Eripa said in relief.

Luxon nodded and smiled as he spotted Thorn and Meric approaching from the city. The King held his sword up in victory.

"For the Light!"

EPILOGUE

The city of Zlegend was in a sorry state. The once powerful walls that had kept the desert tribes at bay for countless aeons were now rubble. Fire had ravaged much of the palace district, and yet despite the damage, it remained beautiful.

Luxon was walking through the gardens of what had been the Shar's royal palace. After the battle, he had passed out and according to Eripa had slept for three whole days. In that time Ferran and Sophia had recovered from their wounds thanks to the healers the Morvan had provided.

He closed his eyes and enjoyed the sound of the fountains tinkling and the birds singing. The smell of jasmine and other flowers filled his nostrils, and for a heartbeat, his worries fell away. He sighed at the sound of footsteps from behind him. He turned to see the Morvan and gasped. She no longer wore the garb of the warrior queen but now wore a dress of flowing silks and her hair was up. The cold hard fighter had been replaced with a stunningly beautiful young woman who smiled knowingly   .

"I thought I'd find you out here Wizard. Come, the Council has gathered."

He blinked.

"What council?"

"Ah, how silly of me. In all the chaos of the last few days, I forgot that you were asleep through it all. We, the leaders of Tulin, have formed a Council of the Continental Coalition. It is through this Council that we will support you in the liberation of your homeland."

Luxon bowed deeply.

"I cannot express my gratitude."

The Morvan had pledged what was left of the Silenzian navy to Luxon's cause. Combined with the Imperial fleet they now had enough ships to transport the coalition armies across the Boundless Sea.

"No. It is we who owe you everything. Without you, the N'Gist would have seized control of our realms one by one and Tulin would have fallen to darkness. Helping you is the least we can do."

She took his hand in hers, and together they walked inside the palace.

*

The Shar's throne room was packed with the leaders of the Coalition. More ships were arriving with every passing hour and messages had been dispatched across the continent requesting warriors and mercenaries of all nations to take up the fight against Danon. A large table had been found and installed in the centre of the room around which were twelve chairs. The leaders of each of the Coalition members sat in them with two empty chairs remaining. Luxon made a move for the one next to Thorn, but the Morvan caught his arm and steered him to a chair next to Alderlade.

"No. **You** are our leader. You sit at the position of prominence," she said with a smile. Luxon gulped and sat in the chair. As he did so, the others banged on the table to signal their approval. A silence fell over the room as all eyes settled on   him. He placed his hands on the table's smooth surface. Alderlade smiled at him, and at the side of the room, Ferran winked.

He cleared his throat.

"I pronounce this meeting of the Continental Coalition begun."

*

The End

ALSO BY M.S. OLNEY

The Sundered Crown Saga-

Heir to the
Sundered Crown

War for the
Sundered Crown

Quest for the
Sundered Crown

Voyage for the Sundered
Crown

Heroes of the Sundered Crown

The Sundered
Crown Boxset

The Nightblade
Danon

The Crimson Blade
The Empowered Ones-

The First Fear

The Temple of
Arrival

The Empowered Ones Boxset

ABOUT THE AUTHOR

Matthew Olney is the #1 Amazon best-selling author of *The Empowered Ones and The Sundered Crown Saga,* among others. He lives in Worcester, England with his wife. Matthew loves history, fantasy, and all things sci-fi.

Learn more about Matthew at https://msolneyauthor.com/

Sign up to Matthew's mailing list

One Last Thing...

Thank you so much for reading. If you enjoyed this book, I'd be very grateful if you'd post a short review. Your support really does make a difference, and I read all the reviews personally so I can get your feedback and make my books even better.

Thanks again for your support!

9 798215 396414